Bound for Murder

Also available by Victoria Gilbert

Blue Ridge Library Mysteries

Past Due for Murder

Shelved Under Murder

A Murder for the Books

Bound for Murder

A BLUE RIDGE LIBRARY MYSTERY

Victoria Gilbert

NEW YORK

Published in the United States by Crooked Lane Books, an imprint of The Quick Brown Fox & Company LLC.

Library of Congress Catalog-in-Publication data available upon request.

ISBN (hardcover): 978-1-64385-243-0
ISBN (ePub): 978-1-64385-244-7

Cover illustration by Griesbach/Martucci
Book design by Jennifer Canzone

Printed in the United States.

www.crookedlanebooks.com

Crooked Lane Books
34 West 27th St., 10th Floor
New York, NY 10001

First Edition: January 2020

10 9 8 7 6 5 4 3 2 1

Dedicated, with thanks, to all librarians, archivists, and library assistants everywhere.

I have always imagined that Paradise will be a kind of library.

—Jorge Luis Borges

Chapter One

There are two times in a woman's life when complete strangers think it's appropriate to offer unsolicited advice—when she's obviously pregnant, and when they discover she's planning a wedding.

"I'm telling you, Amy, don't make the mistake my grandniece did and spend a fortune on one of those fancy cakes dripping with inedible geegaws." My eighty-year-old neighbor, Mrs. Dinterman, tapped the pitted wooden surface of the library circulation desk with one ruby-painted fingernail. "I know that bakery over in Smithsburg likes to show off their cakes like they're sculptures or something, but I sampled one at my grandniece's wedding, and lord-a-mercy, it tasted like sawdust." Stepping back, the older woman patted her hair, which was dyed blue-black as a raven's wing. "You want a delicious cake, you just ring up my cousin Arletta Shober. She makes a divine vanilla cake with just a hint of almond. Looks pretty too, if I must say so myself."

"I'm sure," I said, casting my gaze over her plump shoulder. A tall, white-haired man browsing the art section of the book stacks caught my eye. *Help*, I mouthed at him.

He raised his bushy eyebrows before strolling over to the desk.

"Hello, Mr. Kendrick, can I help you with something?" I asked, silently adding *please*. Mrs. Dinterman, who was focused on the image of Patrick Stewart on the READ poster behind me, ignored Kurt as she continued to extol the merits of her cousin's wedding cakes.

"Yes, thank you, Ms. Webber," Kurt Kendrick replied, loud enough to cut through Mrs. Dinterman's monologue. "I was looking for something on Caravaggio. Would you have any books on that artist?"

"I'm sure we have something," I said, raising my voice to match his volume. Making my excuses to Mrs. Dinterman, I followed Kurt to the shelves. "Caravaggio?" I muttered as we walked. "Couldn't you think of something a little less obscure?"

Kurt shrugged. "I thought perhaps your rather loquacious patron might recognize a more popular artist and wonder why I, an art dealer and collector, needed help finding information on them." He glanced down at me, his blue eyes bright with amusement. "You did want me to rescue you from that endless prattle about cakes, I gather."

"Yes, and thank you." I ran my fingers across a row of book spines. "Let's see what we can find in this one," I called out in a voice loud enough to carry to the desk. Mrs. Dinterman, obviously sensing that I might be stuck helping another patron for quite some time, waved her hand in a cheery goodbye before turning and bustling toward the exit.

"Everyone and their cousin has an opinion on weddings, it seems," Kurt observed as the main doors closed behind Mrs. Dinterman. Stepping back to look me over, he tapped his broad chest with one finger. "Except for me. I've never given such celebrations much thought."

"Me either," I said, gazing up into his craggy face. Kurt dwarfed me, but unlike when we'd first met, I no longer felt intimidated by his commanding presence. Most of the time, anyway.

"You mean to tell me that you haven't been planning your wedding since you were but a wee bairn?" Kurt ran one hand through his thick white hair. "What kind of woman are you, anyway?"

"The sensible kind." My smile acknowledged the sarcasm lacing his words. I studied his face, still handsome despite his seventy-two years. "Why would I be worried about details at this point? Richard and I only got engaged a few months ago."

"I certainly don't blame you for being irritated by that sort of unsolicited advice. You haven't even set a date yet, have you?"

"I'm sure you'd know if we had," I said dryly. Kurt ran an informal network of spies who kept him informed on most activities in our small town of Taylorsford, Virginia, among other locales. "I expect your little birds would've tweeted something like that to you by now."

"Indeed, they would have. Besides, I'm expecting a special invitation. I am a friend of the family, after all. Both families, if it comes to that."

"Are you?" I wrinkled my nose at him. "Aunt Lydia might dispute that claim."

"I doubt it. We've put aside many of our differences over the past year."

"Then why haven't I seen you at our house since back in May? Your absence has been noted. Richard mentioned it just the other day. I told him you'd probably been out of the country on one of your art-buying trips, but I confess I've also wondered why you've become such a ghost."

Kurt stared at the row of books above my head. "It's true, I've been traveling a lot, but . . ." He cleared his throat. "There is another reason. Most of those gatherings included a certain art expert who asks rather probing, and often unwelcome, questions."

"Ah, Hugh." I pressed two fingers to my lips and considered my sixty-six-year-old aunt's significant other, Hugh Chen, for a moment. "You're not worried about him uncovering some shady dealings on your part, are you? I mean, not that I suspect you of engaging in such activities."

Kurt's lips curled, baring his large, white teeth. "I'm sure the thought has never crossed your very inquisitive mind, but yes—I prefer to keep some of my activities to myself. You know Hugh Chen has confessed to a long-term interest in my dealings in art acquisition and sales. So"—Kurt spread his hands wide —"I thought discretion was the better part of . . . well, not valor, I suppose."

"Expediency?" I suggested, widening my eyes and fluttering my lashes.

"Let's say prudence." Kurt shot me an amused smile. "And, just so you know, those innocent doe eyes don't quite work. That tactic might work for your friend Sunny, but for you . . . not so much."

I grimaced. "I've heard that before."

"I'm sure." Kurt glanced toward the circulation desk. "Where is Ms. Fields, by the way? Off today?"

Sunshine Fields was the only other paid library staff member, as well as my best friend. Although we typically covered the library hours together, there were times when we traded off, especially when our library volunteers were scheduled to work.

"No, but she told me she'd be in late. She had to run some errands for her grandparents. Do you know Carol and P.J. Fields?"

Kurt looked away, although not before I noticed his lashes lower to shadow his bright-blue eyes. "Of course, although we're not personally acquainted. But I'm aware that they run an organic farm outside of town. My chef often buys fresh fruits and vegetables from them. The farm has a picturesque name, as I recall."

"Vista View. It's been in P.J.'s family for generations and, unlike most land around here, has been continually farmed. Sunny's told me the whole story—P.J. inherited it, along with enough money to run the place, from his grandparents after his parents refused to move back from the city. People in Taylorsford thought P.J. would sell Vista View, since he was only eighteen at the time, but he surprised everyone and decided to take it on and turn it into an organic farm, although he and Carol also ran it as a commune for a few years back in the early sixties." I tipped my head and examined Kurt's rugged profile. "Were you still Paul Dassin's foster son when Carol and P.J. started up the commune? I think that was in 1962 or '3. It was the talk of the town, according to Aunt Lydia, so I bet you would've heard something of it."

"No, I left Paul's house in the early sixties, right after I turned eighteen, so I wasn't in the area at that point." Kurt took a deep breath. Turning back to face me, he offered up a smile that once again reminded me of the wolf in one of the library's picture books. "Do you think your assistant will be in soon? I only ask because I actually dropped by the library expressly to see her."

I drummed my fingers against my thigh. "I wondered what brought you here. I knew it wasn't for resources on art. We have a decent collection for a small public library, but having been to your home, I'm well aware that your personal collection is more extensive than what we could ever hope to shelve on that subject."

"It is, and I even own numerous tomes on Caravaggio." Kurt winked before tugging the sleeves of his tailored woolen jacket over his crisp white shirt cuffs. "No, as you guessed, I'm not here for the library resources. The truth is, I was in town on other business and just dropped in to see if I might talk to Ms. Fields."

I examined his expression for a moment but couldn't read anything there. Which didn't surprise me. What concerned me was what Kurt wanted with Sunny. I couldn't imagine why he'd want to talk to her, and given some of my previous encounters with the art dealer, it made me a bit uncomfortable to guess. "Really? What about?"

"I want to make a contribution to her mayoral bid."

"That's very generous of you," I said, continuing to eye him, now with suspicion. Somehow, Kurt Kendrick supporting a political campaign seemed out of character.

"Not really. I heartily dislike the current mayor—probably for the same reasons you do. I can't imagine Sunshine Fields doing a worse job running Taylorsford than Bob Blackstone. In fact, I expect her to make some much-needed improvements."

"I'm sure she will, if she gets elected. Anyway, you can talk to Zelda Shoemaker about contributions. She's Sunny's campaign manager."

"Ah yes, I'd heard something about that."

Of course he had. I leaned back against one of the bookshelf posts. "I'm surprised you didn't already think to make your donation through Zelda."

Kurt shrugged. "I prefer not to be trapped by Ms. Shoemaker's quite entertaining, but often endless, chatter."

I grinned. Zelda Shoemaker, Taylorsford's former postmistress, was my aunt's best friend. She possessed a warm, generous nature, and I loved her dearly, but I had to admit that she did relish sharing gossip. "There is that. But if you want to hand over a check, you'll have to deal with her. Sunny isn't accepting any money directly. She says she doesn't want to touch any of the contributions, just in case that could be misconstrued as improper handling of funds."

"Quite right." Kurt flashed a toothy smile. "You see, she *does* have the smarts for the job, even if she is a little on the young side."

"Her intelligence was never in doubt, was it? And as for being young, she's a year older than me and I'm thirty-five. Hardly a babe in the woods."

Kurt looked me up and down. "A mere child, compared to me, although I admit that you and your friend occasionally display a surprising amount of common sense for your age."

"Occasionally?" I wrinkled my nose at him, but he ignored me, his attention apparently captured by something on the opposite wall.

"You convinced Emily Moore to do a reading and signing? How did you manage that coup?" he asked.

I turned to face the flyer posted near the main doors. An older woman, her square face framed by a sleek bob and her dark eyes encircled with large tortoiseshell eyeglass frames, gazed owlishly back at me.

"Oh, that was no trouble at all. She moved to Taylorsford recently, you know."

"Did she?" Kurt's thick white eyebrows came together over his nose. "I'm surprised. She always seemed like such an urbanite. All her novels and poetry give that impression, anyway."

"Well, you're pretty sophisticated, and you live here," I pointed out.

"Yes, but not exclusively."

"Anyway, Ms. Moore is quite nice and very sweet . . ."

"Unlike me," Kurt said.

"Unlike you. And, also unlike you, she didn't hide out for a few years before introducing herself around her new town. She actually came in and offered to do something to benefit the library before I even had the chance to visit her. She said she wanted to get involved in the community and thought the library was the best place to start." I glanced up, noting Kurt's stoic expression. "I thought surely you would've heard that she bought that Craftsman only a few blocks from here—the one that needed so much work. But I guess, like you, she has the funds to take on a fixer-upper."

"I'm sure." Kurt gave his jacket sleeves another tug. "It seems my little birds have failed me this time. I'd heard that she was teaching a few courses at Clarion University, but I honestly didn't know she'd moved to Taylorsford."

"You'll have to give your spies a talking to," I said with a smile. "By the way, I was trying to purchase copies of all her books for the collection, but there's one I just can't buy. Her first book of poetry, the one that made her famous. Or infamous, I suppose you could say."

"The one that was only available as a special printing issued by Andy Warhol's Factory back in 1965? No, I don't suppose you can afford to purchase one of those."

"You wouldn't happen to have one in your collection, would you? As I recall from my research, the book did include illustrations."

"Not by Warhol, although it's still quite valuable due to the association. But no, I don't have a copy of that particular book. I wish I did, honestly. So few were produced that it's quite a rarity."

"Apparently. Even Clarion couldn't get one. I checked with the university library, and they told me that all they have is a photocopy, and that's only used for research, not circulated." I looked back at the poster, examining Emily Moore's square, strong-jawed face. "I'm surprised that she hasn't had the poetry itself reissued in another format, but apparently she's never bothered to do so. With the popularity of her later poetry and novels, you'd think it would sell."

"Perhaps she prefers to keep an air of mystery about her beginnings. Some people do."

"As you should know," I said, as a clatter made me turn toward the circulation desk. "Looks like your mission might prove successful after all. There's Sunny now."

The noise I'd heard was Sunny dropping her keys onto the hard surface of the antique wooden desk. Kurt shortened his long stride to keep pace with me as I walked over to meet her.

Sunny shoved her keys into the macrame pouch she often used as a purse before sliding the pouch under the desk. "Sorry I'm so late, Amy. I didn't think completing all the errands on the grands' list would take so long."

"Not a problem." I stepped behind the desk to stand beside her. "It's been fairly quiet in here today. In fact, Mrs. Dinterman and Kurt have been the only patrons in the building for the last half hour."

Sunny flipped her shining fall of golden hair behind her slender shoulders. "Oh hi, Mr. Kendrick. How are you? Checking out some books?"

"No, I actually stopped by to see you. I was planning to give you a check for your election campaign, but"—he shrugged—"Amy tells me all the contributions must go through Zelda Shoemaker."

Widening her blue eyes, Sunny cast him a bright smile. "Thanks so much, and yes, Zelda's handling all that. You know how it is—things can get unpleasant during an election. I decided early on that I didn't want to touch a cent. Can't have Mayor Blackstone claiming that I mishandled any campaign funds. He's always digging for dirt on me as it is."

"Or making it up," I muttered. Despite the fact that our current mayor had been embroiled in scandals of his own, he seemed determined to paint my friend in a bad light.

"I agree. Knowing the man as I do, he'd be likely to take any opportunity to spread rumors. Without checking first to see if there's any truth in them." Kurt gave Sunny a little nod. "I applaud your wisdom."

"It helps to know who I'm dealing with. But I refuse to lob any dirt at Blackstone in return, although I have much more ammunition." Sunny grinned. "As my grandma often says, never get in a stink match with a skunk."

Kurt's laughter rose up to the wooden rafters of our 1919 library building. "Indeed," he said at last, after wiping his eyes with a cotton handkerchief. "Excellent advice."

"Well, if I have to smear my opponent to win rather than get elected on my own merits, I don't want the job," Sunny continued.

Kurt shot me a quick glance before turning his piercing gaze on Sunny. "Speaking of jobs, what will you do about this one if you do win the election?"

"I hope to keep working here. That is, if Amy will have me." Sunny absently spun her enameled metal bracelets around her wrist as she looked up at me from beneath lowered lashes. "We haven't really worked all of that out, but I do want to stay in the library job. I think I can handle both, although . . ."

"I know, you might have to drop back to part-time," I replied, releasing a gusty sigh. "And I'll have to find someone to work your other hours."

"I'm sure there are several people in town who'd like a part-time job."

"Yeah, but they could never replace you," I replied with such vehemence that Kurt raised his eyebrows and Sunny's cheeks flushed. "You know these collections better than anyone. Better even than me. I'm not going to find someone else who possesses that extensive knowledge."

Sunny leaned in and patted the hand I'd pressed against the countertop. "Maybe, but I'll still be around, I promise."

My foot, resting next to the macrame purse, vibrated from the loud music blaring from Sunny's cell phone. "You want to get that? I realize the rule is no phones at the desk, but since there's no one here right now . . ."

Kurt coughed.

"No one who will care, I mean." I cast him a smile before grabbing Sunny's purse and handing it to her. "Go on—I know that ring."

"Yeah, it's the grands. Again." Sunny pulled a comical face as she fished her phone out of the pouch. "They aren't usually this needy, but ever since the county started that dredging work on the creek, they've been calling nonstop. They're so worried about damage to the trees and shrubs along the stream bed."

"Of course." I'd heard plenty about this from Carol and P.J., who were irate over the heavy equipment that had recently descended upon their quiet organic farm. The fact that the county had a right-of-way to the creek, which was part of a larger watershed, did nothing to appease their anger.

"Government barreling in and taking over, like usual," P.J. had told me, his thin lips quivering with repressed rage. "Didn't even inform us ahead of time. Just showed up one day and proceeded to rip up my fields with their equipment. Well, they'd better not destroy our trees along the creek, that's all I've got to say."

I shook my head. "Can't say I blame them." I directed my words to Kurt as Sunny listened intently to her phone. "The county's been tearing up the stream banks all along its route."

Kurt's expression betrayed no emotion, but his jaw tightened. That was odd. The art dealer rarely appeared tense, even in the direst of circumstances, yet the mention of dredging a creek seemed to have distressed him. It piqued my curiosity.

Or maybe I was imagining things. I shook my head to clear my thoughts. "They say it benefits the environment because it allows for better runoff from nearby rivers and ponds. But I don't know. It seems rather destructive to me."

When Kurt replied, his voice was as calm and charming as ever. "I knew that the dredging work was ongoing but didn't realize it involved that farm."

"Yeah, unfortunately." I glanced at Sunny and noticed that all the color had fled her face. "Anything wrong?"

Sunny's fingers clutched her cell phone so tightly I worried she might crack the plastic case. "Yes. Not with the grands, thank goodness, but dredging crews found something on the farm."

"Buried treasure?" I asked, with a quick glance at Kurt.

"No, not anything like that." Sunny's voice shook. "According to the grands, an operator swung his Bobcat bucket the wrong way and dug deep into the bank, up and away from the stream. And that's when they found it."

"Found what?" I asked, my gaze flitting from Sunny's trembling lips to the carved-in-stone stillness of Kurt's face and back again.

"Bones," Sunny said. "Human bones." She stared at me, her eyes as glazed as glass. "An entire skeleton."

Chapter Two

After I sent a frazzled Sunny home, I waited until Kurt left the library before dashing to the computer to poke around on the Internet. I hoped to find some historical reason for human bones to turn up at Vista View. *It's possible,* I reasoned, *that was once the site of a Native American settlement, or part of some long-abandoned homestead.*

Unfortunately, I found nothing to back up such suppositions. Most of the hits on Vista View either discussed the conversion of the property to an organic farm or announced special events the Fields family had held at the farm over the years. The only other mention was buried in a missing-person report in the digitized version of Taylorsford's now-defunct local paper.

I peered at the computer screen. The article was from 1965, and the farm had merited only one sentence: ADAMS BRIEFLY LIVED ON A COMMUNE ON THE LOCAL VISTA VIEW PROPERTY, BUT HE LEFT SEVERAL MONTHS BEFORE HIS SUPPOSED DISAPPEARANCE, ACCORDING TO THE OWNERS OF THE PROPERTY, CAROL AND P.J. FIELDS.

Printing out the article, I shoved it into the pocket of my linen slacks just as a group of high school students entered the library.

Assisting them with their history homework and checking out books to other patrons kept me busy for the remainder of the day. I was thankful this was a Tuesday, one of the days when the library closed at five o'clock. Not only was I tired, I was also anxious to get home and query my aunt about the nineteen-year-old man mentioned in the report.

Adams. I knew someone with that last name, but warned myself not to jump to conclusions about any connection to Walter Adams, who was my aunt Lydia's friend and Zelda Shoemaker's significant other. It was a common surname, after all. But I'd certainly question my aunt about this nugget of information. If there was a familial relationship between Walt and the missing young man—I stared at the printed article to remind myself of his full name—this *Jeremy Adams*, Aunt Lydia would know.

As soon as five o'clock rolled around, I ushered out any lingering patrons, closed up the library, and hurried home. I'd walked to work that day, as I often did. Since the library was close enough to allow me to walk on all but the worst weather days and Aunt Lydia didn't drive that much, it made sense for us to share a car rather than pay for the gas and upkeep on two vehicles. Walking to work allowed my aunt access to the car most days.

I honestly didn't mind the trek from the center of our historic town to our family home. My walk led from a downtown district that featured small businesses and church properties through a few residential blocks. I'd always enjoyed my stroll in this charming section of town, which was dominated by elegant turn-of-the century Victorians. There were also several Craftsman-style bungalows, and even a few more modern homes, all of which boasted well-kept front yards that were typically enclosed by rose- or vine-covered fences. As a gardener, I found the ever-changing flowers and shrubs along the route a delightful diversion on my walk to and from work.

On this September day, the air was heavy with the spicy fragrance of late-season flowers, blooming profusely as if staking a valiant stand against the oncoming frost. I gazed up into the canopy of trees that lined the sidewalks. As it was still so early, autumnal color barely tinged the tips of the green foliage.

Stubbing my toe on a broken piece of concrete, I swore and dropped my gaze to the sidewalk. Our current mayor, Bob Blackstone, had vowed upon being elected to replace the crumbling concrete with brick pavers, but despite his ten years in office, he had never fulfilled this promise.

Sunny could do better, I thought. *Give her a mission and she'll accomplish it, come what may.* Squaring my shoulders, I increased my pace and vowed to contribute more time to my friend's campaign.

When I reached the Queen Anne Revival home that I shared with my Aunt Lydia, I paused with my hand on the front-yard gate. The house had remained in our family since it was built in 1900, passed down from my great-grandmother Rose Baker Litton to her granddaughter, my aunt, Lydia Litton Talbot. I shaded my eyes and studied the three-story structure. Despite having been proclaimed one of the most beautiful homes in Taylorsford, it was showing its age. Although the gingerbread trim had recently been repainted, its crisp white sheen now sadly highlighted an issue with the fieldstone body of the house. I sighed, absently brushing a lock of my dark-brown hair behind one ear as I lowered my hand. The mortar needed repointing, but that would have to wait. Painting the trim had exhausted Aunt Lydia's meager upkeep budget, and my library director's salary, while enough to cover my personal needs, was hardly extravagant. I could help Aunt Lydia with general expenses, but my savings were insufficient to fund any extensive renovation projects.

As I opened the picket fence gate, I glanced at the house next door. Its neatly trimmed lawn was separated from ours by a taller section of fence draped in climbing roses. Our neighbor's copper-colored car sat in the driveway next to his renovated 1920s farmhouse. The sight brought a smile to my face. It seemed that, for once, Richard hadn't been required to work late.

My fiancé as well as our neighbor, Richard Muir was a contemporary dancer and choreographer. He was also an instructor at nearby Clarion University and often got corralled into helping with the technical aspects of his dance colleagues' student recitals. The other instructors took advantage of his talent for hanging lights and running the light board. As I'd told him more than once, he needed to learn to say no. But Richard, who was sometimes too nice for his own good, usually agreed to help, no matter how many extra hours it added to his workday.

I closed the gate behind me before bounding across the small front yard and up the stone steps that led to our wraparound covered porch. Clucking my tongue, I pushed open the wooden front door with its inset antique windowpanes. It was unlocked, which merited another lecture to Aunt Lydia about security. Of course, she'd claim she was "perfectly safe, thank you," especially if Richard had already arrived home, but I'd still admonish her. Taylorsford had seen more than its fair share of crime, including murders, over the past couple of years.

"Hello," I called out as I dropped my keys into the ceramic bowl on the hall table. "Anybody home?"

"In the sunroom," Richard responded, his clear baritone voice sailing out from the back of the house.

I shrugged off my light jacket and hung it on the hall tree. "I hope you have some wine uncorked," I said as I made my way down the center hall to the back porch, which had been enclosed to form an all-season sunroom.

Richard sprang up from the metal-framed glider as I entered. "We even saved you a glass or two." He crossed to me in three long strides. "How was your day?"

"Interesting," I said.

He kissed me before stepping back to study my face. "Interesting? That sounds ominous."

"Yes, nothing good ever comes after *interesting*." Aunt Lydia sat up in her rocker and motioned toward a tall, narrow table that held a few bottles of wine and one empty glass. "Help yourself. I think the Chardonnay is still cold."

"It's chilled enough for me, I'm sure." I crossed to the table and poured myself a full glass before waving the bottle at Richard. "Are you drinking red or white? There seems to be more red left, if that affects your decision."

"Red, and don't worry, I brought over extra bottles of both." Richard flashed a grin before joining me at the table to refill his empty glass. "What about you, Lydia?"

"I'm fine." My aunt swirled the white wine in her crystal goblet.

"So how was your day?" I asked, meeting her inquisitive gaze. "I smelled the lovely aroma of apple pie when I came in, so I assume you've been testing some more recipes?"

"Yes, trying some different proportions of ingredients to see what works best."

Richard carried his wine glass over to the glider. "Is there a reason for all this pie baking?"

"The county fair is coming up at the end of the month." I followed Richard, setting my wine glass on one of the tile-topped side tables that flanked the glider. "Three weeks from this Saturday, to be precise. Aunt Lydia always participates in one of the baking competitions. This year she's concentrating on pies," I said as I sat beside him.

"I see. Trying to win some blue ribbons, I suppose." Richard used his glass to salute Aunt Lydia.

"Yes, and the competition will be stiff, so I need to make sure I have the best recipe," she said. "I don't know everyone who plans to enter, but I know I'm going up against Jane Tucker and Carol Fields for sure, and they are tough to beat."

"I'm sure they feel the same about you," I said.

"Maybe. Anyway, it's all in good fun." My aunt took a sip of wine before speaking again. "But enough about my mundane activities. You've piqued my curiosity, Amy. What was so interesting about today?"

"Nothing to do with the library, fortunately." I pulled the printout from my pocket. "It has to do with what the county workers discovered at Vista View. They found something shocking where they're dredging out the stream."

Richard cradled his glass between his hands. "Buried treasure, I hope. Or at least something that will benefit Carol and P.J. Fields."

"Sadly, no."

"It was something unpleasant, then?" Aunt Lydia took a long swallow of her wine.

"Unfortunately, yes. They apparently dug up some human bones. Actually, from what Sunny told me, an entire skeleton."

Richard paused with his glass at his lips. "Seriously?" He took a drink before setting down his glass.

"Yeah. I don't know if they're ancient or relatively recent or what, but it's a bit unnerving, either way." I unfolded the paper and waved it through the air. "I think it could be connected to this old story."

Aunt Lydia's blue eyes narrowed. "What's that?"

I smoothed out the folds of the paper. "I did a little online sleuthing to see if I could figure out why human bones might turn up at that location. I figured that maybe it could be something archeological, but . . ."

Richard draped his arm around my shoulders. "You found something else?"

"I did, but I don't know if it's connected in any way. It's simply the only reference I could find to Vista View that wasn't directly related to selling organic produce." I tapped the paper with one finger. "It seems someone who lived on the commune disappeared. According to this article, he'd left the farm several months before he was reported missing, but it just seems odd . . ."

Aunt Lydia stood up and set her wine glass on the side table near the bank of windows offering a view of her garden. "Not Jeremy Adams?"

"You knew him?"

"I knew of him." My aunt's somber expression took me by surprise. "He was Walt's first cousin. He was older by about nine or ten years, but Walt talked about Jeremy incessantly when we were kids. He idolized him." Aunt Lydia, obviously lost in thought, stared over our heads as if transfixed by the stone wall behind the glider. "Jeremy Adams was a musician. He could play almost any instrument, although he was particularly brilliant on guitar. He sang and wrote songs as well. When we were children, Walt often talked about Jeremy becoming the next rock superstar."

I squinted at the small type of the article. "According to this, the family didn't file a missing-person report immediately. They waited until early 1965, claiming they'd hesitated because they'd lost contact with Jeremy at least a year before. They'd known he was living at Vista View, but since he'd never contacted any of them during that time, they didn't know exactly when he'd left the commune or where he'd planned to go."

Aunt Lydia sat back down in the rocker. "Walt always thought he ended up in LA. He said Jeremy had often talked about moving out there to pursue his music career."

I dropped the paper into my lap. "But he never contacted Walt or any of the family again?"

"Only once, and early on, right after he left the commune. Walt was pretty broken up about that when we were kids. He couldn't understand why his beloved cousin would cut all ties, but . . ." Aunt Lydia frowned and twisted the hem of her raspberry silk blouse between her fingers. "Walt later found out Jeremy had a pretty serious drug problem. After that, Walt decided Jeremy must have died out in LA from an overdose, or from violence connected to a drug deal, or something like that."

I slid closer to Richard. Aunt Lydia looked distressed, which didn't surprise me. Her husband—my uncle Andrew Talbot, who'd died back in the late seventies—had also struggled with a drug habit. Although the drugs hadn't been what killed him, I knew the memory of his addiction still troubled my aunt.

Richard, obviously on the same wavelength, stroked my shoulder blade. "That had to be hard for the family—never knowing."

"It was tough. In fact, Walt still mentions Jeremy occasionally, questioning what really happened to him. I mean, it was the sixties, and there was a lot of racial tension back then. I got the feeling from Walt that, as one of the only black families in Taylorsford, they always assumed the sheriff's department wasn't too invested in the case. So maybe not as much was done to find Jeremy as it might've been if he'd been white. But after all this time, you have to assume the person is dead." Aunt Lydia crossed one slender ankle over the other. "Anyway, I doubt those bones discovered today have anything to do with Jeremy, because Walt did hear from him after he'd already left Vista View. Just one phone call, but Walt said Jeremy told him he was on the road, headed west."

"So, unless he was lying to Walt, he wasn't likely to turn up as a skeleton at Vista View." Richard glanced at me. "I know that's where your inquiring mind has wandered, Amy."

"Can you blame me, after the other murders and suspicious deaths we've encountered over the last few years?"

"No, I can't. By the way, speaking of suspicious"—Richard slid his arm away from me and straightened—"my mother's been sending texts about various locales that are 'suitable for an elegant reception,' as she puts it. You haven't been encouraging her, I hope?" The smile he gave me before picking up his wine glass took the sting out of his question.

"Hardly. And, for your information, she's been bombarding me with the same sort of texts." I scooted over to the other side of the glider to grab my own glass. "I think she's afraid we're going to wait until it's too late to line up an appropriate venue."

"It's not her wedding," my aunt observed.

"Try telling her that." I chugged my drink.

"She does like to manage things." Richard took a swallow of wine before adding, "It usually doesn't work on me, so I guess she's widening her net to include Amy."

I slid back beside him. “She’s in for a disappointment, then. I really don’t want to hold our reception in an echoing ballroom in some overly lavish hotel. For one thing, there isn’t anything close to Taylorsford that fits that description, and I refuse to force our guests to navigate city traffic just to attend our reception.”

“She did mention that there’s a winery the next county over that has a banquet hall,” Richard said. “But even that’s a drive.”

Aunt Lydia drummed her fingers against the arm of her wooden rocker. “Were you considering holding the ceremony at Holy Trinity?”

I sipped my wine before meeting her piercing gaze. “Maybe.”

“Mom does approve, shockingly.” Richard flashed a wry smile. “I guess, being Episcopal, it’s ‘high church’ enough for her. Although she did question whether it would hold enough people, since, as she told me, ‘it’s probably small, being out there in the country.’”

I tightened my lips before I could express my thoughts about that comment.

Aunt Lydia had no such qualms. “Honestly, does Fiona think we’re all bumpkins? Her own uncle lived here for decades, for goodness’ sake.”

“She considered that a mistake,” Richard said. “She used to complain about inheriting Great-Uncle Paul’s house, saying it was impossible to find decent renters. She even tried to sell it a couple of times but never received an offer big enough to suit her.”

I leaned over him to set my empty glass on his side table. “Thank goodness, or she and your dad would never have signed the house over to you and we wouldn’t have become neighbors.”

“True. I’m grateful for that stroke of luck.” Richard pulled a comical face before leaning in to kiss my temple. “Extremely grateful,” he whispered in my ear before straightening.

"Me too." I lifted my hand to admire my engagement ring. It dated from the late 1800s and featured a square-cut diamond sunk into a filigree setting of white gold studded on all sides with tiny diamond chips. "I'm still shocked that Fiona offered this to you when she heard about our engagement."

Aunt Lydia sat forward in her rocker. "It is beautiful. I've always preferred vintage rings over the newer styles. I'm not fond of the ones with the diamond just perched in a pronged setting." She rose to her feet and turned to the side table. "And as for Richard's mom being gracious for once, well, that doesn't seem so odd to me. From my conversations with her, I can tell that Fiona's quite enamored of preserving family history. Since the ring originally belonged to Richard's great-grandmother and he's an only child, it made sense for him to inherit it."

"It was actually bequeathed to my great-uncle Paul first," Richard said, standing and striding across the porch to help Aunt Lydia collect items from the table. "I imagine my great-grandmother thought he'd eventually marry, but he never did, and since he didn't have any children, it was eventually passed down to my mom."

"Paul Dassin did have a foster child." As I crossed to join them at the table, my thoughts leapt to a mental image of Kurt Kendrick, known as Karl Klass back when he had been fostered by Richard's great-uncle Paul Dassin.

"That's true, but I suppose Paul decided to bequeath the ring to Fiona after Kurt left town when he was eighteen." Aunt Lydia walked past me, an empty bottle in each hand. "I can certainly understand why, since Kurt never contacted Paul again after he left. Besides," she said, pausing in the doorway, "even without the disappearing act, I suspect Paul Dassin wouldn't have given Kurt the ring. He probably assumed Kurt was unlikely to marry."

"He could today." Richard crossed the room with the corkscrew dangling from his fingers and my aunt's wine glass clutched in his other hand. "But yeah, back then I guess it wouldn't have occurred to my great-uncle that it was a possibility."

"Thank you," Aunt Lydia said, as Richard met her at the door. "Just bring those things along to the kitchen, dear. And Amy, if you could collect the other two glasses . . ." My aunt sailed out of the room, followed by Richard.

"Sure thing," I replied, but lingered for a moment, staring out the tall windows that lined the back wall of the sun porch.

Aunt Lydia's entire backyard was a garden. Vibrant beds filled with vegetables, herbs, and flowers were set in a grid pattern, separated from one another by paths of gleaming white pea gravel. At the far edge of the yard, a narrow grove of trees created a living backdrop in shades of green, while the gently rolling Blue Ridge Mountains rimmed the tops of the trees with dusty purple.

The jangle of our landline phone shook me out of my reverie. "I'll get it," I called out. As I jogged into the hall, I made a mental note to go back for the wine glasses.

The voice on the other end was a surprise. "Hello, Amy," Chief Deputy Brad Tucker said. "Sorry to bother you at home, but I just wondered if you'd be willing to help me with a little research. Nothing major; just a little digging into the past."

"You had me at *research*," I said. "Are you going to reinstate my temporary deputy status too?"

"I was thinking more along the lines of using you as a consultant."

"Unpaid, of course."

"Of course." A hint of humor infused Brad's deep voice.

"What do you need?"

"Well—and this is strictly off the record, you understand—our forensic experts have noted that the skeleton's skull was bashed in, most likely by some heavy object. Which suggests foul play. Of course, they're now working on the identification. It will probably require dental records, and that means canvassing all the dental offices in the region. Which might not even help, especially if the bones belong to someone from outside the area. But we have to start somewhere."

I wrapped the long phone cord around my free hand. "What can I do?"

"Maybe nothing. But if you could do a little research in the town archives and any other places you think appropriate and look for mentions of disappearances in the sixties or early seventies, it might narrow down the list of possibilities. It helps if we can target specific people and then focus on a likely dental practice or two, rather than having to go through hundreds of records from numerous dentists."

"Sure, I can do that." I glanced toward the kitchen. "Should I keep this under wraps?"

"If you don't mind." Brad cleared his throat. "Especially from Sunny."

"Because you're afraid her grandparents might've had some involvement in this case?"

"No comment on that."

I frowned. I didn't like keeping secrets from my friend, but I understood the reason for Brad's request. If Carol and P.J. had had any involvement in the events that had resulted in a skeleton being found on their property, he couldn't risk involving their granddaughter. "All right, I'll see what I can find."

"Thanks. Just contact me directly if you discover anything."

"I expect you already know about that Jeremy Adams case," I said.

Brad paused and exhaled before answering me. "Yes, of course. Thanks again, Amy," he added, before saying goodbye.

I stared at the phone receiver for a second, wondering if the sheriff's office already suspected that the bones might belong to Walt's cousin.

Walt Adams had claimed that Jeremy had headed out west immediately after he left the commune. But Walt had been a child blinded by a major case of hero worship. Jeremy could've lied about being on his way to LA and Walt would've believed him.

I walked back into the sunroom, my mind a jumble of conflicting thoughts. I wanted to help Brad, and the investigation, especially if doing so would remove any suspicion from the Fields family.

But I also knew it might not. In fact, I was afraid it could easily produce the opposite effect.

Chapter Three

The following day, the news about bones being found at Vista View was all anyone at the library wanted to discuss.

At least most of the library patrons had the common decency not to say anything in front of Sunny. But as I walked to the back door, I caught a glimpse of a slight blonde woman in the children's room. I paused to listen to the gossip Elspeth Blackstone, the mayor's wife, was sharing about Carol and P.J. Fields and their farm.

"It was a commune back in the sixties, you know," Elspeth told Samantha Green, one of our regular patrons. "Heaven only knows what went on there. Strange rituals and lots of sex and drugs, I bet."

Samantha shot a quick glance at me before grabbing her daughter's hand. "I doubt that. Come on, Shay, you have enough for now, and I still need to look for some books before we check out." She pulled a protesting Shay away from the shelves that housed our middle-grade fiction.

"It wouldn't surprise me. Those two old hippies are still a little odd," Elspeth said.

Samantha ignored her and guided Shay, whose arms were laden with books, toward the French doors that led to the main part of the library. She rolled her dark eyes as she walked past me.

I stared at the mayor's wife, noticing the self-satisfied smile that had twisted her thin lips. Only in her forties, Elspeth had already resorted to plastic surgery or at least Botox, if the tightness of her skin at the corners of her hazel eyes was any indication. "How's that? You weren't even alive when the commune was active."

Elspeth flashed me a haughty look as she placed her hands on her narrow hips. "True, but my parents were. And they've told me plenty of stories."

I bet they have, I thought. I'd dealt with Elspeth's mother, Sheila Pembroke, when she'd been active with our Friends of the Library group. Having quickly decided that a more opinionated and judgmental person would be difficult to find, I hadn't been upset when Sheila left the group following the rather traumatic events of the previous fall.

"I think it's best to wait for an official report from the sheriff's office before jumping to any conclusions." I eyed the other woman with suspicion. It wouldn't be out of character for the Blackstones to use this discovery to sabotage my friend's mayoral race. "And now, if you'll excuse me, I'd better go. I have some work to do in the archives."

I turned on my heel and left the room before Elspeth could reply.

Making my way outside, I crossed the gravel parking lot to reach the archives, which were housed in a small stone building behind the library. Once the home of the original library director, it had been converted to hold town records and memorabilia.

Before unlocking the door, I brushed my fingers over the new bronze plaque that had been installed on the side of the building. The larger inscription read THE GREYSON-FRYE ARCHIVES. It was followed by smaller script that declared: HONORING TOWN RESIDENTS ADA FRYE AND VIOLET GREYSON, WHO TRAGICALLY LOST THEIR LIVES IN 1879.

Entering the single-room building, I immediately flicked on the overhead fixture. There was no natural light, as shelving stuffed with archival-grade banker's boxes lined the walls of the interior, covering the windows. This was no mistake, as the lack of sunlight also protected the archival materials from harmful UV rays.

I'd come out to the archives to follow a hunch that had occurred to me that morning, over a plate of Aunt Lydia's delicious French toast. Brad needed information on missing persons, and I wanted to make certain Jeremy Adams had actually left town after departing the commune. To help with both goals, I'd decided to examine the town's historical photographs collection.

I pulled down a box labeled 1963–65 and lifted out one of the smaller interior boxes that held photographs. Slipping on a pair of white cotton gloves, I flipped through the pictures, hoping to find photos of Jeremy Adams from around the time he'd disappeared.

It might've seemed odd to anyone else, but I knew a clear photograph would aid my search for further information. To successfully conduct online image searches, I needed a better starting point than the grainy newspaper photo I'd discovered with the missing-person article. With a clearer picture for reference, it would be easier for me to pick out Jeremy from any photographs I might find online. I'd already bookmarked some archival collections documenting the LA music scene in the 1960s and planned to start there.

Although I knew I still needed to check our other records for any additional disappearances around the same time, if I could at least prove that Jeremy Adams had left for LA, as Walt claimed,

I could tell Brad to eliminate any connection between him and the skeleton found at Vista View. *Not an easy task, but perhaps possible*, I reminded myself as I examined the photographs. Sure, it would be like sifting through all the sand on a beach to find a tiny diamond. But that was often the case with research—hours, days, or even months invested in digging through information just to discover one essential gem.

I wouldn't be deterred, even though I knew such searches often ended in futility. The less-than-stellar odds never quelled my desire to sleuth for answers. The miniscule chance for success was part of the joy of the hunt.

Searching through the files, I noticed that many of the photos had been taken during the Heritage Festival, which had been held in Taylorsford every October since the 1940s. I squinted, carefully examining every photo from the mid to late sixties. Despite the helpful identifications of local residents that had been jotted across the backs of some of the pictures, there were also many unknown visitors. But one photo that included a tall African-American man with a guitar slung over his shoulder caught my eye. I flipped it over.

Swallowing back a whoop of excitement, I read the inscription, which identified the young man as Jeremy Adams. I glanced at the date—October 1964.

Placing the photo on the large worktable that dominated the center of the room, I pulled the printout of the article on Jeremy's disappearance from my pocket. A quick read confirmed my memory—Jeremy had supposedly left the commune, and Taylorsford, in August of that year.

I frowned as I picked up the photograph again, aware that I might be holding the proof Brad needed. Despite Walt's recollection of a phone call from the road, his older cousin had not immediately headed out to the West Coast. I tapped the beveled edge of the photo against my gloved palm. Or, even if he'd told Walt the truth, Jeremy had obviously returned to Taylorsford that fall. Without informing Walt or any of his family.

I studied the photograph more closely. Jeremy Adams had been a handsome young man, with an intelligent expression and an infectious smile. Even in a photograph he exuded charisma.

Wish I could've known you, I thought, before shaking off a strange feeling that Jeremy was reaching out to me over the years, trying to convey some important information.

But that was just another one of my odd fancies, like the feeling that long-dead artists were at my elbow when I studied their works. It was something I'd felt before, although not, I had to admit, simply upon seeing a picture. I sighed and slipped the photograph into an acid-free folder, then slid the folder into a plain manila envelope.

Locking up the archives, I returned to the library. Crossing behind Sunny, who was busy checking out stacks of books to Shay Green and her mother, I hurried into the workroom and placed the manila folder under some statistical reports piled on one of my work shelves.

I forced a smile as I joined Sunny at the circulation desk.

"Have a great day," Sunny called out as Samantha and Shay headed for the exit.

"I'm done searching the archives for today," I told her.

"Did you find what you were looking for?"

"Not entirely. But I'll wait and do more digging later." I busied myself straightening a batch of flyers promoting our literacy programs so I wouldn't have to meet her eyes. "Oh—avoid the children's room, unless you like swimming with sharks."

Sunny arched her feathery golden brows. "As in the mayor's wife? Yeah, I saw that she had popped in there. But she's gone now."

I picked up some scattered bookmarks and shuffled them into a neat pile. "Good, because she was bending Samantha's ear with some of her nonsense. Fortunately, Samantha wasn't buying her rumors."

"Glad to hear it." Sunny tapped a pencil against the edge of the desk. "But I'm afraid a lot of people in town will be more receptive to Elspeth's particular brand of gossip."

"I don't know. Bob Blackstone isn't that popular, and neither is his wife."

"Maybe so, but something like this might sway undecided voters." Sunny jammed the pencil into a black metal cup that held other writing implements. "This discovery on our property is just the sort of scandal that could tip the race in Bob Blackstone's favor."

"Don't worry," I said, finally offering her what I hoped was an innocent smile. "It'll probably turn out to be something archeological. Those bones could've been buried there since before the town was incorporated."

Sunny frowned. "Alison doesn't think so. She told me—in confidence, of course—that they didn't appear old enough to have been in the ground that long. 'Seventy-five years, tops,' is what she said."

"You're besties with your ex's girlfriend now?" I twitched my lips. Alison Frye was a deputy in a neighboring county. She was also Brad Tucker's new girlfriend. "Anyway, how would she know that? She isn't assigned to Taylorsford."

"They called in some extra people to help with this case, and since Alison once worked in our county, she was one of the lucky ones." Sunny made a face. "And no, we aren't best friends, but we get along just fine. I saw her when I popped into the diner to grab a muffin this morning. She was meeting Brad for breakfast and he was late, so she and I chatted a bit."

"But Alison's no expert on such things. The state forensics team will have to give the definitive answer on the age of the skeleton."

"And maybe tell us who it is." Sunny twirled a long strand of golden hair around her finger. "That might be the crucial factor. If they can link it to someone from the area, I mean."

"I suppose." I hoped my face hadn't flushed from the knowledge of what I was hiding in the workroom. My brain warned me that I had to share the photograph with the chief deputy first, no matter what my heart said. "How are your grandparents doing?"

"Fine, I guess. They really haven't said too much." Sunny turned to me. "Oh, by the way, would you mind stopping by the farm after work today? The grands want to talk to you about something. I don't know if it has to do with the bones, but they insisted they needed to speak with both of us as soon as possible."

"Okay, sure," I said, mentally rearranging my plans. "I'll just text Aunt Lydia before I leave."

Sunny looked me over, her forehead furrowed. "And Richard, I assume?"

"Of course, but we weren't planning to see each other this evening. He has a late rehearsal at Clarion, so he's going to crash there tonight." I made a face. "I knew putting that folding cot in his office was a bad idea. Now his dance department colleagues just assume he'll stay as late as they want, whenever they want."

"What production is happening this early in the semester?"

"Some sort of charity thing to benefit the dance program's scholarship fund. No students involved—the instructors are dancing instead."

"Even Meredith Fox?"

I twitched my lips. Meredith had once been Richard's fiancée, and even though they'd broken up before we'd met, Sunny occasionally expressed concern over the beautiful auburn-haired dancer having been hired for a full-time position in Richard's department.

But then again, that might be because she's still conflicted over her own recent breakup with Brad, especially since he's already dating someone else.

I studied Sunny's drawn face. I knew how such disappointments could affect one's outlook, even if the breakup had been mutual, as it had been in Sunny and Brad's case. Given her close friendship with both of us, it wasn't surprising that Sunny would be concerned about anything affecting my relationship with Richard.

But I wasn't worried. I knew Richard no longer harbored any feelings for Meredith. "Yeah, although she and Richard aren't performing together this time. He invited Karla to dance with him instead."

"Cool, but she doesn't teach at Clarion, does she?"

"He was allowed to bring her in as a guest artist." I couldn't help but smile at the thought of Richard dancing with his favorite partner from his high school and conservatory days. Since Karla had disappeared from his life after college, it was something that hadn't happened for years. Fortunately, when they'd finally reconnected, they'd rekindled both their friendship and a new dance collaboration. "They'll be spectacular, of course. That might put Meredith's nose out of joint."

"Which you don't mind, despite your constant declaration that you're not worried about her working with Richard," Sunny said.

"Which I don't mind, but not for that reason." I shrugged. "I just find Meredith's superior attitude a little annoying. I mean, she *is* beautiful and talented and all, but"—I cast Sunny a warm smile—"so are you, and you don't act entitled."

"I had an advantage, being raised by the grands. Since they're some of the most down-to-earth people on the planet, they never put up with any superior nonsense from me." Sunny spun her stack of silver bracelets around her wrist. "They never allowed me to become a diva."

"Which is to their credit. Okay, unfortunately I need to work on some statistics for a town council report. Can you hold down the fort out here?"

"No problem," Sunny said, her bright eyes shadowed by her golden lashes.

I walked into the workroom and took a deep breath before I pulled the folder off the shelf and carried it over to the computer I used to compile statistics, write reports, and complete other library-related business.

After grabbing a pair of gloves from a cubby above the workstation, I slipped the photo out of its acid-free envelope and studied it again.

Jeremy Adams's handsome face smiled back at me, unaware of his fate, whatever it had turned out to be.

I pursed my lips and pulled my cell phone from my pocket. Brad Tucker needed to know about this photo, despite the possibility that it might focus the spotlight of suspicion on Carol and P.J. Fields.

Because if Jeremy had ended up dead, and had been ignobly buried in a forgotten grave, he deserved justice. No matter whom that implicated.

I took a deep breath and pressed the key that dialed the chief deputy's number.

Chapter Four

The wooden sign that identified Sunny's family farm as Vista View included a brightly colored graphic of a cornucopia filled with vegetables and fruit. Sunny had hand-painted the sign a few years earlier to replace a battered metal nameplate on one of the gateposts.

As I pulled into the driveway, I ignored the knot of people waving their cell phones. Reporters, no doubt lured by the mystery of the bones found on the property. *At least they had the decency to stay at the end of the lane rather than trespassing on P.J. and Carol's property,* I thought, as I lowered my head and refused to make eye contact. One female reporter stepped out into the lane, forcing me to stop my car, but a tall, loose-limbed man pulled her back onto the side of the road. As I headed away from them, I glanced in my rearview mirror and caught him admonishing the woman.

Driving up the gravel lane that led to the farmhouse, I calmed my nerves by admiring the neatly cultivated field of vegetable plants on my left and the meadow of orchard grass on my right. Carol and P.J. didn't believe in raising animals for meat, so they didn't use much of the hay they bailed from their fields. That allowed them to make a tidy profit selling it to area horse farms, supplementing their income from sales of organic fruits and vegetables.

I parked my car in a small gravel lot next to Sunny's canary-yellow Volkswagen Beetle and sat for a moment, my gaze fastened on the house but my thoughts drifting elsewhere. I'd dropped by Brad Tucker's office to show him Jeremy Adams's photo on my way to the farm. He'd thanked me for my help but had also asked me to continue my research, since he was not convinced the skeleton belonged to Jeremy, even if I seemed to think that was the case.

Why I felt so strongly about this, I couldn't really explain to Brad, or even to myself. Somehow it was as if Jeremy's photo had spoken to me, telling me it *was* his body that had been discovered at Vista View. It was irrational, of course, but I'd experienced enough strange sensations like this over the past few years to listen to that mysterious voice in my head. Especially where murders were concerned.

I sighed as I opened my car door. Brad had also asked me to share anything I might hear that could have a bearing on the case. I'd agreed, even knowing that I might have to make a difficult choice if Carol or P.J. said anything that could connect them with the investigation. I climbed out of my car, not sure I had made the right choice in agreeing to meet with my friends today.

The two-story farmhouse was a square box of a building, its simple wooden-siding facade enlivened by vivid yellow paint and delft-blue shutters. As I made my way to the front porch, I dodged a cluster of free-range chickens. Carol didn't believe in cooping up her hens, except at night, so stumbling over a few in the front yard was something I'd learned to expect.

"Hello," I called out as I entered the house through the unlocked front door. "It's just Amy."

An older woman hurried from the back of the house to greet me. "Nonsense. You're not *just* an anything," Carol Fields said. "Now come along, dear. We're all in the kitchen. I've put Sunny to work making pies."

"You too? I must warn you that Aunt Lydia is testing out recipes as well." I followed her short, plump figure down the hall. Sunny had inherited Carol's fair complexion, light hair, and blue eyes, but she'd gotten her slender frame and height from her grandfather. Carol was even shorter than me, and I was slightly below average height for a woman.

"Well, Lydia is a tough one to beat, and then there's Jane Tucker. They seem to alternate wins from year to year. I think Jane took home the largest number of blue ribbons last year, so I imagine Lydia is determined to best her this go-round." Carol shot me a smile as we entered the kitchen. "But maybe I'll be the dark horse this year and spoil both their plans."

"Hello, Amy, thanks for stopping by. I hope that flock of vultures at the end of the lane didn't pester you too much," said P.J. Fields, who was standing in the doorway that led to the pantry.

"No, but I'm sorry to see them camped out on your property," I replied. "That has to be nerve-racking."

With the swift efficiency of someone practiced in changing the subject, Carol spoke up, her voice so bright it was brittle. "So how goes the wedding planning?"

"Don't ask," I replied, a little more sharply than I'd intended.

Sunny, who was using her thumb and forefinger to create a scalloped edge on a pie crust, paused midpinch. She wrinkled her flour-dusted nose as she glanced from me to Carol. "Uh-oh, you've touched a sore spot, Grandma."

I shook out my tensed hands and joined Sunny at the yellow Formica-topped kitchen table. "Here, let me help." I grabbed a wooden rolling pin to flatten a ball of dough sitting on a piece of waxed paper. After a few moments spent exorcising my demons by rolling out the pastry, I looked up at Sunny's grandmother. "And sorry, Carol, I didn't mean to snap at you. It's just that everyone seems so concerned about my ability to handle my own affairs. It's like, just because I'm engaged, they think I've lost all capacity for logical thought."

Carol shoved a short strand of white hair behind her ear before crossing to one of the kitchen's aqua-blue counters. "No need to explain, dear. I know how nosy people can be." She glanced over at the pantry door, where her tall, skinny husband still had his back pressed against the doorjamb.

"Who's telling you how to arrange the wedding now?" P.J. asked, hooking his thumbs around the straps of his loose denim overalls.

"You mean besides my future mother-in-law, who keeps sending cryptic texts about choosing gold or silver chargers, as well as photos of far-too-expensive venues?" I grinned as Sunny made a face. "Mrs. Dinterman at the library yesterday, and someone at church on Sunday."

"Really?" P.J.'s gray eyes widened. "Not during the service, I hope."

"They weren't quite that bold. Aunt Lydia and I were just leaving when Mrs. Jordan cornered me and laid out all the rules for using the sanctuary for weddings. I found out later that she's just been elected as a deacon. I guess she assumed I'd want to get married at Aunt Lydia's church, but really"—I pressed the solid wood rolling pin with so much force that dough squeezed out between the edges of the waxed paper enclosing the pastry—"I don't have any idea how she even knew I was engaged."

Sunny's eyes sparkled with good humor. "Amy, this is Taylorsford. Surely you realize that everyone in town knows you and Richard are getting married." She tossed her long blonde braid behind her shoulders. "It's the most interesting news in Taylorsford since that last murder. Two thirty-something neighbors getting engaged, and one of them is Lydia Talbot's niece and the other is Paul Dassin's great-nephew? It's like a fairy tale. So darned romantic." Sunny shot me a roguish grin.

I frowned as I peeled the waxed paper away from my circle of dough. Sliding the translucent crust over the sugar- and cinnamon-dusted apples in the pie pan would be tricky. "Of course, what was I thinking? If nothing else, I'm sure Zelda spread the news far and wide."

Carol grabbed a pair of oven mitts off the counter. "No doubt about that."

"But at least it's good news. Now"—P.J. straightened and flashed a toothy smile—"we need to find a match for you, Miss Sunshine Fields."

Sunny shook her head. "As I've told you guys more than once, I don't want to marry anyone. Especially now that Amy's snagged the best guy in town."

I squinted in concentration as I maneuvered the pastry dough over the mound of fruit filling the bottom crust. "You had your chance, but as you informed me early on, you were only interested in Richard as a friend. I'm sure if you'd actually made a play for him, things might've turned out differently."

Sunny snorted. "Like that would've happened. He only had eyes for you from the moment he met us at the library. Anyway, right now I'm more interested in getting elected mayor than in dating." She cast me a significant glance. "I actually just received a rather magnanimous campaign donation."

"Oh, who from?" Carol asked as she crossed to the oven and popped open the door. "Darn it, I forgot again." She slapped her forehead with her mitt-covered hand. "I should've moved these racks around before I preheated the oven. It seems like I'm always doing stuff like that these days."

"Too much on your mind, I guess," I said, eyeing her with concern. Carol and P.J. were only in their midseventies, but I sometimes wondered if the effort required to run Vista View was taking a toll on their health. *And now with all this furor over the bones found on the farm . . .* I lifted my filled pie tin and carried it over to the counter next to the stove.

Sunny handed her own completed pie to Carol. "The donor was Kurt Kendrick, of all people. A pretty healthy sum, too. It will help a lot with our advertising."

I thought I saw Carol's shoulders tense as she slid the pies onto the rearranged oven racks. "My goodness, is that so? I must admit, he's the last person I would've expected." She straightened, but kept her back to us as she set the oven timer.

Walking past P.J. to head for the sink to wash my hands, I noticed how tightly his fingers clutched his overall straps. "Anyway," I said, "It's not that surprising. Kurt actively dislikes Bob Blackstone, so it isn't such a stretch."

"Maybe." P.J. strode over to the kitchen table and yanked out one of the chrome-framed chairs. "But you have to admit, it's odd. Never met the guy, but from what I've heard, that Kendrick fellow doesn't really seem like the type to get involved in ordinary town business." He dropped into the chair and motioned to the seat next to him. "Come and take a load off, Sunny-girl. You've earned a little break."

"And you want to talk to me about something," Sunny said, dusting the flour from her hands as she sat down.

After drying my own hands on a gingham kitchen towel, I leaned back against the weathered pine cabinets that lined one wall of the kitchen. "Me too, according to what Sunny told me. What's up?"

Carol fanned her flushed face with both hands. I couldn't blame her. Although it was September, the weather was stuck in summer mode. "First, can you adjust the temp on that thing, Amy?" She pointed at the air conditioner filling the lower half of a kitchen window. "I wish we could put in central air, but the ductwork would cost a fortune."

At the window, I fiddled with the knob on the clunky window unit. It rumbled ominously for a moment before cold air blasted my face. Carol and P.J. could really use a new air conditioner, but that wouldn't happen. They had a mantra—*Make do with little, make things last, don't give capitalists the cash.* I'd heard them express that sentiment so many times, I could've repeated it in my sleep.

"I'm guessing you need our help with searching old records or something," I said as I joined them at the kitchen table.

"Yeah, what's the deal?" Sunny fiddled with the tassels decorating the ends of the braided ties on her peasant blouse.

Carol traced a crack in the yolk-colored tabletop with one finger. "Well, P.J. and I just thought, you two being such great researchers and all, that maybe you could help us with a little investigation."

I took a seat at the table next to Carol, across from Sunny and her grandfather. "Related to that skeleton?"

"Yes, but not directly," P.J. replied. "We're actually more interested in tracking down some former members of our old commune."

I slid to the edge of my seat, my curiosity piqued. "Why's that?"

"To warn them, of course." Sunny sat back, looking from Carol to P.J. "That's what you want to do, right?"

"Yes," P.J. said. "We don't want them to be blindsided, especially if the authorities start poking around in the past."

I arched my eyebrows. "In case they have something to hide?"

Carol tapped the table with her short fingernails. "No, and don't you go putting that idea in anyone's head. We don't suspect our old friends of anything. We just don't like the idea that the cops might catch them unaware and interrogate them over something they don't have a clue about."

I managed to meet Sunny's amused gaze with a smile, but inside my stomach did a little flip. Carol and P.J. were playing innocent, but I could see the tension tightening their lips and jaws, even if Sunny was too blinded by her trust in them to see it.

They are definitely hiding something. I twisted my hands in my lap, wondering if they already had an inkling that the authorities suspected foul play in Jeremy's death.

"We have a list." P.J. pulled a folded piece of notebook paper from his pocket. "There's a lot of names on here, but we're only really interested in the starred ones. They were the folks that lived on the commune for any length of time. There's only about six of those—a few are dead, and the rest were transients, just staying for a night or two. I don't think there's any way to track that group down, and I expect most of those gave us fake names anyway. But all the starred ones lived here for at a least a year."

I took the worn piece of paper from him and carefully unfolded it. The ink was faded, but I could read the names. "Some of these people still live in the area, don't they? I recognize Pete O'Malley and Ruth Lee, who apparently called herself Rainbow back then, according to your notes on this list."

"Yes, and I suppose we could reach out to them ourselves, but . . ." Carol's blue eyes glistened with welling tears. "The thing is, we know the authorities are probably keeping tabs on us right now, and those horrible reporters are definitely watching our every move. We thought it would be better if you could help Sunny track them down—and then, Amy, you could go alone and speak with them." She pulled a tissue from the pocket of her apron and dabbed at her eyes. "Sorry. This isn't the way I ever pictured a reunion of the old commune crowd."

"What do you want me to say?" As I passed the list to Sunny, I thought about that photo of Jeremy Adams. But I couldn't say anything, despite our friendship. It was true that Brad had sworn me to secrecy, but there was another, more forceful reason for my silence. It was my desire to reveal the truth. *And you're not sure, are you, that these two people, who you've known and loved for years, would be happy if you did that?* I shook out my cramped fingers.

P.J. leaned forward, his hands on the table with his fingers tightly entwined. "Just let them know about the investigation into the bones, in case they haven't heard about it. And warn them to expect a visit from the sheriff's office."

I rolled the edge of my blouse hem between two fingers. "Why are you so sure the authorities plan to interview your former commune members?"

"Because"—P.J. straightened in his hard-backed chair—"we all have records. Minor stuff, mostly, like getting arrested during protests."

"But that sort of thing shouldn't affect an investigation into a . . ." I closed my lips over the last word, not wanting to betray Brad's suggestion of a possible murder. "Into this case," I finished, as the image of Jeremy Adams's sweet smile flitted through my mind.

"Maybe not, but we don't totally trust the authorities." Carol shrugged. "Old habits die hard."

Sunny sat back and crossed her arms over her chest. "So that's why you weren't too keen on me dating Brad?"

Carol waved that aside with one hand. "No, he just wasn't right for you, dear. As you discovered, soon enough. This other thing"—she shared a conspiratorial glance with her husband—"isn't about us, really. We weren't too caught up in the drug scene, but unfortunately some of the other commune members fell prey to some serious habits. That was honestly one reason we shut the commune down after only a couple of years."

Sunny's gaze slid from her grandmother's tense expression to her grandfather's stoic face. "You're afraid they might have other stuff in their pasts that they wouldn't want investigated?"

P.J. nodded. "It's possible. Which is why we want to give them a heads-up. It won't change the past, but Carol and I think they should have a chance to come clean, if necessary. I mean, we think they should have the option to share their secrets with family or friends before some cop comes around and airs any dirty laundry."

"I guess that makes sense," Sunny said. "And I can see why you want us to find them. But why only ask Amy to talk to them? I'm happy to help with that."

"Because you're likely to be under observation too, baby girl," P.J. said. "The authorities, and the media, are less likely to be concerned about Amy's whereabouts, while I suspect they'll track your movements along with ours."

"Oh great," Sunny said, dropping her arms to her sides. "Just what I need in the middle of my campaign."

I offered her an encouraging smile. "I promise to be discreet. The mayor and his minions won't get any information out of me."

"Just promise to be careful." Carol sent P.J. a swift glance before staring down at her hands, which were clenched together on the tabletop.

I raised my eyebrows as my stomach took another nose dive. "Why? Are any of these people dangerous?"

"No, of course not," P.J. said, a little too quickly. As if sensing my growing concern, he added, "Anyway, we know how resourceful you are. I'm sure conversations with some harmless old folks won't pose any problems for you."

"I've encountered a few dangerous senior citizens," I said, as images of Kurt Kendrick and a few other older people flashed through my mind. "But I'm happy to talk to your friends, if they'll allow it."

"Good, it's settled then." Carol rose to her feet. "Now, who wants cookies? I just happen to have made a batch earlier today."

Raising my hand, I noticed P.J.'s troubled expression and made a mental note to be on my guard when speaking to anyone on his list of "harmless old folks."

Chapter Five

During a lull in activity at the library the next day, Sunny and I shared notes.

Sunny, arriving around eleven, was brighter-eyed than me, even though we'd both stayed up late the evening before to comb the Internet for any information pertaining to the former commune members. But since Sunny was scheduled to work until eight in the evening, she'd been able to sleep in, while I had been required to get up early to open the library.

Motioning toward the list I'd unfolded and placed on the circulation desk, Sunny pointed out a name. "Okay, that one—'Stanman' Owens. I did locate someone named Stanley Owens who's around the right age. He became a lawyer, specializing in environmental cases. Seems like he retired a few years back, though. Last known address is in Baltimore."

"I found him too," I said. "Could be the right guy. But if it is, I don't think I'll need to inform him of anything. According to an obituary I found, he's dead."

"Really?" Sunny wrinkled her brow. "The grands didn't mention anything about that."

"Yeah, it's pretty recent. Some sort of accident." I tapped the list with one finger. "According to the info I found, he fell off a footbridge over some gorge up in the mountains. No one knows why, or can figure out what he was doing up there alone."

Sunny's eyes widened. "They suspect he jumped?"

"No, it seems to have been an accident. He had a camera with him, so the authorities assume he was leaning too far over the edge to get a photo or something. Anyway, he's obviously off our list. But there are a few others I can talk to fairly soon. Like Peter O'Malley. Your grandparents already confirmed that he's the same guy who owns the equipment repair shop in Taylorsford. You know, the one that's out on the eastern end of town, near the strip mall and car dealerships."

"That surprises me, to be honest." Sunny popped her aqua-blue-framed glasses off the top of her head and put them on before peering at the notes I'd scribbled on my list. "He seems like such a good ol' boy. Not someone I'd ever have pictured belonging to a commune."

I shrugged. "People change. Anyway, as far as I can tell, a couple other of these folks have died. And this one"—I ran my finger across one line, which identified someone called Belinda Cannon—"is missing, according to something I read in an old newspaper article. She wasn't linked to the commune in that report; I only found info on her when I was doing more research on missing persons from the area. Maybe she left Vista View before her own disappearance and her family didn't want her involvement with the commune mentioned or something."

"So, two former members went missing?" Sunny frowned. "Because from what I've found, Jeremy Adams disappeared soon after leaving the commune too."

"Yeah, I suppose that wasn't uncommon back in those days especially among the hippie crowd. They often lived like gypsies, I guess," I said, keeping my tone light. I'd wanted Sunny to make that connection on her own, so I technically wasn't betraying anything Brad had told me in confidence.

"I also unearthed a few obituaries." Sunny leaned in and tapped the list with one brightly painted fingernail. "But Ruth Lee, who my grandparents knew as Rainbow, is definitely the lady who owns the consignment and antique shop in Taylorsford."

"That means I can talk with her and Pete O'Malley easily enough." I stepped back. "Did Carol or P.J. say anything about this Daisy Miles they listed? That's one that's eluded me."

"Only that she was a writer, or wanted to be or something." Sunny took off her glasses and stuck them in the pocket of her pleated navy skirt. "Of course, *Daisy* probably wasn't her real name. Most of the commune members used nicknames."

"We don't even know if her last name was real, so . . ." I shrugged. "Could be tough to find her."

"I'll ask the grands if they have any more information on her."

"Fortunately, most of these people didn't bother to change their last names." I tapped the paper. "So, while I don't have an address yet, I did find a Dean Bodenheimer living in Frederick, Maryland. From what I gleaned from his social media, it seems he could be this guy on the list. He's the right age and was involved in the music industry when he was younger. In fact, it appears he still plays percussion with a retro rock band."

Sunny's blue eyes brightened. Like me, she savored the thrill of the hunt. "That would make sense, since the grands knew him as *Drummer*."

"Yeah, a musician. Like Jeremy Adams." I shot Sunny a quick glance. "Do your grandparents ever talk about him?"

"Not much. I know he was Walt's older cousin, and that he went missing after he left the commune, but that's about it."

"Aunt Lydia says he was a very talented guitarist and singer-songwriter. He supposedly headed out to LA to pursue his musical dreams but then disappeared."

Sunny frowned as she tugged on a strand of golden hair that had escaped the confines of her sleek ponytail. "They've never mentioned him being a musician."

"That's odd, but I suppose, since he left maybe not on great terms . . ." I caught a glimpse of the concern in Sunny's eyes and lightened my tone. "You know, if he abandoned the commune to chase after money and fame. Something like that could've upset your grandparents."

"I suppose they might've seen that as a betrayal of their principles," Sunny said, her expression still troubled.

I wanted to ask about other information her grandparents might have shared on the former commune members, especially Jeremy, but thought better of it. Such questions could keep for another day. "Are you guys still being harassed by reporters?"

"Yes, and it's gotten worse since someone at the sheriff's office slipped up and leaked the fact that the skeleton's skull was bashed in. Now everyone's talking murder." Sunny pressed one hand to her forehead. "It's enough to give me a headache, honestly. The phone rings constantly. Of course we don't answer it, but the grands refuse to turn off the ringer. They're concerned that the authorities might need to get in touch with them and they don't want to appear uncooperative."

“That makes sense, but it must be unnerving to hear that jangling all day and night.”

“Tell me about it. And then there’s this one reporter who won’t take no for an answer. Last night she just lurked in her car at the foot of our driveway, but this morning she actually climbed the fence and started wandering the property. Granddad found her in the old barn and chased her off, but I bet she’ll be back. Even though he warned her that she was trespassing and he’d have to take legal action if she showed up again.”

I shook my head. “Some people . . .”

“But we’d better shelve this discussion for later, because it looks like we’re about to be inundated.” Sunny pointed at the patrons approaching the desk

I straightened and greeted the group, one of whom had a reference question for me, while the others toted stacks of books for checkout.

My questions about the Adams case would have to wait. Customer service always came first.

* * *

Spurred on by Sunny’s obvious anxiety, I took a little extra time at lunch to head over to an old cement-block garage that sat on the edge of town. The gas pumps I remembered from childhood were long gone, the ramshackle building having been converted into a workshop years ago. As I parked in the small lot and climbed out of my car, I mentally rehearsed the warning the Fields had asked me to relay.

A pitted tin sign swinging from a rusted iron bracket declared that the shop belonged to Peter O’Malley and promised “speedy repairs” on lawn mowers, boat motors, and other small equipment.

The faded image of a grinning tortoise seemed to belie the swiftness of the repairs, but I assumed it was the sort of joke that seventy-five-year-old Pete—known around town for his sarcastic humor—enjoyed.

"Hello, anyone here?" I called out as I picked my way through the tangle of mechanical parts that littered the plank floor of the shop.

A weathered baseball cap emblazoned with O'MALLEY REPAIRS popped up behind a jumble of cardboard boxes.

"Yep, hold yer horses. Just tightening a bolt. I'll be right with you."

I leaned over and brushed dust from the hems of my slacks. When I straightened, Pete O'Malley stood in front of me, clutching a metal wrench.

Like a weapon, I thought, then chased that image from my mind. Pete was known to be irascible, or "downright ornery," as Zelda liked to say. But I'd never heard any rumors about him being violent.

Besides, he was a small man. He barely topped my height, and unlike me, he was as skinny as a fence post. *Although*, I warned myself, *those ropy muscles in his arms might give him a distinct advantage in a fight.*

"What do want, miss?" Pete's cornflower-blue eyes narrowed as he looked me over. "Got a lawn mower you want repaired or something?"

"No, nothing like that. Is there somewhere we could sit down and talk for a moment?" Glancing around the shop, I spied a small plastic table and two folding metal chairs. "Over there, maybe?"

"I don't usually take time out of the workday just to jabber with strangers," Pete said, eyeing me with interest. "But I suppose you're not entirely a stranger. You're Lydia Talbot's niece, aren't you?"

"Yes, I'm Amy Webber." I met Pete's inquisitive stare with a lift of my chin.

"That's right, you're the younger sister's kid. You run the library now, from what I hear."

"I've been the library director for a few years now, actually."

Pete studied me, concentration deepening the lines on his weathered face. He slapped his hip with the hand not holding the wrench. "I see it now. You're the spitting image of Lydia's grandmother, old Mrs. Litton. Couldn't forget that face, especially those dark eyes." His chapped lips twitched as he stared at me. "She used to chase us kids out of her garden by threatening to call the sheriff, even though we was only using her yard as a shortcut into the woods. Quite the high-and-mighty lady, that Rose Baker Litton. Always acted like she was better than anybody else in town, but I hear she got her comeuppance. Went a little batty in the end, didn't she?"

I grimaced, not happy to be reminded of my resemblance to Rose. "Yes, she was my great-grandmother and, sadly, developed a form of dementia later in life." I cleared my throat. "Anyway, I'm actually here as a friend of Carol and P.J. Fields. They sent me to talk to you."

The humor on Pete's face drained like water down a grate. "Now what do they want with me? We haven't spoken in years." As he turned away, he motioned toward the table and chairs. "But go ahead, take a seat."

At the table, I stared dubiously at the chairs. Pete grabbed a roll of paper towels from a nearby shelf and tossed it to me. "Might want to wipe that off before you sit down. Don't want to ruin those nice gray pants of yours."

I rubbed as much dust and grime from the chair as possible before balling up the paper towel and sitting down. "Carol and P.J. told me that you lived on their commune back in the sixties."

"Yep, I stayed out there on the farm for a year or two. Back when I was young and stupid." Pete's lips curled into a sneer. "They did all right with that property after we all left, it seems. Turned it into a going concern."

"They've worked hard," I said mildly. "The thing is, Mr. O'Malley, that Carol and P.J. feel you should be warned . . ."

"About any connection I might have to those human bones discovered on their land? Heard the rumor that the poor devil's skull had been smashed. Messy business."

"Yes." I examined his weathered face. "Do you have any idea why someone would bury a body at Vista View? I mean, of course you probably don't, but can you imagine any reason why those bones might have turned up there?"

Pete reared back, lifting the front legs of his flimsy chair off the ground. "Can't say I do. But honestly, the time I spent out there is mostly a blur to me."

I pursed my lips as I examined his lined face. "Because it was so long ago?"

"Because I was doing drugs at the time. Come on, you know that wasn't uncommon back in the day. We was all experimenting with stuff. Trying to expand our consciousness, some said. Me, I just liked the way it made me feel."

I leaned forward, resting my arms on the tabletop with no regard for the sleeves of my white blouse. "But you were all pretty mellow, right? I've heard Carol and P.J. talk about those days, and they always sound nostalgic. They've told me it was a simpler, sweeter time."

Pete snorted and dropped the front legs of his chair to the floor. "They must've been still wearing their rose-colored glasses to spout that nonsense." He pulled the baseball cap from his head, revealing wisps of gray hair plastered across a bald spot. "It wasn't no Shangri-la. Sure, we had a decent place to sleep and plenty to eat and all that. But you take a bunch of young people—most of us were barely twenty—well, you throw that age group together, with their hormones raging, and free-flowing drugs, and you see what happens."

I drew a heart in the dust on the tabletop with one fingertip. "The commune members had problems with one another?"

"Some did. Some just had issues with themselves. But we had plenty of arguments and differences of opinion, let me tell you. Then you add in free love . . ." Pete shook his head. "I shouldn't go into all that. It was a long time ago. Doesn't matter now. You should just know there was some hookups, and not all of them worked out so well. Jealousy, ya know. It can turn even the most enlightened pacifists into beasts."

Feeling I was falling too far down a very trippy rabbit hole, I straightened and fixed my gaze on Pete's sardonic smile. "You included?"

"Maybe, but like I told you, I don't remember much about that time. It's all hazy. Although"—Pete jammed the hat back onto his head—"if someone's looking for a killer, maybe they ought to be checking out the dealers who were operating around here at the time."

"Drug dealers?"

"Yep. A few of them would've killed in a heartbeat. Someone didn't pay up for a delivery, and . . ." Pete swept his finger across his throat in a slicing motion.

"You should tell the authorities that, if they do question you. Or even if they don't. It might be useful information."

"Eh, not sure what good it would do. Most of those fellas disappeared by the seventies. Not to say new dealers didn't replace them, but the ones operating in the sixties didn't hang around very long."

"But you knew some of them?"

"Only by their nicknames." Pete's grin displayed coffee-stained teeth. "It wasn't like they were sharing their real IDs with us. I do remember there was a skinny little guy who called himself Weasel, and man, was that ever an accurate description from what I heard. And then there was this other dude everyone called the Hammer. He supplied most of the commune, except for me. I had my own sources—ones I'd done business with before and trusted. I wasn't about to deal with strangers. Fact is, I never met either guy, but I did hear plenty about the Hammer. Seems he was a favorite with the others because he never shorted them and didn't seem inclined to work with a gang."

"So he wasn't really the dangerous type?" I frowned, considering the commune's possible connection to violent criminals, and whether Carol or P.J. had known all the details about such activities happening on their farm.

"I didn't say that." Pete yanked his cap farther down his forehead. "He was a big guy, from what I heard. Intimidating. I think the others didn't dare cross him 'cause they weren't inclined to find out what he'd do. Who's to say a guy like that didn't kill somebody and bury them out there at Vista View? That makes more sense to me than anybody from the commune being involved in murder."

I stared at him, my mind registering his immediate jump to that conclusion. Maybe he knew a lot more than he was saying.

His supposedly hazy memory might prove more convenient than true. "We don't actually know it *is* a murder yet."

Pete sniffed. "Seems likely, don't you think? People don't generally smash their own skulls and then bury themselves."

"The bones could be much older. Someone from back before Taylorsford was even a town." I didn't believe that theory at this point, but thought it might elicit more information from Pete.

"Doubt it. We dredged that creek in the early days of the commune. By hand. Good ol' P.J. told us it would help with an irrigation system, but we never got that built." Pete tapped the side of his beaky nose. "I think P.J. just wanted to give us something to do. He didn't like us sitting around too much. Thought it led to trouble. He was always assigning the commune members chores. Claimed it would improve our characters." Pete snorted. "P.J. was a great one for building character."

"Sounds like you didn't like him all that much."

"He was all right. Carol too. They was the real thing, you know. True believers. Committed to peace and love and changing the world. Not like some of the rest of us." Pete lowered his head, staring at the heart design I'd drawn on the tabletop.

I couldn't read anything in his eyes but sensed tension in the hands he'd clasped together on the tabletop. "They're good people," I said.

"Seem to be. I haven't seen them in forever. When I was living with them . . . Well, I guess I was too rebellious for their taste. I was more into the drugs and free-love stuff than what they called the true meaning of communal living. But I will say this—with all the bed-hopping that went on, those two never participated. They were always devoted to each another."

"And you admired them for that." I met Pete's sharp gaze as he lifted his head.

"I did. It wasn't something I was used to. Didn't have very good role models at home. So, sadly, I never really learned how to have a decent relationship with a woman. Even now, as you see"—Pete lifted one arm and indicated his shop in a sweeping motion—"I'm alone. Just never trusted in all that true-love stuff, I guess."

"It's tough to do that sometimes," I admitted, pushing back my chair and standing. "I'm afraid I need to get back to work. Thanks for talking with me, Mr. O'Malley. I hope this will at least give you a heads-up if the authorities come poking around. That's all P.J. and Carol wanted."

Pete rose to his feet. "But you wanted more from me, didn't you? Some extra information to tuck away in that inquisitive brain of yours." He tipped his head and examined me, a little smile playing about his lips. "I did know exactly who you were when you walked in here, Amy Webber. I may be old and a bit of a loner, but I'm up to speed on the local gossip. I've heard how you've gone and gotten tangled up helping the authorities solve a couple of criminal cases over the last few years."

I inhaled, swallowing a sharp retort. "You already knew about that?"

"Come on," he said. "This is Taylorsford. How could I have lived here and remained ignorant of such stories? Now"—he spread his grease-stained hands—"it looks to me like you've stumbled smack-dab into another murder investigation."

"Oh, I hope not," I said in a fervent tone.

But as I told him goodbye, I had to admit he was probably right.

Chapter Six

As soon as I walked through the library staff door, I was greeted by an unexpected commotion from beyond the workroom. Shoving my purse onto a shelf, I dashed across the room to reach the circulation desk.

A thirty-something-year-old man wearing khakis and a forest-green Henley shirt stood in front of the desk, facing off with Sunny. I looked from Sunny's beet-red face to the stranger's implacable stare before noticing that a few library patrons were clustered off to one side of the desk, clutching books to their chests.

"Look, I just want to talk to you. Get your side of things," the man said. "Especially now that the authorities have identified that skeleton as Jeremy Adams."

My fingernails dug into my palms. It seemed likely, given the speed of the ID process, that the photo I'd found had encouraged the sheriff's office to immediately check with the local dental practice that held Jeremy's old records. And apparently they'd made a match.

"And I said no." Sunny slapped a rolled-up magazine against the surface of the desk. "You might as well take yourself and your questions out of here, Mr. Danish."

"Dane," the man said, running a hand through his light-brown hair. "Daniel Dane, as I've already told you several times."

I realized this was the reporter from the other evening—the one who'd stopped that woman from blocking my access to Vista View's driveway.

Sunny tapped the rolled magazine against her palm, as if testing its usefulness as a bludgeon. "Well, Mr. Dane, since you don't actually need assistance from the library staff and I refuse to answer your questions about my grandparents, why don't you march your nosy self out of here so I can get back to doing my job?"

"What's all this?" I reached over and pried the mangled journal from Sunny's tensed fingers.

Sunny glared at the stranger and tossed her long plait behind one shoulder. "This guy's poking into my family business. I've asked him to stop, but he keeps pestering me."

The man, who was tall and thin, with a hawk nose and eyes as gray-green as the Atlantic Ocean, lifted his hands in a conciliatory gesture. "Sorry, Ms. Webber. I didn't mean to cause a commotion. Just doing my job."

"Which is?" I shot him a questioning stare, curious how he knew my name.

"Investigative reporter." The man thrust his hand over the desk. "Daniel Dane, but you can call me Dan."

"I can call the sheriff's office if you're actually harassing my employee," I said, ignoring his proffered hand.

"What he's doing is keeping other patrons from checking out books." Although the high color had faded from her cheeks, Sunny's tone was as jagged as a tin-can lid.

"I was simply asking a few questions. I don't know if you've heard, Ms. Webber, but that skeleton found at Vista View has been identified as Jeremy Adams, who once lived on a commune out on Carol and P.J. Fields' farm. As a journalist, I'm just trying to gather some facts from the people who might actually know the truth." Dan Dane pulled back his hand and patted the small notebook that poked out of the pocket of his navy windbreaker. "I'm not recording anything on audio; just making a few notes."

"Perhaps this isn't the time or place," I said, gesturing toward the milling patrons. "There are other people who need Ms. Fields' assistance."

The reporter nodded. "I appreciate that, and I really don't want to be a bother. But I did tell Ms. Fields that I'd be happy to make an appointment for another time."

"And I told you no," Sunny said, turning her head. "I'm done with you, Mr. Dane."

As I processed the confirmation of my suspicions concerning the connection of the skeleton to Jeremy Adams, I examined Dan Dane's intelligent face. "I'll tell you what—why don't you meet me outside? There are a couple of benches out front where we can sit and talk. Perhaps I can answer a few of your questions while we allow Ms. Fields to get back to doing her job." I pointed toward the front doors. "That way. I'll meet you in a second."

Sunny sputtered something unintelligible as Dan Dane flashed me a smile and loped off.

"I just plan to give him some harmless information and get him out of your hair," I told Sunny when the doors had closed behind the reporter. "Do you think you can focus on checking out books for a while, or do you need a break? I can always call Dawn over. Her volunteer shift doesn't end until we close today, and she's just shelf-reading right now."

"No, I'm fine." Sunny smoothed down the front of her finely pleated cotton tunic. "Just watch what you tell that man. He seems to know an awful lot about Taylorsford, and my family, for a stranger."

"Don't worry, I plan to be careful, especially since I'm a bit unsettled that some random reporter knew my name." I offered her an encouraging smile. "I'll just give him enough innocuous information to send him merrily on his way. Maybe that will satisfy him and he won't bother you again," I added, laying my hand on her arm.

"Okay, thanks." Sunny ducked her head. "I apologize for letting my anger get the best of me. Shouldn't do that at work, I know, but after hearing that news about Jeremy Adams, I was already on edge."

I gave her arm a pat before lifting my hand. "I totally understand why that guy would upset you, so let's forget it. And by the way," I called over my shoulder as I circled around the desk, "remind me to tell you about my lunch conversation later. There's some info you might want to share with the grands."

Sunny gave me a thumbs-up signal before motioning for the waiting patrons to approach the desk.

Remembering Brad's words, I considered what I should or shouldn't share with Sunny as I made my way outside, where Dan Dane had already taken a seat on one of the stone benches placed under a maple tree.

I sat on the opposite end of the bench. "Now be honest, Mr. Dane, what really brings you to Taylorsford?"

"Please, call me Dan. And, as I already explained to your assistant, I'm writing an in-depth article on people who went missing from this area in the sixties. And, full disclosure—this is not something brought on by the discovery of that skeleton at Vista View. I've actually been working on this piece for some time, long before that news broke."

"Is that actually a viable topic for an article? I doubt we've had that many cases around here."

"You'd be surprised." Dan crossed his lanky arms over his chest. "There are at least ten young people who disappeared without a trace from this and the two adjoining counties between 1960 and 1970."

"I guess if you've been looking into this for a while, it must've started as a cold-case investigation," I said, as my mind raced with the possible connection between the reporter's research and the former Vista View commune members. "Are you working with the authorities?"

Dan shook his head. "Not officially. Until this latest revelation about the Adams kid, no one was really interested, except me and a few family members. In fact, the cases I'm investigating are so old, the sheriff's departments, and even the feds, have given up on them."

I flicked a fallen twig off my shoulder. "What makes you so interested, then?"

"Personal connection," Dan said.

I turned my head to stare at him. "Some friend or relative of yours went missing?"

"Yes, from the next county over, but still in this general area. It's my aunt, who was eighteen back in 1964. I never knew her, of course, since my mom was only fifteen when her sister disappeared." Dan met my gaze with a sad smile. "It's always tortured my mom, what happened to her sister. And, since investigative reporting is what I do . . ." He lifted his hands. "But even though this started as a personal quest, I soon discovered there were other people who'd disappeared around here during that time period."

"I'm sorry to hear about your aunt. That must've been tough for the family."

"Yes, it was," Dan said sharply. He took a breath and gave me an apologetic smile. "Sorry. It's just that my mom . . . Well, she's never really gotten over losing her sister. I'm just trying to get her a little closure."

"So you decided to look into all the cases instead of just one." I couldn't help but give him an understanding smile. It was the sort of mission I would've felt compelled to pursue too, if I'd been in his shoes.

"On my own time, since this is a freelance article. My regular news venues don't mind, just as long as I turn in my assigned copy on time."

"Okay, I get it. You're on a mission. But how about this—maybe instead of bothering Ms. Fields or her family, you allow me to assist you with gathering more information. As you observed, I'm a pretty decent researcher."

"I've heard that." Dan tapped his temple with one finger. "I did a bit a sleuthing on Taylorsford already, and your name popped up. Something to do with assisting the authorities on recent murder cases?"

"Hmmmm . . ." The maple tree's limbs, spreading above our heads, were still full and green. I stared up into the canopy of fluttering leaves. "I don't want to get too heavily involved in anything like that again, to be honest. But I'd be happy to give you access to our town archives. You might find some helpful info in the files."

"That sounds great." Dan rapped the bench with his fist to draw my gaze back to him. "But I do want to talk to Ms. Fields again. And her grandparents. I wouldn't even mind if you were present, if that made them feel more comfortable."

I frowned. "Why are you so determined to speak with Carol and P.J. Fields? I doubt they had anything to do with any disappearances."

"Because Jeremy Adams lived on their commune right before he went missing."

"Actually, now that you mention it, there were really two people who went missing after they left Vista View. The second one was a young woman named Belinda Cannon." I examined Dan's face for any evidence that he recognized the name, and did notice a flicker of recognition. "Did you find anything on her in your research?"

"Just her name," Dan said, his eyes clouded as if he were lost in thought. "But a lot of young people were very transitory at that time, so it's hard to track them all." He glanced back at me. "Trust me, I'm not saying that Carol or P.J. Fields was involved in any criminal activity. But they could still know something, maybe even something they wouldn't consider relevant. Some little fact they've never shared with anyone, for their own reasons. Sometimes those little facts are what will crack a case wide open. That's really why I want to talk with the commune members—to see if they remember anything that could implicate anyone involved in the various disappearances." He held out his hands, palms up. "It's crossed my mind, given the times, that maybe Jeremy Adams was killed by a drug dealer or even a group of people involved in the drug trade in this area. Maybe P.J. and Carol Fields or their friends could provide a lead I could follow related to that theory."

I thought about the list, now refolded and stashed in my purse. I didn't want to stand in the way of Dan Dane's pursuit of the truth, but I also needed to fulfill my promise to Carol and P.J. and give their friends a heads-up before both the law and the news media landed on their doorsteps. "How long will you be around?"

"As long as necessary," Dan replied, getting up and moving to stand before me. "I'm not from the immediate area, but I'm close enough that I can drive out fairly often, and I'll just get a motel room somewhere if my research takes more than a day at a time."

"I was just going to suggest that you return tomorrow or Friday morning. I should be able to adjust my schedule to give you some assistance in the archives on one of those days." *That should keep him away from Carol and P.J. a bit longer*, I thought, rising to my feet before adding, "We open at nine."

Dan Dane thrust out his hand again, and this time I accepted his firm shake. "Thank you, Amy. Friday would be best for me, so I'll meet you then. But if you could also put in a word with your assistant for me . . ."

"See you Friday," I said, and turned on my heel to head back into the library.

With the identification of Jeremy Adams's body, the authorities would undoubtedly question Carol and P.J., but I knew they were unlikely to share the existence of the list they'd given me and Sunny. *They'll probably say they have no clear memories of that time*, I thought, with a grim smile. *Just like Pete O'Malley.*

The problem was, despite my wish to believe their stories, I couldn't be sure any of them had truly forgotten as much as they claimed.

Chapter Seven

Richard and I had planned to have dinner at his house that evening, so I rushed home after work to grab a shower. I stared into my closet as I towel-dried my shoulder-length dark hair, as if willing a new outfit to appear. Not that Richard was overly concerned about my wardrobe, but I did like to occasionally dress up for date nights. Fortunately, the weather was still stuck in summer mode, which expanded my options. Except when it was warm enough for bare legs—or truly cold, and tights and boots could come into play—I tended to avoid wearing dresses or skirts because I despised wearing panty hose.

Another point where my future mother-in-law disagrees with me, I thought, my lips curling in distaste. *She finds bare legs tacky, while I find them liberating.* Finally settling on a comfortable but flattering red knit dress, I thrust my bare feet into some ballerina flats and ran downstairs. I waved a goodbye to Aunt Lydia, who was whipping up something in the kitchen, and headed out the back door.

Just a month earlier, Richard had installed an arched arbor in the fence that separated his yard from our garden. I pushed open the gate, pausing to thread one of the trailing rose vines through the white latticework of the arbor.

As I approached the door to Richard's back porch, I was startled by a small creature zipping past my legs. I jumped back in time to see it dive into the shrubbery that flanked the concrete stoop. Its tail, striped marmalade orange and yellow, disappeared with a flick.

Another stray kitten. I spied a couple of butter tubs nestled next to the shrubs and sighed.

"You have a visitor," I said, as Richard opened the screen door.

"He's been hanging out for a while." Richard stepped back to allow me to enter before taking me in his arms. "Hello, sweetheart, how was your day?"

"Interesting. I will tell you all about it in a minute." I waited until after he kissed me before I added, "And that kitten might not have lingered quite so long if you hadn't set out those little bowls of cat food and water."

Richard stepped back and hung his head. "He just seemed so hungry."

"That is how it starts." I followed him into the kitchen, where a tortoiseshell cat lounged on the tall, narrow oak table that functioned as a kitchen island. "What does Loie think about this situation?"

Seven-month-old Loie opened one emerald eye and stared at me before tucking her head beneath her black-and-orange leg.

"She's not a fan," Richard admitted, lifting the cat and gently placing her on the floor, an action she protested with a piercing meow. "I have to keep her off the back porch these days. She goes ballistic when she spots the kitten through the door."

"Not surprising. It's moving in on her turf." I studied my fiancé. Of average height for a man, he appeared taller due to his lean dancer's physique and perfect posture. "What's for dinner? Do you need help with anything?"

"No, it's all prepared." Richard grinned as Loie swiped at my bare leg as she strolled past me and sauntered into the hall. "It's mainly cold salads. Hope that's okay."

"Sure, sounds good," I said. "And what sounds even better is a glass of that wine I spy over there."

Richard reached the soapstone counter in three long strides and opened one of the whitewashed cabinets lining the upper wall. "Coming right up," he said as he took down two wine-glasses. "Why don't you grab a seat on the sofa? I'll bring you a glass."

I headed down the short central hallway to the front of the house—a single open room split between a comfortable living area and a small dance studio, complete with a barre, wall of mirrors, and shining expanse of wooden floor. Richard had carefully renovated the farmhouse he'd inherited from his great-uncle to complement its original 1920s style, so the dance studio stuck out as an anomaly. But I was glad he had a place to train and practice away from his university studio. *Otherwise*, I thought, with a wry smile, *I'd never see him.*

"Now tell me what was so interesting about today." Richard crossed to the sofa and handed me a full glass of white wine before sitting beside me. "I did hear about the identification of that skeleton, of course. It was all over the news."

"Yeah, unfortunately for Sunny's grandparents. But I also have other news." I settled back with my wine and filled him in on my conversations with both Pete O'Malley and Daniel Dane. "The weird thing is," I said, finishing off my wine, "both of them suggested that perhaps some dealer or drug gang operating back in that time might've been involved in killing Jeremy and burying his body."

"That would make sense." Richard leaned back against the sofa cushions just as Loie strolled over and sat at his feet. "Hopefully they're all long gone from the area, though."

"I suppose that would be safer for everyone concerned, although it won't help solve the case. But perhaps I can find out something from the former commune members that will prove useful. And yes"—I held up my hand in a *stop* gesture—"I will immediately notify Brad or someone else in the sheriff's office if I discover anything that makes me feel the least bit nervous."

"I should hope so." Richard absently patted his thigh with his free hand while keeping his gaze fixed on me. "You do tend to tumble into trouble a little more than I'd like," he added, as Loie leapt into his lap.

I crossed myself with mock solemnity. "Cross my heart and hope *not* to die, I promise to be careful. And really, it's just talking to a few older folks. Which reminds me—there's one person on the list I haven't been able to locate. Not for certain, anyway. A Daisy Miles. She was supposedly a poet, or at least that was her ambition, according to P.J. and Carol."

Richard kept his gaze on me as he petted Loie. "That could be anyone. No luck with the Internet sleuthing?"

"Not so far." I took a long swallow of my drink. "I imagine Daisy was a nickname, which complicates things."

Richard set his glass on the coffee table and grabbed his phone, causing Loie to cheep in protest. But she stayed on his lap, despite shooting him a baleful glance. "Wait a minute, did you say Daisy?"

"Yeah. What's up?" I placed my glass beside his and leaned in as he tapped something into the cell phone.

"Rang a bell. Clarion put out a news release just the other day profiling Emily Moore. I mean, she is a poet, and about the right age too."

"Okay, but what . . ."

Richard handed me the phone. "Take a look. There's a reference in there that might interest you."

I scrolled through the article, pausing when a certain name jumped out at me. "Wow, her nickname at Andy Warhol's Factory was Daisy?"

"Yep." A self-satisfied smile lit up Richard's face as his fingers stroked Loie's silky head. "See—I can play detective too."

"That you can." I gave him a peck on the cheek before placing the cell phone back on the coffee table and grabbing my wineglass. "So our elusive Daisy Miles could really be Emily Moore. If that's true, who would've thought she'd end up buying a house back in the same area where she once lived on a commune? If she really is the same woman, that is. I guess if Emily is Daisy, she must've left Vista View not long before she went to New York. I wonder how that all came about?"

"Looks like you might be able to ask her, and confirm she really is the same person as the Daisy Miles from Vista View. If she'll talk to you, of course."

"I doubt that will be a problem. She seems pretty friendly and open, especially for someone with her fame." I polished off my wine before sliding closer to Richard. "Now—enough of this sleuthing. Instead, why don't you tell me about this vagrant kitten.

Is today the first you've actually seen him, or have you been keeping quiet about this for a few days, hoping to spring him on me as a fait accompli?"

Richard stared at the large wall-mounted TV on the opposite wall as if there were something playing on its flat black screen. "Full disclosure—I've caught glimpses of him off and on for the past couple of days."

"Aha!" I placed my wineglass on the coffee table and tapped Richard's arm to force him to look at me. "The plot thickens."

Richard widened his eyes. They were a beautiful gray, fringed with thick black lashes, and I had to admit, he knew how to use them to good effect. "It's all been quite spontaneous, I promise. Anyway," he said, his fingers caressing Loie's sleek fur, "Loie could use a pal, don't you think? A companion she can cuddle up with when we're not around. Besides, if she has a buddy to play with, maybe she'll stop attacking my legs while I'm practicing. I think Fosse could be the ticket."

I arched my eyebrows. "Wait a minute, you've already named him? And"—I leaned in, stroking Loie as I gazed up at Richard from under my eyelashes—"how do you know it's a boy?"

"I might have picked him up once or twice." Richard grinned. "Okay, you've got me. I've already considered adopting him. I've even scheduled a vet appointment so he can be checked out and given his shots." Richard grabbed his glass and took a swallow before adding, "To be honest, the only reason I haven't let him in the house yet is because I didn't want to expose Loie to any diseases or fleas."

I sat back. "Looks like you're getting a brother, Loie. I hope you'll eventually learn to get along with him." When I leaned in to pet her head, her eyes opened to little emerald slits. “Fosse—named after Bob Fosse the dancer and choreographer, of course.”

Richard grinned. “Yeah. The little guy has the appropriate swagger.”

“I think you’re going to have your hands full, making sure Loie doesn’t go into full attack mode.”

“I know I’ll have to keep them apart at first.” Richard examined my face with a hint of trepidation in his gaze. “I hope you don’t mind.”

“Of course I don’t mind. I love this silly creature,” I said, as Loie meeped and curled into a tight ball, her little black nose touching the tip of her tail. “I guess one more won’t hurt. But I draw the line at more than two at any one time. I don’t want to turn into one of those infamous old cat ladies.”

“I doubt that will happen. Aren’t they usually depicted as living alone? You share a house with Lydia now and will be living with me soon. Although”—Richard lifted Loie and placed her on the sofa beside him—“not soon enough, as far as I’m concerned. When are we going to set a date?” His lips were suddenly at my ear.

“Whenever you want,” I replied, trying to maintain my concentration while Richard kissed my neck and shoulder. “We could try for May. That would make it a year since we got engaged.”

“It is a beautiful season,” Richard said, sitting back. “But that’s eight months from now.”

“Yes, which will give us time to get everything together. Despite your mother’s machinations, I don’t want anything elaborate, but even the simplest wedding will require some planning.

Besides"—I snuggled closer to him—"it's not like you won't see me almost every day."

Richard slid his arm around my shoulders. "True. Oh, and speaking of planning, is it okay if I invite Karla to Sunday dinner sometime soon?"

"Sure, I'm always happy to see her. When?"

"Definitely after the scholarship recital performances. I won't have time to clean the house or prepare any food until that's all over. I was thinking two weeks from this Sunday. Mainly because"—he sat back, dropping his arm —"that will also allow me to celebrate my mother's birthday. It's not the exact day, but close enough, and since my dad is going out of town for a work conference the entire weekend . . ."

"Okay, okay," I said, startling Loie by throwing up my hands. "But if Fiona is going to be there, can I also invite Aunt Lydia and Hugh? You know, for reinforcements on my side?"

Richard's guffaw sent Loie scurrying off his lap and under the coffee table. "Of course. I'd like them to get to know Karla better anyway. I want her to meet some more people in the area."

I watched Loie's tail switch fiercely back and forth as I considered his words. "Hold on—are you plotting to get her to move to Taylorsford? I thought her dance studio was doing well."

"It is, but she doesn't own the space, and her landlord wants to jack up the rent. She's worried about that, so I've been scouting some places near Clarion." Richard shrugged. "Figured it couldn't hurt to look into the possibilities of her living and working a little closer."

"Which would mean you two could collaborate more often. Which"—I clasped one of his hands—"I wholeheartedly approve of, by the way."

Richard gave my fingers a squeeze. "You've guessed it. I want to collaborate with Karla as much as possible. And, to be honest, I'd like to work with her studio. She does such great things with kids with mental and physical challenges. I'd like to help with that effort."

I groaned. "More time away? All right, as long as it's for a good cause."

"It's actually a bit selfish. I'd love to set a piece on those kids. Or more than one. I think it would be an interesting challenge, and maybe something that could be used in other, similar, studios." Richard swung my hand up and kissed my knuckles. "I knew you'd understand. Which is one of the many reasons I love you."

"All for art," I said, sweeping my other hand across my brow in a dramatic gesture that made Richard laugh again.

"And there's that," he said. "You being silly. I love that too."

"Good, 'cause you're likely to experience it a lot."

Richard used our clasped hands to draw me closer to him. "Sounds like fun. But not as much fun as this," he added, before pulling me in for a kiss.

"Okay, so maybe we'd better call a halt if we're ever going to have dinner," I said several minutes later, after coming up for air.

"For now." Richard rose to his feet.

"For now." I followed him into the kitchen.

"You can grab a chair at the table while I pull stuff together. But first"—Richard strode over to the pantry—"I'll need to take care of the cat. Loie's giving me the *look*. You know, the one that demands food. I'd better deal with that first."

"You'd better," I said with a smile. "And put some kibble out for Fosse while you're at it."

"That's the plan." He paused in the doorway to cast me a grin. "I may even eventually feed you, if you behave yourself."

"Me? Behave?" I crossed over to him and tapped his chest with one finger. "Is that what you really want?"

"No, not really," he admitted, and kissed me until Loie's howls brought us back to our senses.

Chapter Eight

The following day, I decided to kill two birds with one stone by visiting Ruth Lee at her consignment and antique shop. I figured I could fulfill Carol and P.J.'s request while also searching for a birthday gift for my future mother-in-law.

Knowing Fiona, I assumed she might prefer some interesting objet d'art to the typical bottle of perfume or silk scarf. "Besides," I told Sunny, when I informed her that I needed to take the afternoon off, "I wouldn't have any idea what she'd like and would probably choose the wrong thing. But I know she loves old china. Maybe Ruth's shop has something interesting to offer along those lines."

Sunny shook her head. "Have you ever been in there? It's more like a collection of junk, in my opinion. Although I know my grandmother has scored a few inexpensive treasures there. But you really have to dig."

"Well, I need to talk to Ruth anyway, so at least I'll accomplish that task, even if I can't find a gift." I slid my purse strap over one shoulder before heading out of the workroom. "Are you sure you don't mind covering the library this afternoon?"

"No, it's fine." Sunny looked me over. "Besides, you're helping out the grands by talking to Ruth Lee, so I'm happy to do a little extra here."

"Okay. Bill's arriving any minute, so he can spell you on the desk." I crossed around the desk, heading for the door. "I'll give you a call later and let you know if Ruth tells me anything useful."

"You'd better!" Sunny called after me.

I didn't have to walk far, as Ruth Lee's shop was only a few blocks away. Housed in a building that sat between an old stone house occupied by a realtor and the wooden-framed post office, the shop was surrounded by a narrow lot overgrown with shrubs and spindly trees. Three stories tall but only one room wide, the building looked like it had been sliced from a larger structure, an impression its sheer brick sides did nothing to allay. With its small cement stoop topped by a battered wooden door, only the shop's huge picture window—filled with an assortment of odd but colorful objects—leant the building any charm.

Its general unkept air—the same sense of neglect that had made me walk past without stopping every time I'd been downtown—gave me the sinking feeling that I wouldn't find a gift for Fiona inside. I pushed back my misgivings and entered.

"Hello," I called out, as a bell attached to the door gave off a clanking sound. "Anyone here?"

I surveyed the shop, my gaze at first captured by the dust motes dancing in the light falling from the front window. It was the only natural light filling the space. Shadows veiled the back of the building, where narrow shafts of light fell from metal fluorescent fixtures dangling from chains attached to the high, beadboard ceiling.

As my eyes acclimated to the dim light, I noticed that both side walls were covered by unpainted wooden shelves, which stretched from lower cabinets to the chipped crown molding. The shelves were filled with items that appeared to be arranged in no discernible order, with plastic baby dolls perched on top of wooden cigar boxes and rusted hand tools spilling out of hand-painted terracotta pots. Running down the center of the room, a motley collection of display cases boasted glass so cloudy it was impossible to tell what was inside. The mismatched styles and colors of the cases brought to mind a row of old train cars abandoned on a side rail.

"Hello," I called out again. "Ms. Lee, are you here?"

"Coming!" A reedy voice sailed from the dim reaches at the rear of the shop. "Just take a look around. I'll be with you in a minute."

I leaned over the first display case and peered past the smudged surface of the glass. Nestled in swathes of faded crimson velvet, pieces of costume jewelry sparkled with the unnatural brilliance of rhinestones and colored glass.

Definitely not anything that would appeal to Fiona Muir. I straightened as a figure materialized from the shadows.

"Good afternoon," said the woman, tugging on a strand of crinkly gray hair that had escaped her long single braid.

"Hello, are you Ruth Lee?" I examined her. She was taller than I'd expected, and large-boned, but so thin that she appeared fragile. She had the appearance of someone who had once been robust but had lost too much weight due to age or illness. Her face was so hollow that it looked like it had been scooped out with a spoon.

"Yes, that's me." Ruth's eyes were small and dark and surrounded by a fan of wrinkles. "Were you looking for anything in particular, Miss . . . ?"

"Amy Webber," I said, extending my hand.

She reached over the case to clasp my fingers. "Are you Lydia Talbot's niece? I've seen you around town, but I don't recall you ever coming into the shop before."

"No, this is my first time." I pulled my fingers free of her surprisingly strong grip. "And while I'm looking for a gift for someone who likes old china, that's not my only mission. I'm also here to relay a message from Carol and P.J. Fields."

Ruth Lee blinked rapidly and took a step back. "Really? Now why on earth would they send you as a messenger? They should know where to find me. They've been to the shop plenty of times."

"Yes, but right now they don't want to draw attention to your . . . connection."

"What connection is that?" Ruth turned aside and plucked a mosaic glass paperweight off the shelf behind her. "I did briefly live on their farm, but that was so long ago . . ."

"When Jeremy Adams lived there," I said. "You must've heard the news about his body being found at Vista View."

Furiously polishing the paperweight with the hem of her long cotton tunic, Ruth didn't meet my inquisitive gaze. "Yes, I couldn't escape that story, what with all the media reports and the town gossips going crazy. But again, it was all so long ago. Nothing to do with me now."

"It's just that Carol and P.J. thought you should be warned about the authorities looking into the matter. They wanted to give you a heads-up." I circled around the display case to stand beside her.

"Is that right? Imagine that." Ruth set the paperweight back on the shelf. "I suppose you should convey my thanks, although they needn't have bothered. I have nothing to hide from the sheriff's department, or anyone else."

"They just wanted to be sure you weren't blindsided. You know how they are—always thinking about others."

"Yes, yes. The ultimate do-gooders, bless their hearts."

Knowing what that phrase actually meant to anyone south of the Mason-Dixon line, I fixed Ruth with a hard stare. "I know they're under suspicion, since Jeremy's body was discovered at Vista View, and in a condition that indicates foul play. And I admit that maybe they just want to cover all their bases, but be fair—you should realize they just want to protect you, and the others from the commune."

"Don't get riled up. I have nothing against P.J. and Carol. They were always decent to me, which is more than I can say for some of the commune members." As Ruth turned to face me, I noticed her shaking fingers. She caught my gaze and immediately clutched the faded purple fabric of her tunic to hide her hands. "I didn't care much for most of the others, to be honest. Which is why I've only stayed in touch with P.J. and Carol. I haven't talked to anyone else from those days in years."

Ruth turned back to the shelf and picked up a rose-patterned teacup. She held it up to the cold fluorescent light as if inspecting it for flaws. "Perhaps this is something that would appeal to your friend? You mentioned wanting a gift." Ruth waved the cup at me. "It's Haviland. Just one piece, but with the matching saucer. No? Well, something else then." As Ruth set down the cup, her trembling fingers made it rattle against the saucer.

I tried to catch her gaze but failed. "So, if you don't mind telling me, how well did you know Jeremy Adams?"

Ruth sighed and stared at a point over my shoulder. "Very well, actually. In fact, as you'll probably find out if you talk to any more of the commune members, we were romantically involved."

Here is a possible motive, I thought, even though something in Ruth's eyes seemed to belie such an idea. *Whatever impression she gives now, back then she could've been a woman scorned, and possibly angry enough to kill the lover who'd abandoned her.* "So you loved him?"

"Oh yes, desperately, as only a young girl can. Fortunately, I've grown wiser as well as older, and I've put all that behind me." When Ruth dropped her gaze and looked into my eyes, I was shocked by the pain I saw on her face. "You see, I loved Jeremy, but he never really loved me. He used a lot of pretty words to promise me things, but even before he left Vista View, I'd discovered he had another lover. Then he left both of us without a word." She shrugged. "I had to suck up my pain and get over it, and I did. Faster than Drummer got over his anger, that's for sure."

This is something new. I pressed my palms against the smooth glass of the display case. "Why would Dean Bodenheimer be angry with Jeremy?"

"Because he believed Jeremy was planning to let him tag along when he went out to LA." Ruth exhaled a derisive sniff. "Drummer really thought he was going to be part of Jeremy's new band, or so he used to tell me. He'd brag about Jeremy selecting him as a partner in his quest for fame and fortune. Of course, Jeremy had no intention of including Drummer in any of his plans, but what I don't know"—Ruth brushed back another errant tendril of her gray hair—"is whether Jeremy actually promised Drummer any such thing. Knowing Jeremy, he may have. He was rather glib with his assurances."

"Which means Dean Bodenheimer could've also felt betrayed when Jeremy left without him."

"Absolutely. Whether or not promises were made, Drummer was furious when Jeremy left without a forwarding address."

"Angry enough to kill?" I asked gently. It was obvious that, for all her disclaimers, Ruth Lee was still deeply affected by Jeremy's disappearance.

And now the discovery of his death, I reminded myself.

Ruth gnawed on her lower lip for a moment. "Perhaps. Who knows? I did hear rumors that one of Drummer's ex-wives had to take out a restraining order against him after their divorce."

"What about Pete O'Malley or Stanley Owens? Or Belinda Cannon, who also disappeared, and not long after Jeremy left the commune? Or even Emily Moore? You would remember her as Daisy Miles, I suppose. Did they display any violent tendencies?"

"Not so much, although both Daisy and Pete certainly had flashes of temper, and the strength to hurt someone, given the right circumstances. Belinda was so strung out most of the time, and actually she was . . ." Ruth tightened her thin lips and cleared her throat before continuing. "Never mind about that. Water under the bridge. Who else? Oh yes, Stan. Honestly, I can't picture him harming anyone. I'd believe Carol or P.J. as killers before Stan."

I picked up the teacup she'd shown me and examined it. Perhaps I would buy it, even if I later decided to give Fiona a different gift. It was the least I could do to make up for this interrogation. "Why's that?"

"He was so meek and easily frightened," Ruth said. "Even the farm animals spooked him. Imagine, being scared of a calf or a lamb. But that was poor Stan." Ruth's eyes glazed, as if she was lost in a memory. "He was so terrified of heights that it was absolute torture for him to climb up into the hayloft. P.J. finally had to release him from any chores that involved being even inches above the ground."

I shot her a questioning glance. "Really? But he died . . ."

"From a fall from a high footbridge. Yes, I heard that." Ruth rubbed her temples. "It's very strange. I was baffled when I heard about it. Although perhaps he decided to, you know, do away with himself."

"The authorities don't think so. I guess something about the way it happened doesn't indicate that," I said. "At least from what I read in the news reports."

"Yes, but . . ." Something secretive flickered in Ruth's eyes. "He had a nervous breakdown, you know, right before he fled the commune."

"Really? Do you know why?"

"Not for certain. But when I tried to comfort him one night before he left, he admitted he was tortured by something that had happened. I had my suspicions, but he would never confirm them one way or the other."

I cradled the cup between my hands. "If he killed Jeremy . . ."

Ruth twisted the hem of her tunic between her fingers. "I can't believe that. Any of the others, yes. But not Stan. No, I always thought it had something to do with a failed relationship. I think that's why he connected with me in that moment. I was obviously deeply hurt by Jeremy's abrupt departure, and Stan had apparently been rejected by someone too. He did confess that much to me, although he would never say who it was that he'd loved and lost." Ruth lifted her chin and met my inquisitive gaze squarely. "We bonded over our mutual heartache, I suppose."

I set the cup down on the top of the display case and reached for the saucer. Sliding it under the cup, I carefully considered my next words. "Forgive me for pouring salt in the wound, but I do want to ask you something else about Jeremy Adams." I kept my gaze fixed on my hands as I spun the cup around on the saucer. "I suppose, hearing the news of his death, you could feel quite differently now, but before that . . . Well, not to be rude, but you did say that you were terribly hurt when he originally disappeared. I assume you were angry too?"

"Of course. He promised me we'd always be together, and then he was gone." Ruth swept one finger under her right eye. "Sorry. I still tend to tear up about that, after all these years."

"He betrayed you," I said, sympathy infusing my voice. I knew all too well how the betrayal of a lover could bring forth fury as well as tears.

"He did, and I reacted badly. I can see why the others might suspect me of killing him. I was that angry. But"—Ruth shook out her tensed fingers and dropped her hands to her sides—"I swear I didn't. Despite everything, I loved him. And anyway, I had something of his that made me think he loved me too, or at least trusted me more than anyone else. A promise that, despite everything, maybe he'd return to me one day."

The triumphant look that suffused Ruth's face took me by surprise. "Oh? What was that?"

"A copy of his demo reel." Ruth's thin lips curved in a tremulous smile. "He left it with me before he headed to LA. Only a cassette, of course. He took the actual reel with him. It contained all his original songs. He always played covers when he performed for us at the commune, but for his demo reel he only wanted the music he'd created."

"And he entrusted you with a copy?"

"Yes, and that's why I never thought we were completely done." Ruth touched her fingers to her lips, as if remembering a long-lost kiss. "I don't think anyone one else at the commune knew anything about it. Certainly not that girl . . ." Ruth shook her head and gave me a triumphant look. "He told me he'd worked on it in secret, writing both the lyrics and the music in order to show the true depth of his talent. He planned to shop it around as soon as he made the right contacts."

"You still have the cassette?"

"Yes, although I eventually copied it over to a CD before the original tape wore out. I listened to it too many times, I suppose." The sudden shyness flickering over Ruth's face made me catch a glimmer of the young girl she'd once been, madly in love with a brilliant musician.

I knew that story. My version, like hers, had not ended well. But it seemed she'd clung to the dream much longer.

"Maybe that's something you should share with the authorities," I said. Although I wasn't sure what Jeremy's original music could've had to do with his death, it seemed like an important puzzle piece that Brad and his team might need.

"I'd rather someone else do that." Ruth met my questioning look with a lift of her hands. "Carol and P.J., of course. I don't know—I just thought if they were the ones to turn it over to the sheriff's department, it would be weighed in their favor. Like, if the authorities believe Jeremy trusted Carol and P.J. enough to let them keep something so valuable to him, maybe they wouldn't look so suspicious?" She shrugged. "As I said, they were always decent to me, so I don't mind helping their cause."

"I don't think that's exactly legal . . ."

Ruth cut me off with a wave of her hand. "Oh, come on. It's not like the cops always play fair. Anyway, it's actually a bit selfish of me. I'd rather not be too involved in this investigation, and that CD might drag me in too deep. You'd be doing me a favor, as well as helping P.J. and Carol."

I knew I should refuse this request. It would disrupt the chain of evidence if I accepted Ruth's CD. But I had to confess, for some inexplicable reason, I wanted to hear Jeremy's music. Perhaps it was the image of a vibrant young man—smiling at me from a photo that spoke to me across the years—that convinced me to agree.

"All right," I said. "But you keep the original. Carol and P.J. can say they copied it to the CD and then tossed the cassette. That way you'll still have a copy, no matter what happens."

"Sadly, the cassette fell apart long ago. Now all I have is the CD."

"Are you sure you want to give it up?"

"Yes, I'd rather see it help my old friends instead of just sitting on a shelf. I'm sure Jeremy would've wanted that too," Ruth said before heading toward the back of the shop. "Wait there—I'll be just a minute."

I sucked in a deep breath. Why was I doing this crazy thing? It was out of character for me, but for some reason I felt compelled to comply. *By a photograph*, I thought, with a snort of derision. *You really are losing it, girl.*

Musing over this foolish compulsion, I crossed to the front window and stared out into the street. A tall, lanky figure caught my eye. Someone standing at the window, peering in.

P.J. Fields.

I rubbed my eyes. *No, that can't be right*, I told myself. It was a weekday afternoon. I knew P.J. was usually too busy with farm chores and direct sales of his produce to come into town.

And why would P.J. be lurking around in front of Ruth's shop? Or if he'd planned to drop in, why would he scurry off as soon as someone noticed him?

"Here you go." Ruth's voice cut into my thoughts.

I turned to face her and took the slim plastic case from her hand. "Okay. But if the sheriff's department really starts questioning you . . ."

"I can handle them." Ruth spoke with a confidence she'd not displayed up to that point. She gave me a little smile. "I've dealt with situations like that before, back when I had a few run-ins with the law over my activism."

"All right, then," I said. "And thanks for sharing so much information with me. But before I go, I do want to buy that teacup and saucer. It might be just the thing."

Ruth smiled again and wrote up the sale in her old-fashioned receipt book. Fortunately, she also had a credit square on her phone to take my payment, since the cup and saucer were a bit more expensive than I'd imagined.

But I didn't complain. I simply slipped the CD case into the bag with the gift box and left the shop, promising to stop by again soon.

On the street, I looked around for P.J. Fields, but he was nowhere to be seen.

Chapter Nine

The next morning, I asked Sunny to watch the desk so I could head out to the archives.

"I want to check on a couple of things before I assist that reporter with his research," I told her, grabbing my keys. "And by the way, Mr. Dane should show up around ten. Could you escort him out to the archives when he arrives? Bill's scheduled to volunteer all morning, so you can ask him to cover the desk."

Sunny made a great show of rolling her eyes. "Sure, I'll be happy to interact with that guy again."

"Come on, he isn't that bad. Just tell him 'no comment' if he starts getting too nosy."

Sunny grumbled over this before finally agreeing. "But you owe me one," she said as I headed for the back door.

"I owe you a lot more than that," I called back over my shoulder.

After carrying the envelope containing Jeremy Adams's photo back out to the archives with the clear intention of refiling it, I instead extracted the picture and laid it on the worktable.

"You wrote some fine music," I told the face smiling up at me. "I wish other people could hear it."

I drummed my fingers against the tabletop as I considered this conundrum. When I'd gotten home the evening before, I'd popped Ruth's CD into my computer and ripped it to the music app on my cell phone before sliding the CD back into its case and hiding it under a pile of socks in one of my dresser drawers.

Honestly, I'd fully intended to drive out to Vista View to give the CD to Sunny's grandparents, but two things had changed my mind. First, when I'd called the farm, I'd reached Carol, who at the start of our chat informed me that P.J. had been over in Smithsburg all afternoon, haggling over the rent for the booth he hoped to set up at the new farmers' market there. I knew this was a lie, but because I couldn't be sure Carol was in on the deception, I decided to say nothing about Ruth's CD.

Then, after listening to all of Jeremy's songs on repeat, I wanted more time to consider my best course of action. Deep in my heart, I felt they should be shared with the world, and I wondered if that would be possible if they were relegated to the evidence locker in a murder case.

Considering this, I lifted the photo and stared into Jeremy's dark eyes. "You've put me in quite a dilemma," I said, somehow not feeling foolish while talking to a photograph of a dead man. "Maybe I should check with a lawyer first, to see what the ramifications might be. Then I'll talk to Ruth again and see whether she wants to help me find a way to get an album made. Even if it takes a Patreon site or a GoFundMe page or something, I bet we could do it."

Strangely, I felt a rush of joy, almost like Jeremy approved of this idea. *Which is crazy*, I thought, reminding myself that I didn't believe in ghosts. Although . . . *Admit it, there were those incidents in the recent past that had you questioning whether Hamlet was right about there being more things in heaven and earth . . .*

Lost in my thoughts, I jumped when the door to the archives opened. I shoved Jeremy's photo back into the folder and forced a smile as Sunny ushered Daniel Dane into the room.

"Good morning," I said, ignoring the guarded expression on Sunny's lovely face.

"Hi." Dan's sea-green eyes focused on the worktable. "I see you started without me."

"I just wanted to pull a few things beforehand," I said. I'd already decided not to mention my work for the sheriff's department. I didn't entirely trust the reporter yet, especially where Carol and P.J. were concerned. "I still need to grab a few more boxes, though. Sunny, could you retrieve the town council records for 1964 and '65? Maybe there's some mention of unsolved disappearances in the notes."

"Okay." She made a beeline for a metal file cabinet. "But I shouldn't linger. I don't want to leave Bill on his own at the desk for too long."

I swept this aside with a wave of my hand. "Oh, he'll be fine. And he knows where to find us if he needs assistance."

Sunny cast me a suspicious side-eye glance as she riffled through the cabinet.

"There wasn't much about any of the missing people in the area papers," Dan said, circling around the table to stand beside me.

"I know. That's why I suggested checking the town records. They might've recorded a discussion that wasn't shared with reporters." I glanced up at Dan. "Not everyone trusts the news media, you know."

Dan's smile lit up his long-boned face. "Only too well."

"Here you go." Sunny slapped several acid-free file folders down onto the table. "I think I'll head back." She turned on her heel and marched to the door.

"Wait a minute, Ms. Fields," Dan said, stopping her in her tracks. "I want to apologize again for badgering you the other day. I'm afraid I was too aggressive. I hate that we got off on the wrong foot."

"Wrong entire leg," Sunny replied, but she allowed her fingers to slip off the doorknob. She turned to face us.

Dan, who'd sat in one of the room's wooden chairs, scooted it closer to the table. "I also want you to know that I don't actually suspect your grandparents of any wrongdoing." He kept his gaze focused on the file folders. "My research has revealed their solid commitment to nonviolence."

"Glad to hear it," Sunny said, stepping away from the door. "They don't even kill animals, you know. We just raise chickens for the eggs, and cows and goats for their milk."

Dan looked up and flashed her a warm smile. "I know. I read that in an article about the farm. Now, where do you suggest I begin?"

"Just take a look through all those papers and see what you can find," I replied, handing him a pair of gloves. "You don't have to put these on for the files, as a lot of that material is comprised of copies, but please use them when you get to the photos."

Sunny, who'd inched farther into the room, leaned back against the file cabinet. "Since you say you don't suspect my grandparents, what's your theory about who killed Jeremy Adams, Mr. Dane?"

"Please, call me Dan." He perused a stack of town council minutes, his brow furrowed with concentration. "And, to answer your question, Ms. Fields . . ."

"Sunny." She wrinkled her nose when I shot her an amused look.

"Okay, Sunny it is."

"And Amy," I added.

Dan set aside one stack of the papers and sat back in his chair. "At this point, my working theory is that Jeremy, like some of the other missing people, got tangled up in the drug trade. There was a pretty serious illicit drug scene around here in the 1960s and '70s. Underground, of course. From the outside, Taylorsford and the surrounding counties appeared to be idyllic country locales. Havens for those who wanted to escape the turmoil of the city. But appearances can be deceiving, and I've discovered that there was a lot more going on beneath the surface."

"I can certainly believe that." I thought about the secrets I'd uncovered in previous investigations. Since drugs had figured into some of those cases as well, I was aware that Taylorsford had not escaped that particular blight.

Dan's gaze slid from me to rest on Sunny. "I suppose you know there was drug use among the members of your grandparents' commune?"

"Yes, of course." Sunny fiddled with a strand of her hair, twisting it around her finger. "But the grands weren't heavily into it, or so they've told me. They mostly smoked weed."

"Perhaps that's true." Dan crossed his lanky arms behind his head and leaned back in his chair. "But some of their friends, including Jeremy Adams, apparently had pretty serious habits—ones that included the hard stuff. Which meant they had to be involved with hard-core dealers. Who were not, as you can imagine, model citizens."

"You think Jeremy and the other missing people ran afoul of drug dealers?" The image of Jeremy's smiling face flitted through my mind. I frowned, hating the thought that he'd met his untimely end in some particularly gruesome fashion.

"Some of them, anyway." Dan stretched his arms above his head before dropping them back to his sides. "Which would explain why they were never seen again."

"Even your aunt?" I glanced at the reporter. "I hope you don't mind me sharing that information with Sunny, Dan."

"Not at all." His gloved fingers riffled through the photo box for a moment before he looked up and caught Sunny's eye. "As I told Amy the other day, it's what started my current investigation. Back in the sixties, my mother's sister also disappeared from this area."

"I'm so sorry. I'm sure that was extremely painful for your family." Sunny offered him a comforting smile. "But, getting back to Jeremy, do you think it's possible that some criminal buried his body on our farm? Without my grandparents' knowledge, of course."

"It's a possibility." Dan motioned to the chair next to him. "Have a seat, Sunny. I imagine you've been on your feet most of the morning."

I looked from Sunny to Dan and stifled a smile. The reporter hadn't asked me to sit down, but then, he wasn't gazing at me with that intent expression either.

Sunny's made another conquest. And she doesn't even know it yet. I studied her face, noticing the softening of the lines bracketing her lips. *Maybe.*

"In all honesty, I suspect it would've been more than one lone dealer," Dan said, pulling the extra chair away from the table so Sunny could sit beside him. "Probably a gang of some kind, or at least a dealer who was in league with a larger organization. That would explain how people could be made to disappear so easily."

A thought popped into my head, and I crossed to the shelves to hide the conflict undoubtedly mirrored on my face. I knew someone who had worked as a drug dealer in this area back in the sixties. Someone clever enough to make people disappear.

But just the other day Kurt claimed he'd left the area before Jeremy went missing. I yanked a box of miscellaneous materials from the sixties off the shelf. *Still, everyone also thought Jeremy left, and he obviously returned. Who's to say Kurt couldn't have come back as well? Not to mention, you know that Kurt Kendrick sometimes lies . . .*

After plopping down the box, I backed away from the table. "I think I may leave you guys here and go back inside," I said. "Trust me, Dan, you're in good hands with Sunny."

"I'm sure of that," he replied with a smile.

Sunny, pouring over a few of the documents from the files, did not respond. That was enough to tell me how obsessed she'd become with proving her grandparents' innocence. Normally, my flirtatious friend would've returned Dan's interest by now.

"But, before I go, Dan, I'm just curious about one thing." I paused at the door, turning back with a nonchalance I didn't feel. "Have you discovered the names of any of the dealers who worked this area?"

"A few. But mainly just nicknames. Or street names, I guess you'd say." Dan looked me over, one eyebrow quirked.

Maybe my tone hadn't been as casual as I'd hoped. "I just thought it might help us in the search for more information."

"Well, anything to help the cause. Okay, there was a woman they called Esmerelda, and some dude called the Weasel, but the one that really sticks out is some guy they called the Hammer."

Sunny glanced at Dan, a little line creasing her smooth forehead. "With that name, he must've been one scary dude."

"I'm not sure about that. I haven't heard any stories of him being overly violent. But he did work the area, and had a good-sized clientele, including some people at the Vista View commune."

"I heard the same thing from Peter O'Malley," I said, earning sharp glances from both Sunny and Dan. "When I talked to Pete the other day, he mentioned both the Weasel and the Hammer."

Sunny gave a mock shudder. "Sounds like a bad rock band."

"It does, but there wasn't anything funny about those guys." As Dan leaned across to grab more papers from one of the files, his arm brushed Sunny's. "Oh, sorry," he said, pulling away.

"No problem." Sunny turned, scooting her chair to the side so she could face the reporter. "And I guess it's my turn to apologize. Honestly, I thought you were digging for dirt on my grandparents to write an exposé or something. That's why I was so rude to you at first—I was afraid you planned to cast unsubstantiated suspicion on them just to bolster your own readership."

"I understand, and honestly"—Dan offered her a smile that would've melted a far stonier heart—"I admire your loyalty, and understand your desire to protect them. It's what we should all do for family, isn't it?"

"Absolutely," Sunny said. "So how about we let bygones be bygones." She held out her hand.

As Dan smiled and clasped her fingers in a firm grip, I called out a "See you later" and made a hasty exit.

* * *

An hour later, Sunny and Dan approached the circulation desk, chattering away like they'd known each other for years.

"You seem to have gotten very friendly," I observed after Dan left the library and Sunny joined me behind the desk.

"He's actually a pretty interesting guy."

"I'm sure. Not too hard on the eyes, either."

"A little skinny for my taste, but"—Sunny shrugged—"that really isn't relevant if you're just going to be friends. And like I told the grands, I'm not looking to date anyone right now." She lifted her chin and met my amused gaze with a defiant stare.

"Right." I pointed to my temple with one finger. "Totally got that vibe. Anyway, flirting aside, did you find any useful information for Dan's article?"

Sunny tapped her painted fingernails against the pitted surface of the desk. "For your information, we weren't flirting. And yes, a few things. Dan had to head off to work on another project, though. He said he'd come back soon to dig a little deeper into the files."

"I'm sure he will." I couldn't resist a little smirk. Turnabout was fair play, and Sunny had pushed me to pursue relationships often enough in the past. Now it was my turn to encourage her.

"Look, Miss Intrusive, if you must know—we had a very serious discussion. In fact, I shared the story about my mom. I thought it would help to explain why the grands are so sensitive on the subject of missing persons."

"Really?" My expression instantly sobered. Sunny rarely spoke about her mom, Heather, who'd run away from home when she was sixteen, only to show up again right before she gave birth to Sunny. I knew Carol and P.J. had hoped Heather would agree to live with them and raise her baby in their home, but soon after Sunny was born, Heather had disappeared once again.

Carol had once told me in confidence that she suspected Heather was dead, since she'd never again contacted them or attempted to see her daughter. P.J. refused to believe this, and Sunny . . . Sunny always claimed she didn't care.

"Dan is easy to talk to," my friend said, keeping her head down as she sorted through some past-due notices I'd printed out and stacked on the desk.

"Being a reporter, I imagine he's been trained to listen. But he does seem like a decent guy. And he strikes me as rather intelligent, too."

"Oh yes," Sunny said, immediately covering her enthusiasm by arranging the notices into a neat pile. "Anyway, he has a master's in creative writing, along with his journalism degree."

"Ah, an author." As I examined Sunny's profile, I couldn't help but notice the rosy color rising in her cheeks. "Just your type."

"I do love books."

"Along with intelligent men who are easy to talk to?"

Sunny gave me a grin. "Maybe. But I swear I'm not going to date Dan. At least not seriously. I have too much going on right now to try to squeeze in a romance."

"Okay, fair enough. But don't push him too far away."

Sunny tossed her gleaming golden hair. "You know me better than that. But I'm keeping it on strictly friendly terms for now. Besides, if I help him uncover the truth about these disappearances and how his aunt or Jeremy Adams might've been the victims of drug deals gone wrong, it could benefit the grands. So there's that, too."

"There's definitely that." I looked her up and down. "You know he's going to fall in love with you."

"Not necessarily. And I don't intend to encourage him."

I shook my head and cast her a rueful smile. "Oh, Sunny, don't you realize by now that you don't have to?"

Chapter Ten

Having left the house without bothering to prepare a lunch, I told Sunny I'd cover for her from one to two if she'd hold down the fort at noon.

"I think I'll just walk down to the Heapin' Plate and grab a sandwich to go," I said as she poked her head into the workroom.

"Oh, could you get me something too?" Sunny rummaged through her macrame pouch and pulled out a ten-dollar bill. "Just get me a sandwich; I have a bottle of water in the break-room fridge."

"What do you want?" I asked, slinging my purse strap over one shoulder.

"Anything vegetarian is fine. But tell Bethany to substitute an extra pickle for the chips, would you?"

"Watching your girlish figure?" I asked, raising my eyebrows.

Sunny grinned and patted her hip. "No, I just like their dill pickles."

"Okay, see you in a bit," I called out to her before exiting through the staff door.

The Heapin' Plate, the diner run by Bethany Virts, was only a short stroll away. Located in a historic turn-of-the-century building that had once been a general store, the restaurant had retained its original pressed-tin ceiling and marble-topped walnut counter but was decorated in a vintage 1950s style. Round, chrome-edged tables and metal ladder-back chairs filled the black-and-white-tiled floor, and the large front windows were framed by yellow-checked gingham curtains.

I surveyed the dining area, noticing with dismay that Elspeth Blackstone was holding court at one of the tables.

Spreading more salacious stories about Sunny and her family, no doubt. I frowned and crossed to the counter without looking in Elspeth's direction. But before I reached the line for takeout orders, I heard someone call out my name.

"Amy, please join us." Zelda Shoemaker waved me over to a table by the far wall.

A short, plump woman whose rosy, unlined face and expertly dyed blonde cap of curls made her look younger than her sixty-six years, Zelda was the polar opposite of my self-contained aunt. Yet they'd been best friends from childhood.

Across the table from Zelda sat Walt Adams, a tall, lanky sixty-five-year-old and another of my aunt's childhood friends. He was also Zelda's significant other, although they'd only recently gone public with their relationship. Walt, who was one of the few African-Americans who'd lived in Taylorsford before the 1970s, had been hesitant to announce their relationship to the town, despite the fact that both he and Zelda had lost their spouses years before. It was only after some recent traumatic events that they had resolved to face whatever friction they might encounter from any less enlightened residents of the town.

Fortunately, there'd been no backlash, at least from what I'd heard. "Just let me order first," I told Zelda, motioning toward the counter.

After a few minutes, with takeout orders placed for both me and Sunny, I crossed over to their table. "How are you two doing today?" I asked, taking the third seat at the table.

"Just fine, dear," Zelda said. "Although I am keeping my eye on that viper over there." She pointed toward Elspeth and her small group of friends.

"Now, Zel, let's not get into that," Walt said, his gaze wandering to follow a man who'd just entered the diner. "Look—there's that investigative reporter I was telling you about. The one who's been looking into the disappearance of people from this area in the sixties."

"Daniel Dane?" I turned in my chair as the reporter made his way to the counter.

Catching my eye, he waved.

"You know him?" Zelda asked, her tea-brown eyes widening. "Walt's been following some of his articles, and when we heard Dane was in Taylorsford, he hoped to meet him. Do spill the beans about how you made his acquaintance so fast, dear. From what Walt told me, he's only just appeared in town."

"He stopped by the library yesterday," I said, sharing a *What can you do?* look with Walt. "He wanted to question Sunny, but I hooked him up with the archives instead. Although, honestly, he and Sunny . . ."

"Yes?" Zelda bounced in her chair.

Uh-oh. Better backtrack if I want to keep her from proclaiming them a couple. "Oh, it's nothing. He seems like a nice guy. Devoted to the facts, which is always good. He claims he's determined to uncover the truth but isn't going to throw anyone under the bus to do so."

"Sounds like my kind of guy." Walt, stroking his chin with his long fingers, appeared lost in thought. "Maybe you could introduce us? I've been waiting for years for someone to really look into Jeremy's disappearance."

"Didn't the authorities do that back when he was declared missing?" I held up my finger when I heard Bethany call out my ticket number. "Hold that thought. Let me grab my order and I'll be right back."

At the counter, I paid for the sandwiches and asked Dan, who was waiting, to join me at Zelda and Walt's table once he had his own order.

"Now, Walt," I said, as I sat down beside Zelda again. "Tell me more about the investigation into Jeremy's disappearance. I don't think I've ever heard you talk about it before."

"I don't usually say much." Walt ran one hand over his closely cropped black-and-silver hair. "Honestly, there isn't that much to say."

"Walt thinks the authorities botched the case," Zelda said, giving his other hand a pat. "Don't you, dear?"

"Unfortunately, yes. I admit they didn't have a lot to go on. My aunt didn't even report Jeremy missing until several months after he supposedly disappeared. I'd gotten this call from him, you see. A month or so after he apparently left that commune out at Vista View."

I knew this but gave him a questioning look anyway. Not knowing whether it was supposed to be a secret, I didn't think I should tell either Walt or Zelda that Aunt Lydia had shared this story with me.

"The truth is," Walt continued, "Jeremy hadn't stayed in touch after leaving home. He pretty much flew the coop right after his high school graduation and only contacted the family once or twice before I got that call from him. We knew he was living on the commune, but he never came to see us during that time and discouraged us from visiting him. So not hearing from him for a while wasn't that odd."

"But then you didn't hear from him at all?"

Walt nodded. "That's right, and after he had told me to be sure and let my aunt know he'd phone her on her birthday. When that day came and went and there was no call, she started to get worried. He may not have been one to stay in touch, but Jeremy would never have promised something like that and not followed through."

I clutched the white paper takeout bag between my hands. "That's when your aunt reported him missing?"

"Soon thereafter." Walt looked up and over my shoulder. "Well, how about that—just the man I wanted to meet."

I scooted over as Dan Dane pulled out the fourth chair at the table. "Sorry to intrude, but Amy invited me over. Daniel Dane," he added, thrusting out his hand.

Walt clasped the younger man's hand and gave it a firm shake. "Walter Adams. Very nice to meet you, Mr. Dane."

"Call me Dan, please. And I'm happy to meet you too. You're Jeremy Adams's first cousin, aren't you?"

"Yes, he is." Zelda lifted her chin and met Dan's inquisitive gaze. "And I'm Zelda Shoemaker. I never met his cousin, but I heard a lot about him when Walt and I were kids."

"Pleasure," Dan said, leaning over the table to shake her hand as well.

"Walt was just telling me about the initial investigation into Jeremy's disappearance," I said as Dan sat back in his chair.

"What little there was of it." Walt's bitter tone made me glance over at him with surprise.

"Sadly, they didn't do much," Dan said. "Of course, he was a young hippie with no permanent address. I guess they thought it wasn't that odd for him to be out of contact with his family."

"And he was poor, and black." Walt leaned forward, resting his arms on the table. "From what I can tell, the search was pretty cursory. At least, I've never seen evidence that they did much more than ask a few people about his possible whereabouts. But maybe you know more about the search than I do, Dan. I've been following your articles about the people missing from this area."

"I've been able to dig up more information on the movements of some of the other missing people, but I'm afraid I've never found out much about Jeremy." Dan poured a small puddle of ketchup onto his plate.

"He called and told you he was headed out to LA, right?" I asked Walt.

"Yes, he claimed he was calling from the road."

The bag crinkled under my fingers. "Which makes it weird that his body turned up here."

"Walt and I think he must've returned for some urgent reason," Zelda said. "To meet with someone, maybe?"

"Who could've been the someone who killed him," Walt said darkly. He narrowed his brown eyes. "Perhaps that's an angle you could investigate, Dan. Why Jeremy returned, and who he came to see. Because I don't think that anything except an emergency involving a close acquaintance would've pulled him away from LA at that point."

Dan finished off a couple of french fries before answering. "Good point. I'll have to look into that."

Walt toyed with his fork. "There was another thing—something I never shared with the authorities. Jeremy told me he'd meant to give me a copy of his demo reel containing all his original songs. He said he'd left too quickly to get it to me, but he would mail it. I know I should've told the sheriff's deputies about that package so they could've checked to see if it was sent, but then it never arrived, and"—Walt looked up, meeting Dan's intense gaze—"well, I was just a kid, and it made me angry, him just forgetting like that. That unfulfilled promise fed into my despair over his disappearance from my life, so I was always too angry to ever mention it. I guess it's far too late to track anything like that now."

I stared down at my white paper bag as if it held all the secrets in the universe. The bag crackled as I tightened my grip. I wanted to tell Walt I could give him his copy, but realized I shouldn't. If Walt thought it was something that could've helped the initial investigation into Jeremy's disappearance, I had to share it, and Ruth's involvement, with Brad Tucker instead. I made a mental note to call and see if I could drop by his office after work.

"That's too bad." Dan placed the uneaten burger he'd lifted to his mouth back on his plate. "I'd love to have been able to listen to it."

"Me too." Walt sat back in his chair.

"But I promise I'll follow up on that lead, even though it is rather tenuous," Dan said, looking around as a wail of sirens filled the street outside the diner.

Elspeth Blackstone leapt to her feet and rushed over to the door, followed by several other customers.

The diner's owner, Bethany Virts, a small, wiry young woman with dark hair pulled back into a tight bun, leaned over the counter and called out, "What's going on out there?"

Mr. Dinterman popped in the front door, his face ashen. "Just down the street. Apparently there's been a robbery or something."

He twisted his bony hands together. "And Ruth Lee . . . Well, she's been shot."

The dining room erupted into chaos, with everyone talking over each other. A couple of older women burst into tears. Moving closer to Zelda, Walt slid his arm around her shoulders.

Camille Blackstone, Elspeth and Bob's older daughter, ran into the diner shouting that Ruth was dead. In the silence that fell after this announcement, Camille added that she'd overheard the deputies say they weren't sure exactly when the break-in had happened.

"Her 'Closed, opening at ten AM' sign was still hanging on the front door," Camille said. "They think the robbery might've happened last night and no one noticed until this afternoon. They said Ruth probably didn't have any customers this morning, and she lived alone above the shop, so . . ." Camille shrugged her narrow shoulders.

I let fly an obscenity that made Zelda shoot me a disapproving look. But I didn't care. My stomach was churning. I'd just spent time with the woman the day before, which made her death feel all too real to me.

And to make things worse, you saw P.J. Fields lurking outside her shop . . . I took a deep breath before tightening my lips. I had to remain calm. Of course I'd have to share that information with the authorities, but I certainly wasn't going to blurt it out in front of Elspeth Blackstone and her cronies.

"She was shot?" one female customer shrieked. "Murdered? Right here in town?"

"That's enough. We don't know all the details, so please, let's not discuss this anymore." Bethany's narrow face was pinched with dismay.

I cast her a sympathetic glance. Bethany, whose mother had been murdered only a year and a half before, undoubtedly still had a hard time hearing this type of news.

"Didn't I tell you?" Elspeth's sharp voice rang out. "I bet it's that hippie-dippie Fields family again, mixed up in more criminal activities."

"Now, wait a minute." I took two strides forward before Walt grabbed my arm.

"Let me handle this," he said under his breath. Releasing me, he stepped into the center of the room and spoke to the cluster of diners in a clear, commanding voice. "Let's not jump to conclusions. We don't know what happened."

"It's downright suspicious." Elspeth placed her hands on her slender hips and faced off with him. "I know for a fact that Ruth Lee once lived on that commune run by Carol and P.J. Fields out at Vista View. I bet they're mixed up in her death, as well as that Jeremy Adams business. It's just too much of a coincidence, two commune members dying under suspicious circumstances." She turned to face the group at her table. "And Sunny Fields wants people to elect her as mayor? I say that takes some cheek."

Zelda jumped up so quickly that her chair fell backward and clattered against the hard floor. "Don't you dare turn this into something about Sunny."

"Now, Zel," Walt said, casting her a warning glance.

Zelda bustled around the table to stand beside him. "Some poor woman is dead, and all you can think to do is tear down other people just to help your husband's campaign." She shook her finger. "You should be ashamed of yourself, Elspeth Blackstone."

"I'm not ashamed to speak the truth," Elspeth replied, fixing Zelda with an imperious glare.

"But we don't have all the facts, so we don't know what really happened yet," Walt said in an even tone. He glanced from Zelda's furious face to Elspeth's smug expression. "How about allowing the authorities to do their job before we start spreading tall tales as the truth?"

Dan, who'd moved around to stand right behind me, muttered, "These small-town mobs, always eager to spread lies."

I glanced up at him over my shoulder. "It's not just in small towns."

Dan didn't meet my gaze. "I know. Which is why I like to keep my own counsel and seek justice in my own way."

"Truth and justice do go together," I agreed, before I slapped my forehead. "Oh my goodness, Sunny! She'll hear this news soon enough. Some patron is bound to tell her." I spun around, bumping Dan with my elbow, and grabbed my takeout bag. "Sorry, gotta go. Tell Zelda and Walt goodbye for me, would you?"

I didn't wait for his reply. Dashing out onto the street, I hurried toward the library. I knew I needed to take over coverage of the desk from Sunny, who would certainly want to rush home.

Lunch would have to wait, or not happen at all. But I didn't care. Sunny should go home to stay with her grandparents. After all, whatever their involvement in the case, they had lost someone else they'd once known well, and under tragic circumstances. They'd need Sunny to comfort them.

It seemed I couldn't do much for P.J. and Carol right now, but at least I could give them that.

Chapter Eleven

The nice weather convinced me to spend some time in the garden after work, although I had to wait until I got back from dropping off Jeremy Adams's CD at Brad Tucker's office. Of course, I'd also had to dash home and grab the CD before driving over to the sheriff's department, so I'd ended up missing Brad. But the attendant at the front desk had allowed me to write a note and tape it to the slim black case. He'd also promised he would personally hand-deliver the package to the chief deputy.

Fortunately, the early September days were long enough to allow me some time in the garden before darkness fell. I relished the work, knowing it would clear my head after the events of the day. Swiftly changing into a ratty T-shirt and a pair of well-worn jeans, I headed outside.

September meant deadheading roses as well as pruning some of the early-blooming shrubs and pulling up any vegetable plants that had died. I tackled the roses first. I knew they'd keep producing flowers into October or November if I cut back the dead blooms, but it was a time-consuming task. I had to deal with the climbing roses on the fence as well as the bush varieties in the garden.

Then there were the thorns. It didn't matter if I wore gloves or how careful I was handling the trailing vines, I always ended up getting pricked or scratched. Swearing as another tiny dagger pierced my skin, I didn't hear the footfalls of someone walking up behind me.

"Hello, Amy," said a deep masculine voice.

I spun around, clippers at the ready.

"Whoa." Kurt Kendrick held up his large, knobby-knuckled hands. "Forgive me. I didn't mean to startle you. I rang the doorbell and no one answered, but then I spied you working here along the fence . . ."

"Sorry." I locked and pocketed the clippers. "Guess I'm a little jumpy these days."

"Understandable." Kurt looked me over. "I'm sure the news about your friend's family is unsettling, not to mention that terrible incident in town today."

"Yeah. Anyway, how can I help you? Aunt Lydia is out. She and Zelda are having dinner at some new restaurant over in Smithsburg, and they always talk long into the evening, so I know she won't be back for a while. But if there's anything I can do, just ask."

"It's actually you I've come to see."

I shoved my floppy straw hat back away from my forehead. "Really? What about?"

"Your inveterate sleuthing. Do you really think that's wise? I know you're a researcher, but I believe you're placing yourself in danger, and that is hardly part of your job description." Kurt's blue eyes narrowed. "Yes, I know you're helping the sheriff's office again with some research, and also tracking down some of the former commune members for Carol and P.J. Fields."

"How do you . . . ?" I shook my head. "Never mind; I should realize by now that you know almost everything that goes on in Taylorsford."

Kurt lips curled away from his large white teeth. "Yes, you should. But really, Amy"—his grin immediately faded—"you are treading into dangerous waters with this particular investigation."

"Unlike the others?" I asked, raising my eyebrows.

"Exactly like the others, which is why I'm concerned." Kurt shuffled his feet.

That sign of nerves from the typically self-possessed older man was enough to capture my attention. "Would you like to sit down?" I motioned toward the garden.

"Yes, thank you." Kurt turned and strode over to one of the white-painted benches placed at the edges of the garden beds.

I followed more slowly, pondering what would drive the enigmatic art dealer to issue such a direct warning. "Have your little birds tweeted information that indicates some immediate danger?" I asked as I took a seat next to Kurt.

"No, it's my own specific knowledge." Kurt ran one hand through his thick white hair. "You know I dealt drugs back in the day, before I got into dealing art."

"Yes, and I suspect you were active in this area."

"I was. Before and for a little while after I left Paul Dassin's home." Kurt's head was turned away from me, his gaze focused on the back of Richard's house.

"And I imagine you knew many of the other dealers."

"Obviously. The truth is, despite the times, they were not all . . . adherents of a philosophy of peace and love, if you catch my drift."

I studied his rugged profile. "I do. Are you saying you suspect one of them of murdering Jeremy Adams? I've heard that theory already, from a few of the former commune members."

When Kurt glanced over at me, his stare was so intense that I scooted to the opposite end of the bench.

"You must concede that it's a possibility," he said. "And I'm not just talking about the Adams case. There's also Ruth Lee, whose death could be connected to her relationship to Adams."

"What do you mean? I'm aware they were lovers back in their commune days, but what would that have to do with anything?"

"What if she was somehow mixed up in his death? Or at least knew who had killed him?" Kurt straightened until his back wasn't touching the bench. "Even if Ruth remained silent for all these years, the killer might have grown concerned that the discovery of Jeremy's body would loosen her lips. Perhaps Jeremy's murderer was afraid she knew something about why he was killed. If it had anything to do with his drug use . . . Well, you must understand—dealers face severe criminal penalties if they're caught. Significant jail time is often a consequence. If any of them feared this new investigation into Jeremy's death might expose their current illegal operations, it could drive them to do whatever it took to protect themselves."

"Even commit murder?" I met his fierce glare without blinking but had to clasp my hands in my lap to still their trembling.

Is he talking only about others? Or was he involved in silencing a difficult client or two himself? My fingernails dug into my palms. *It's impossible to tell.*

"Yes," Kurt said shortly. He lapsed into silence as the chirping of an unseen bird filled the air. "And you should know, my dear," he said at last, "that sadly, once one has taken the life of another human being, it's far easier to kill again."

"Hopefully you are not speaking from experience." I fought to keep my tone light.

He looked away without replying. "You should stop helping anyone with this particular investigation, Amy. It is not prudent to take it any further."

"Because you think I might be in danger?" I slid closer and tapped his arm. "I didn't know you cared so much."

His fingers landed over mine and gripped with such force that I squeaked.

"I do, which is why I am giving you this direct warning." He stared at me in a way that made me shudder. "I do care, about you, as well as Richard and Lydia and others. But . . ." He pulled his hand back.

In for a penny . . . "But if we do anything to endanger your interests, you can't promise what might happen?"

Kurt reared back, crossing his arms over his broad chest. "That isn't what I meant."

"Isn't it?"

Twisting his lips, Kurt stared at me for a moment before answering. "No. But you would be wise to avoid digging into the pasts of men like me. They have not all changed as I have. But like me, they *do* all have secrets they do not wish to share."

I noticed that his eyes were glittering like sapphires—brilliant but cold. "If you know something about the dealers who may have supplied Jeremy Adams, you should inform the sheriff's office. It could provide crucial info, especially if the same person or organization killed Ruth to cover up their past crimes."

"Who says I haven't? Or won't eventually. Anyway"—Kurt dropped his arms to his sides—"the bottom line is that you and the Fields family should stop poking around in this particular case. Leave it to the professionals."

"I am leaving it to them. I'm just assisting with some research. It's not like I'm going to track down those former dealers and try to force a confession out of them." I drummed my fingers against the seat of the bench. "Except for you, of course. I might continue to try to pry more information out of you."

"I wouldn't," Kurt said, in a tone that could've frozen mercury. He stood and moved to loom over me. "Now, I've said my piece. I leave the rest to your common sense and discretion."

I couldn't hold back a nervous burst of laughter. "You're sure that's wise?"

"No," he said, as he turned to go. "Which is why I'll continue to keep an eye on you."

He strode away before I could form any decent response.

I sat for a moment considering his warning, before I stood and crossed the garden to reach the arbor—and the entrance to Richard's backyard. Jogging up to his back door, I knocked loudly, hoping he could hear me through the porch and into the house.

The door to the kitchen popped open and Richard rushed out. "Amy! Something wrong?"

"No." I wrapped my arms around him and leaned into his chest. "I just needed a hug."

"Anytime," he said, returning my embrace. "But I thought you said you were working in the garden and wouldn't be coming over this evening." He pushed me back, still holding on to my arms. "You look a little flustered. Sure nothing's wrong?"

"I'm fine." I debated telling him about Kurt's warning.

But if you do, he'll be very unhappy if you continue to help either Brad or Carol and P.J. And you know you will . . .

A yowl pierced the air.

"Not again." Richard dropped my arms and stepped back, glancing over his shoulder. "Loie is not happy."

"I told you she wouldn't welcome the addition of a new cat," I said, biting back a smile. I didn't want to embarrass him over his shock that Loie and Fosse hadn't become buddies the minute he'd brought the new kitten into the house. I knew Richard was unaccustomed to dealing with pets, since his parents hadn't allowed any animals in their home when he was growing up. "Where's Fosse now?"

Richard ran one hand through his short dark hair. "Upstairs, in the spare room. But even though she can't see him, Loie is still ticked off."

"Of course she is, but she'll get over it. You'll see." I followed Richard into the house. "Here, let me entice Loie with some treats while you go and fetch Fosse. Maybe with the two of us supervising, we can keep them from killing each other while they get better acquainted." I pulled the clippers from my pocket and dropped them on the kitchen counter before grabbing a packet of cat treats and heading into the living room.

While Richard jogged upstairs to grab Fosse, I located Loie, who was crouched under the coffee table, her dark pupils almost filling her green eyes and her tail thrashing from side to side.

I sat in an open spot on the floor, near the point where the wooden dance floor butted up against the living room area, and spilled some of the cat snacks into one palm. Leaning forward, I held out my hand. "Come here, girl. You know you want a treat."

Loie eyed me with suspicion.

I wiggled my fingers. "Don't be such a diva. Come out and get a snack."

The tortoiseshell cat twitched her little black nose and inched forward.

"That's right," I cooed, in a voice I used only on pets. "Have a nice little treat and get over yourself, you silly fluffball."

Loie reached me and thrust her face into my palm to nibble on the treats. Just as I leaned in to pet her head, Richard clattered down the stairs.

Instantly, Loie knocked aside my hand and jumped straight up in the air. I fell backward, and cat treats went flying in all directions.

Loie landed on her paws with her back arched and her tail fluffed out like a bottlebrush. Her eyes, slitted into shards of emerald, were fixed on something over my shoulder.

There was a shout and a thud, and I spun around on my backside to see Fosse—who'd obviously leapt free of Richard's arms—racing toward Loie.

Richard pursued the ginger kitten, but stumbled when his bare sole made contact with a couple of the hard cat treats. Swearing, he hopped on one foot, while Fosse stopped short as Loie arched her back higher and hissed.

I scooted to a point where I could place my body between the two cats. "Now Loie, let's not lose our cool."

"I think it's long gone." Richard plopped down on the floor next to me.

My gaze darted from Fosse, who appeared fascinated by this vicious new toy, to Loie, who was growling in fits and starts like a dying car battery. "She just needs to get it out of her system. Once she realizes that the kitten poses no danger, she'll calm down." I sat up and slid closer to Richard.

Danger, I thought. *Far too much talk about danger today.* But the kittens were helping ease my anxiety after my talk with Kurt, so I focused on them.

Richard draped one arm around my shoulders and pulled me to his side. "I hope you're right."

"I am. This happened every time we introduced a new pet to our existing ones," I said. "They have to establish who's in charge, and then everything is fine."

"You mean Loie wants to make sure Fosse knows who's the boss?"

"Of course. Now look—her tail is back to its normal size and she's just staring Fosse down, not hissing at him."

Richard tightened his grip on me. "Because he's not making any aggressive moves."

"Right. Because he obviously isn't stupid." I gazed at the kitten, whose amber eyes were half closed as he leisurely licked one of his copper-and-yellow-striped legs. "He's showing her he isn't going to attack, which is why she's calming down."

Loie's tale was still twitching, but the fear and fury that had vibrated her entire body had ceased. She settled down on the floor, her paws curled up under her, as she stared intently at Fosse.

"If we just sit here a while and let them work it out, I think they'll be okay," I said.

"I don't mind." Richard leaned in and kissed the top of my head. "I didn't think I'd see you this evening, so this is a bonus. By the way, since I won't see you much this next week, what with all the rehearsals for the scholarship recital, I wondered if I could take you home after the performance on Saturday night. If Lydia doesn't mind driving back by herself, I mean."

"Oh, she won't be alone. Sunny's coming along with us. Now look at that." I pointed at the two cats. "They're just eyeing one another now. No hissing or growling."

Fosse lay flat on the floor, his limbs relaxed, while Loie kept her legs curled up under her body. But she didn't back away when the ginger kitten reached out a paw and left it lying just inches from the patch of sleek black fur on Loie's breast. Casually, as if he weren't at all interested in her response, Fosse batted one of the spilled treats toward Loie.

"It seems Fosse is a rather clever devil," Richard said, as Loie sniffed at the treat.

"Just like his daddy," I replied, patting his thigh.

"Now wait a minute, I'm not devilish."

"I meant clever, but now that you mention it . . ." I leaned in and kissed him on the cheek. "Sometimes you can be quite a charming devil, I admit."

"Good to know," Richard said, pulling me into his arms. "Do you think we can take our eyes off the kittens for a moment?"

"Only a moment?" I asked, before he kissed me and we stopped talking for quite some time.

At that point, Loie and Fosse were no longer glaring at each other. They were both gazing at us in fascination instead.

"It appears that they've bonded over the peculiar habits of humans," Richard said, reaching out to pat Loie's sleek back.

I just smiled and petted Fosse.

Chapter Twelve

After breakfast on Saturday morning, I called Emily Moore, hoping to arrange a meeting with her sometime during the upcoming week.

She surprised me by suggesting I stop by that day.

"I'm free this afternoon," she told me. "And I'm always happy to make time to talk with a librarian."

"Well, this has to do with something other than the library," I warned her. "Just to be fair, I think I should tell you that my primary goal is to convey a message from P.J. and Carol Fields. If you are indeed the Daisy Miles who once lived on their commune, which I suspect you are."

I wouldn't have blamed her if she'd hung up on me, but after a long silence she responded. "I see you've discovered my alter ego. Very well, I suppose I should listen to what Carol and P.J. have to say. They were always good folks, so I imagine their hearts are in the right place with this."

"Let's make it after lunch," I said. "I'd hardly expect you to feed me, especially on such short notice."

We agreed to meet at two o'clock, which gave me time to do a little work in the garden before grabbing a shower and changing into some decent clothes.

It was a warm day, so I could get by without a jacket. Donning a copper-colored silk blouse and black jeans, I decided to wear my black leather sneakers instead of my loafers. After my talk with Emily, I thought I might walk to the other edge of town and back, just to fit in a little more exercise.

Reaching Emily Moore's address, I paused on the sidewalk leading to the porch to admire the fine lines of the brick bungalow. Climbing the stone steps, I surveyed the porch, which stretched the full width of the house. It was decorated with an assortment of comfortable outdoor seating and wicker plant boxes filled with geraniums that picked up the pink tones in the brick. I looked up, noticing the fine woodwork evident even in the porch's ceiling. As I pressed the antique bronze doorbell, a melodic chime rang through the house.

Emily opened the door and greeted me with a smile. "Hello, Amy. Please come in."

I offered her an answering hello and followed her into the house. She was a woman of average height, but chunky, with the solid, muscular bulk of someone who participated in sports or worked out. Her hair, cut in a short bob, was dyed a rich brown.

Not the typical image of a poet, for sure. When she stopped in the center of the room and turned to face me, the stereotype was further shattered by the strong line of her jaw and her piercing dark eyes. Dressed in a plain ivory cotton blouse over chestnut-brown pants, Emily Moore didn't fit my imaginary picture of the woman who had risen to fame in the flower-power sixties and psychedelic seventies. No bohemian chic clothes, filmy floral scarves, or long hair. Which was, I had to admit with a mental slap, an example of my own biases. I often railed against the depiction of librarians as skinny older women with their hair pulled up in a tight bun, wearing cardigans, glasses on a chain, and pearls. Yet here I was, making similar snap judgments.

I stepped through the front door, which opened directly onto a large room that obviously served as both a living room and dining area. There was a stone fireplace on one wall. Emily, with another smile, directed me to one of the oversized armchairs flanking the hearth.

"Thanks so much for talking with me today," I said as I sat down. "I know it may have come as a shock, having me mention your connection to Vista View out of the blue."

The poet's wide, dark eyes were soft as pansy petals behind her large glasses. "It did, at first. Few people have ever connected me with the Daisy Miles who lived at Vista View all those years ago." Emily took a seat across from me. "How did you figure that out?"

"Oh, that was my fiancé. He remembered something Clarion had recently published about you in a news release. It referenced you using the nickname Daisy during your time at Warhol's Factory, and when I mentioned that the girl at the commune was an aspiring poet, he put two and two together."

"Who is your fiancé, if I may ask?"

"Sorry, I should've said. It's Richard Muir. He teaches dance at Clarion."

"Ah yes. And of course I know who he is." Emily's smile broadened. "Hard to miss, isn't he?"

A flicker of heat rose up the back of my neck. "Yeah, I guess so."

"Lucky you," Emily said, her tone light as meringue. "I saw him dance once, when I still lived in New York. He was a bit younger at the time, of course. A Twyla Tharp piece at Lincoln

Center, I believe it was. Anyway, he was quite brilliant. And that body. Ooh-la-la, as they say." Emily shot me an amused glance. "No need to be concerned, dear. I'm not going to move in on your beau. It's just a natural admiration for beauty from a woman old enough to be his mother."

"Well, of course, I didn't think . . ." I rubbed at my face with the knuckles of one hand to hide the color that had risen in my cheeks. "Anyway, before I say anything more, I want to tell you again how grateful I am that you're willing to take time out of what must be a very busy schedule to talk with me. Especially on such short notice."

Emily Moore stretched out one leg and stared at her foot, as if examining her expensive leather pumps for scratches. "Oh, I'm not as busy as all that. In fact, I've slowed down considerably in recent years."

"You still write, though. I bought your most recent volume of poetry for the library just last year."

Emily waved one of her ringless hands through the air. "I manage to put out a book every couple of years. But I no longer write for literary magazines, and my teaching schedule has been reduced to two courses." She pursed her lips. "I'm almost seventy, you know. Time takes its toll."

As I recalled Carol and P.J. still planting and harvesting in their midseventies, something in her statement jangled through my mind. "Wait—I actually thought you'd be a few years older. I mean, if you were on the commune back in 1963 and '64 . . ."

Emily Moore's broad smile transformed her rather blunt-featured face, and for the first time I could see why, as a young person, the nickname Daisy might've been appropriate. "I lied about my age."

I shifted in my chair. "You were actually a minor?"

"Yes, I was barely fifteen when I showed up at Vista View. I said I was eighteen, though, because I immediately realized Carol and P.J. wouldn't allow me to stay if I told them my true age. They would've tried to find my parents or called social services. They were sticklers for things like that."

"As they should have been."

"Perhaps. But they didn't know my family. I was better off at the commune, underage or not, believe me." Emily Moore sat back in her chair and surveyed me with a glint of amusement in her eyes. "So now, tell me, what is this information you've been commissioned to share? I believe that's why you're here."

I straightened as much as I could in the nest of soft cushions. "Carol and P.J. asked me to find you, along with some of the other former commune members. They wanted to warn you that the authorities might come calling and asking questions."

"A little late. I prepared myself for that eventuality as soon as I heard they'd found Jeremy's body at Vista View. I assumed it was only a matter of time before I'd be questioned. My old nickname is not as hard to discover as I had hoped. It certainly didn't take you and your fiancé too long to figure it out." Emily leaned forward, clasping her hands together to form a church-and-steeple gesture. "Not that I'm worried. I never really tried to disassociate myself from my Daisy persona completely. I simply reverted to my real name when I embarked on a more conservative career path. At any rate, it doesn't matter. I have nothing to hide."

"I hope finding out Jeremy was dead wasn't too much of a shock." I summoned up a sympathetic smile. "I assume you were well acquainted, since you lived together for a year or so."

Emily tapped the tips of her fingers together. "I knew everyone on the commune fairly well, but you can save your condolences. Jeremy Adams and I were not close friends."

I stared at the poet. This didn't mesh with what I'd already heard. "Really? I talked to Peter O'Malley just the other day, and he seemed to think that most of the commune members were . . . close." For some reason, I decided not to mention my talk with Ruth.

"Oh, Pete." Emily sank back in her chair. "I'm sure he wishes that were true. But that was all in his head. Drug-fueled fantasies."

"So, despite what he told me, there weren't actually a lot of random romantic hookups?"

"Not as many as Pete would've liked, I'm sure. Carol and P.J. discouraged that sort of thing. They didn't mind sex outside of marriage, of course, but they weren't fond of promiscuity. They felt it took away from the real work we were supposed to be doing."

"Which was?"

"Changing the world, of course." Emily offered me a gentle smile. "That was the real goal. Sadly, you can see how well that turned out."

I dug my fingernails into the soft upholstery of the chair. I'd fulfilled P.J. and Carol's request without really trying, but decided, since Emily seemed so ready to talk, that I could pursue a different line of questioning. "I'm just curious. Since you did live so closely at the commune, I'm sure you observed everyone's interactions. Can you think of anyone who might've had a problem dealing with Jeremy?"

"Who didn't? He had the type of artistic temperament that often leads to relationship issues." Emily rose to her feet and faced the fireplace. "If I'm honest, I must confess that he could be a difficult individual, and not just when he was strung out on drugs."

"Yes, I heard he had an issue with that."

Emily leaned forward and straightened an engraved crystal object on the wooden mantel.

Some sort of literary award, I thought, hoping I could get a better look at it later.

"From Pete? That would be quite the pot-and-kettle situation."

"Not just from Pete." I paused, not wanting to drag my aunt into the mix. "But obviously someone had an issue with Jeremy or they wouldn't have killed him."

"Well, other than one of his drug suppliers," Emily said, keeping her back to me. "There's also Rainbow Lee, who was obsessed with him. She called it love, of course, but it was more like idol worship. She was very possessive, and Jeremy was a bit of a cad, really. He was sleeping with another girl at the same time. That didn't go over well with Rainbow—excuse me, *Ruth*—either."

A possibility occurred to me. "Belinda Cannon?" I asked, keeping my tone light.

Emily turned to face me, her dark eyes shadowed behind the heavy lenses of her glasses. "Yes, that was her name.

Anyway, Rainbow and Jeremy had some rather alarming fights about the situation. Then Jeremy just up and left the commune to pursue his fortunes, abandoning Ruth. That could've been a motive for a crime of passion, I suppose. A woman scorned."

I thought about the older woman I'd met recently. Could she really have killed her lover and then continued to mourn him for the remainder of her life? I shook my head. Stranger things had happened. "What about Dean Bodenheimer? I think you knew him as Drummer?"

"He had something of a temper, for sure." Emily looked away, her gaze focused on a side wall covered in framed diplomas and award certificates. "But I always thought Drummer and Jeremy were friends. They were both musicians and jammed together almost daily. Of course, Jeremy also had a temper, so they argued sometimes. To be honest, Drummer was the one who always backed down when things got too heated." She turned her owl-eyed gaze back on me. "In fact, if either one of the two was capable of murder, I would've expected it to be Jeremy, not Drummer."

I mulled over this information for a moment. If Walt's cousin had possessed a temper, perhaps he'd driven another, equally volatile person to murder. Which possibly led the trail back to his drug dealer. That would make sense, especially given the more recent death of Ruth Lee. Perhaps she'd known something about Jeremy's killer—or at least could've given the authorities more specific information about his dealers. Someone involved in a criminal trade, even if they'd left it behind, might be driven to kill anyone who could expose their dark past.

This line of reasoning brought me back to a thought that had been nibbling at my subconscious for days. Kurt might not have had anything to do with Jeremy Adams, or his death, but I had to wonder if he knew more about that tragedy than he would care to admit.

Although, I reminded myself, Emily could also be correct about Ruth Lee. She could've killed the lover who betrayed her, and her death could have simply been a robbery gone wrong. I gnawed at my lower lip for a second before I stood up and moved closer to Emily. "The thing that I find particularly odd is Jeremy leaving the commune without a word, only to apparently return not long after. What's your theory on why he came back to Vista View?"

When Emily turned to me, her expression was almost apologetic. *As if she's sorry to have to keep dragging Jeremy's name through the mud.*

"I'm not sure he did," she said. "I did hear from him once, you know, after he left. He said he was calling from LA, and I had no reason to doubt that. He even gave me a number where I could reach him in case . . ." Emily blinked rapidly before looking away. "Well, he trusted me to be his contact, I suppose, in case anyone else needed to reach him. He said he didn't want to bother Carol and P.J., and that some of the others were probably still furious with him, so . . ."

"But you never shared that number? Not even with the authorities?"

"No," Emily said, before she looked back at me. "As for discussing anything with the sheriff's office, let's just say they didn't do much investigating into Jeremy's disappearance. He was just a young black man who had no job and had broken off connections with his own family. The powers that be saw him as little more than a vagrant, so his case wasn't high on their priority list. They never even talked to me before I left for New York, and well, let's just say that back then I wasn't inclined to seek out any interactions with the cops."

"So you have no idea why or how he ended up back at Vista View?"

"No, and if you think about it—just because his body ended up there doesn't mean that's where he was killed. If a drug deal was involved, I suspect the murder happened elsewhere, and the killer or killers just buried him at the farm." Emily shrugged. "Maybe to do just what's happening now—throw suspicion on members of the commune if the crime was ever to be discovered." Emily studied me with her myopic gaze for a moment. "You seem intensely interested in something that I doubt has much to do with you, Ms. Webber. What's the real reason you're here?"

I shuffled my feet against the thick Oriental rug covering the polished wood floor. "Sunny Fields is my best friend, and I've known her grandparents since I was a teen. They did ask me to notify you, and a few others, about any possible investigation into the commune. But"—I met Emily Moore's gaze squarely—"I'm also conducting a little research on my own. Just following any clues, hoping they lead to anything that might remove suspicion from P.J. and Carol. Or any other innocent parties, for that matter."

"I thought so. I'd heard about you before we met at the library, you know." Emily spread her hands wide. "How could I not, teaching at Clarion? I started working there this past summer, even before I moved to Taylorsford, and there was a recent case involving two professors that was a hot topic of conversation in faculty meetings."

"Oh," I said, cursing the heat rising in my face. "I guess I wasn't quite as clever as I thought."

"I'll tell you a secret, Amy," Emily Moore said, her smile sweet and languid as honey. "Based on what I've seen in my long and rather colorful life, no one ever is."

Chapter Thirteen

When Dan Dane returned to the library several times over the next week, I wasn't certain which was the bigger attraction—Sunny or the archives. But I was pleased that the reporter seemed determined to get his facts straight before he published anything—a trait I had to admire.

I also respected his support of Sunny and her grandparents. Although I was certain Dan wouldn't cover up facts just to protect them, he seemed willing to give them the benefit of the doubt—something many others in town seemed reluctant to do. When I warned him to be careful, given the recent murder of another commune member, Dan simply replied that he was going to do his job. "Discover the truth and achieve some measure of justice for the wronged," he said. "That's all that matters. I occasionally have to take risks to do that, but I think it's worth it."

Emboldened by his courage, I decided to follow his example and take the risk of continuing my quest to locate and talk to additional members of the commune. I made some progress, contacting Dean Bodenheimer and setting a meeting for the upcoming Saturday. As luck would have it, he told me he planned to be in Taylorsford to visit an old friend and would stop by the house to talk to me before he left town. That was fine with me, since it meant I didn't have to drive into Frederick.

Fortunately, Aunt Lydia, who claimed she needed a new outfit to wear to Richard's performance Saturday evening, had planned a shopping outing with Zelda for the afternoon. Her excursion definitely made things easier. I didn't mind Bodenheimer coming to the house, but I didn't want to involve my aunt in my little investigation. It would be best if she could disavow any knowledge of the visit if she was ever questioned by Brad Tucker or anyone else from the sheriff's office.

I saw Aunt Lydia and Zelda off early on Saturday afternoon and then settled into the comfort of the sitting room to read a book. Despite being a librarian, having an uninterrupted stretch of time to read was a luxury. I couldn't read at work—I was too busy answering questions, conducting research, helping with homework, or assisting patrons at the circulation desk. Not to mention all the budget work I was required to do, along with the ordering and processing of new materials. People often assumed that anyone who worked in a library got to read on the job, but sadly, that wasn't true. I always had a towering "to read" stack of books teetering on my nightstand and far too many unread titles filling my e-reader.

The doorbell jangled me out of my delightful reading reverie at precisely two o'clock. It seemed Dean Bodenheimer was nothing if not punctual.

I ran my fingers through my hair and tugged down my Lindsey Stirling tour T-shirt as I crossed the short distance to the front door.

The man standing on the other side of the door was nearly as broad-shouldered as Kurt Kendrick but much shorter. The hair he'd pulled back into a low ponytail was steel gray, but his face was surprisingly unlined for someone in his seventies. Although stocky, he looked quite fit—especially his arms, which were so well muscled that they bulged against the short sleeves of his black polo. *Drummer*, I reminded myself, as I welcomed him into the house and led him to the parlor.

"Please, have a seat." I motioned toward the room's most prominent feature—a monstrous wooden chair whose seat was upholstered in black velvet faded to a coppery brown. "Can I get you something to drink?"

Dean Bodenheimer waved this question aside. "No, no. I just came from a birthday party where there was entirely too much of everything." He stared at the chair, which had a back elaborately carved with a rose-and-vine pattern.

My great-grandmother Rose Baker Litton had acquired that chair to match the rose theme in her parlor. It had been shipped across the Atlantic, which had probably cost a fortune, and was as uncomfortable as it was imposing.

We rarely used the parlor, but as soon as I'd answered the front door, I'd decided to talk with Dean Bodenheimer in there rather than in our homey sitting room. I thought the parlor's stately air of uncomfortable grandeur might be just the thing to keep my guest off-kilter, and me on my guard.

I sat down in a mahogany chair with delicate curved legs and stiff needlepoint upholstery. "That's right, you said you were visiting a friend in Taylorsford. I hope they're doing well?"

"Very good, considering their age. It was one of my former music teachers, as a matter of fact. They just turned one hundred."

"Wow." I shifted on the hard, horsehair-stuffed chair seat. "I can't imagine reaching that age."

"Me either, although it is drawing ever closer." Dean Bodenheimer flashed a wry smile. "Anyway, how can help you, Ms. Webber? Over the phone you said you needed to talk with me. Something to do with Carol and P.J. Fields?"

"Yes, and please, Mr. Bodenheimer—call me Amy."

"Call me Dean, then. I've never liked that 'Mr. Bodenheimer' label."

"Okay, well . . ." I gripped the curved wooden arms of my chair. "I'm actually just passing along some information at P.J. and Carol's request. They wanted to alert the former commune members about the recent discovery on their farm."

"Discovery?" Dean's small eyes narrowed. "What type of discovery?"

"You haven't heard?" I looked him over, noting the tension tightening his heavy jaw. "It's been all over the news."

"I learned long ago to avoid the news. It does nothing to inform me and just elevates my blood pressure."

"Then you haven't heard about the recent discovery of a skeleton that crews unearthed when they were dredging a stream out on Vista View farm?"

Dean blinked twice, while the rest of his body went completely still. "No, I don't know anything about that."

"Based on dental records, the investigators determined that the skeletal remains belonged to Jeremy Adams. His death has been labeled a homicide." I kept my gaze locked on Dean's stony face. "Of course, that means the sheriff's office and others are digging into Jeremy's past association with the commune. That's why Carol and P.J. asked me to talk with you. They wanted me to give you a heads-up before anyone from the sheriff's department came knocking on your door." I considered mentioning Ruth Lee's recent death and decided to hold off on sharing that information. One bombshell at a time might yield better results.

"Very thoughtful of them," Dean said, wiping the back of one hand across his face. By the time he pulled his hand away, he'd forced a tight smile.

"They're thoughtful people." I was intrigued by Dean's obvious discomfort over this news. Emily Moore had claimed Jeremy and Dean had gotten along well, but as musicians, perhaps they'd been engaged in a rivalry the others in the commune hadn't noticed. "You knew Jeremy, of course."

"Yes, although we weren't close."

My lips twitched. It seemed Jeremy hadn't been close to anyone, except perhaps Ruth Lee, if his fellow commune members were to be believed. *But*, I thought, *maybe they aren't.*

Dean turned his head and cast his gaze on the table near his chair. A single framed photograph was perched on the polished cherry surface of the table. "Is that Andrew Talbot as a young man?" he asked, pointing to the picture.

I sensed this was a deflection but decided to play along. "Yes. He was my uncle, although I never knew him. He died years before I was born."

"I remember. It was a terrible car accident back in the late seventies, wasn't it? A shame." Dean looked back at me. "Okay, to tell you the truth, I met Andrew when we were teenagers. We didn't go to the same school, but we were on cross-country teams that used to compete against one another, so I saw him at our meets. I always thought he was a nice guy, but I didn't hang out with him. For one thing, I heard he kept some questionable company."

"Oh?" I asked, keeping my tone light. "Who was that?"

"Some of the druggy crowd." Dean lifted his hands. "Don't get me wrong—I smoked my share of weed back in the day, but I was never into the really hard stuff."

"You were more like Carol and P.J. than Jeremy in that regard?"

Dean's thick eyebrows arched over his light-brown eyes. "Is that what they told you?"

"Well, yes. Me and my best friend, who happens to be their granddaughter."

"In that case, I can see why they stretched the truth a bit." Dean tapped his expensive leather loafers against the rose-patterned wool rug that covered the hardwood floor. "Not wanting to look bad in front of the grandchild and so on. But in all honesty, both Carol and P.J. experimented quite a bit. LSD, mostly. They said it was to expand their consciousness, and I suppose that was their reason, but still . . ."

I cut him off, not interested in hearing anything else about Carol and P.J. from someone I had no reason to trust. "Anyway, it appears Jeremy Adams's death resulted from foul play. All they have is his skeleton, but apparently his skull was bashed in, probably by some heavy object. I was wondering if you could think of anyone who might have wanted to do that, or even someone who had the temperament to do such a thing. Even if you and Jeremy weren't close, you were definitely in a position to observe his relationships with the other commune members. Was there anyone who might've had a motive to kill him?"

Dean reared back. He immediately slid forward again, obviously poked by one of the chair's carved roses, and crossed his arms over his barrel chest. "Not really. Yes, there were a few conflicts between members of the group, what with us living so close together and all. But murder?" He looked up and over my head, as if his gaze had been transfixed by the view through the bay window behind me. "I can't picture anyone wanting to kill him."

"Not even Ruth Lee?" I scooted to the edge of my chair, my hands pressed against my knees. "You might remember her as Rainbow. Others have told me Ruth was in love with Jeremy, often jealous, and might've snapped when he abandoned her."

"I suppose it's possible," Dean said.

His response was a little too eager. I narrowed my eyes and stared into his suddenly animated face. "She had a volatile personality?"

"Definitely. Always losing her temper and throwing tantrums over the least little thing. A drama queen, if you know what I mean." Dean's lips twitched. "I remember her going off on Jeremy over that other girl. What was her name? Bonnie or Bedelia or something."

"Belinda?"

"That's the one. I thought Rainbow was going to kill the girl when she caught her in Jeremy's bed. But"—Dean shrugged—"it ended up as a shouting match and nothing more. Belinda left soon after. If I recall correctly, she took off in the middle of the night without a word to anyone. So the whole thing blew over."

"But you do think Ruth Lee could've killed someone. What about the others?"

Dean leaned forward, his eyes shining. "Honestly, I think any of them could've killed him."

I studied his eager face with suspicion. Was he enthused about sharing some glimmer of the truth, or was he excited to be handed a way to deflect the suspicion off himself?

Dean waved one hand through the air, as if hitting a beat with an imaginary drumstick. "Pete O'Malley always had a firecracker temper, especially when he was high, which was quite often. Even Carol and P.J. had their moments, although that was only if they thought someone was endangering the commune. I heard them get into it with Jeremy a couple of times. He wasn't very discreet with his drug use, or careful about where he bought his stash. That sparked some pretty vicious arguments, believe me." Dean sat back, resting his beefy arms on the chair's carved arms. "If you ask me, all of them had the temperament for murder, except maybe Stan Owens, who we called Stanman."

"Why exclude him?"

"He was too meek and accommodating to get into a conflict with anyone." Dean cast me a cool smile. "I remember we gave him a hard time because he was so fearful. He had all these phobias, especially about heights. He even refused to sleep on the top level of our bunk beds. Always had to have the lower bunk." Dean shook his head. "Come to think of it, you'd better talk to him too, just so he isn't terrified by a visit from the cops."

"He died not long ago. Some sort of accident. I don't know any details," I said, deciding not to share what I did know. "Hadn't you heard that?"

"No," Dean said shortly. "Didn't have a clue."

I let that go, but made a note of his uneasiness with the question. "By the way, Ruth Lee is also deceased. Very recent and quite tragic. She was shot in her antique shop. The authorities are calling it a robbery gone wrong, although there are still some questions surrounding that theory. I suppose you hadn't heard that either?"

Dean shifted heavily in his chair. "I'm sorry that happened, but no."

I eyed him with interest. He was definitely not comfortable discussing the deaths of his fellow commune members. Which might be a result of the shock of hearing such news for the first time. *Or perhaps*, I thought, *from knowing more about those events than he wants to reveal.* "Anyway, back to the list. I notice you left off Emily Moore. You probably remember her as Daisy Miles."

"Naw, she and Jeremy were tight. Not in a romantic sense. But they were both creative types. More so than me." Dean smiled. "I was always more pragmatic about my music than they were about their respective arts. Anyway, she often used to sit with him while he was working on his music. He'd go out to the old barn to compose or practice, and Daisy would keep him company. Or at least, that's what I saw."

I picked at a loose thread dangling from my needlepoint seat cushion. "Really? She told me they weren't that close. She said it was all very casual, like the friendship you've just claimed you had with Jeremy."

Dean's lips thinned. "Well, Daisy always did have a rather loose relationship with the truth. Maybe she was just trying to gloss over that history."

"You mean she lied to me." *Or you did*, I thought, eyeing him. He was a guy who looked strong enough to single-handedly bury a body, even today.

Dean shrugged. "Could be. But I doubt it was for evil purposes. She probably just wanted to brush you off. She always was a bit of a loner."

Studying his implacable face, I decided to take another tack. "You became a professional musician after leaving the commune, right?"

"Yeah. Mostly as an engineer and producer, although I did pick up percussion gigs as a studio musician too."

"And you worked out in LA?"

"LA and Nashville." Dean tipped his head and examined me. "And no, I never heard anything about Jeremy Adams from anyone I worked with."

"I just wondered. He was supposedly such a brilliant musician. I thought if he did make it out to LA before his brief return to Taylorsford, someone might have heard of him."

"Nope. And believe me, after I heard he disappeared, I did ask."

Dean expressed this last statement with such vehemence that I yanked the loose thread from the cushion. *Is he just trying to convince me? Or is his bravado meant to hide a lie?*

After dealing with a few other criminals, I had learned not to trust everything people told me, no matter how innocent they might appear on the surface. But I'd also learned that provoking a possible murderer wasn't a wise choice. I could share my suspicions with Brad Tucker later, but for now, I'd shift the conversation away from Dean. "Both Pete and Emily suggested that perhaps Jeremy's killer was one of his dealers. I do think that's a reasonable theory."

Dean unclenched his jaw as he leaned forward in his chair. "That would definitely make sense. Jeremy had a problem with drugs, as I'm sure you've heard. All of us experimented, but we could take it or leave it. Well, except for Pete, maybe. And Belinda, come to think of it. But anyway, Jeremy was a true addict. I've seen plenty of those over my years in the music business, believe me."

"I'm sure." I stuffed the loose thread into the pocket of my jeans. "Did you know any of the dealers who supplied people at the commune? Pete mentioned someone called the Weasel, and another guy who went by 'The Hammer.' Oh, and there was a woman too. Esmerelda, I think he said."

"Those are the only names I ever heard, and I personally only dealt with Esmerelda. I always felt safer with a woman." Dean's tight smile held no humor. "Although since then I've met some females who could give any male enforcer a run for his money. But at the time I was more naïve about such things."

"You never met the guys?"

"No, but I heard plenty. The Weasel was supposedly just a slimy little runner for a bigger organization. He wasn't dangerous, although the people he worked for certainly were. The other one ran his business on his own. I guess he was intimidating enough to make that work. Big guy, from what I heard. Way over six foot tall, and all muscle. He was nicknamed after that Nordic god. You know, the one with the magic hammer."

I swallowed back a swear word. "Thor?"

"That's the one. Supposedly it fit this guy perfectly. At least from the descriptions the others shared with me."

"Like a Viking," I said, talking more to myself than to Dean.

"Exactly. In fact, Daisy and Jeremy and some of the others may have called him that once or twice." Dean scratched at the light stubble on his chin. "Sounds familiar, anyway."

As I stood up, I had to concentrate to keep my legs from visibly shaking. I knew the man whose youthful nickname had been "The Viking." Kurt Kendrick—who had supposedly left the area before Jeremy disappeared. But whose words and claims were not, as I knew quite well, always trustworthy.

That was an angle I certainly didn't want to share with the man in front of me. Or anyone, for that matter, until I could investigate it a little further. "Well, Dean, I don't want to keep you too long. Thanks for stopping by so that I could fulfill my promise to P.J. and Carol. I appreciate you taking the time."

"No problem," Dean said, rising to his feet and crossing the short distance to stand in front of me. He thrust out his hand. "Nice to meet you, Amy. Please tell Carol and P.J. hello from me. Maybe I'll actually get around to visiting them one day."

"I'm sure they'd like that," I said, although I wasn't convinced it was true. Dean Bodenheimer seemed to have thrown off any convictions he may have held when he joined the commune, judging by the expensive gold watch he was sporting on his thick wrist. No more *Make do with little, make things last, don't give capitalists the cash* for him, it seemed.

My assumption was solidified when I walked him out onto the porch and spied the high-priced sports car parked in front of the house.

"Thanks again, Dean," I said again, after he told me goodbye. "And just . . . be careful, I guess. I mean, Carol and P.J. were concerned that this investigation might dredge up something more than a body, if you know what I mean."

Dean didn't meet my eyes before he turned to the stone steps that led down into the front yard. "Not a problem," he called over his shoulder. "I have nothing to hide."

"Good to know," I called after him as he strode toward his pricy car.

I didn't believe him, of course. Everyone had something to hide, and judging by his evasiveness during our conversation, Dean Bodenheimer might have more skeletons rattling around in his closet than most.

Chapter Fourteen

I was exhausted on Monday, which was my own fault. "Or Richard's," I told Sunny. "You know I attended yesterday's matinee as well as the Saturday evening performance of that dance concert, and then Richard asked me along when he and the rest of the dance faculty went out for drinks . . ."

Sunny swept back the curtain of my hair that had veiled my face when I'd slumped over the circulation desk with my head in my hands. "And you drank too much, because you were surrounded by a bunch of people that you have little in common with and who intimidate you with their perfectly toned bodies and athletic prowess."

"Bingo. I'm such an idiot sometimes."

"Yep, you are." Sunny patted my back. "I'm sure it wasn't so terrible."

I straightened with one palm pressed against my forehead. "Oh, most of them are polite enough. But they were all talking shop and I had nothing to contribute, so I just sat there silent as the grave, drinking like a mourner at a wake."

"You could've just talked about personal stuff. Asked a couple of them how things were going in their life. Told some stories about your own work. You know, made small talk."

"Right, because I'm so good at that. Anyway, they were all so wrapped up in discussing their upcoming choreography projects and professional performances, I didn't think my library stories would thrill them too much. Sadly, Karla had to go home right after the performance, so I didn't have an ally, other than Richard, of course. And I didn't want to force him to entertain me."

"I suppose Meredith Fox was there?"

"Oh, yeah." My eye roll rewarded me with a stab of pain. "She's been hired to do some major revival of a Merce Cunningham piece at Lincoln Center, so of course she constantly inserted that little tidbit into the conversation. Honestly, Sunny, I tried, but I couldn't get a word in edgewise. Which meant I couldn't help but worry that the whole crew thought I was the most boring little mouse ever. I distracted myself by drinking." I groaned and rubbed at my temple. "But I should have stopped before that last martini."

"I just hope Richard was driving."

"Of course. Poor thing, he realized early on that he'd have to limit his drinks because I was going to be incapable of driving him home."

"He took one for the team. Good for him." Sunny clasped her hands together, jangling her enameled bracelets. "And I'm glad you decided to go to the event with him, even if it did mean arriving early."

"It was a double-edged sword, actually. Sure, riding in with him turned out to be a good decision. But it also meant I couldn't escape the evening festivities unless he missed them too. Which I didn't want him to do, so . . ."

Sunny looked me over, her expression filled with mock solemnity. "The things we do for love."

I made a face at her, then grimaced when a spasm of pain shot through my head again. "Yeah, kick me when I'm down. Some friend you are."

"Enough of a friend to tell you what a fool you are to care what those people think. And enough of a pragmatist to know they probably weren't feeling anything negative concerning you." Sunny pointed a finger at me. "In my experience, other people don't think about us as much as they think about themselves. I bet they were all worried you'd find *them* boring, or not on your intellectual level, or something."

I met her amused gaze. "You're probably right. Remind me of that again, like, every day, would you?"

"Sure, boss."

I looked her over, noting the dark circles under her eyes. "What about you and the grands? How are you guys holding up?"

"Oh, we're doing fine." Sunny looked away as she swept back her long hair and swiftly tied it up into a ponytail with the elastic band she'd been wearing on her wrist. "It's stressful, with the media hounding us and the authorities basically staking out our home and asking questions of all the neighbors and so on, but we're hanging tough."

"I'm sure. Just let Carol and P.J. know I'm thinking about them, would you?"

"Of course." Sunny turned back to face me with a sad smile. "They'll appreciate that. Now, given your less-than-clear head, do you want me to show Zelda how to use that new shelf-reading gizmo? She's over in the stacks, waiting to start her volunteer hours."

"No, no. I said I would train her and I will. I just hope she doesn't talk my ears off."

Sunny's peal of laughter rang through the quiet library. "Zelda? Not talk? What planet are you living on?"

"Hangover world," I muttered.

I grabbed a tablet computer and the new handheld device I'd recently purchased with some funds donated to the library back in the spring. It was the same contribution that had allowed us to name the archives and install new carpeting and furniture in the children's room—an unanticipated windfall from an unexpected source.

I was certainly grateful to be able to afford this new device, which promised to be a real time-saver. Waved over a shelf of books, it could read the bar codes inside the volumes and transmit that information to our integrated library system, or ILS. Using a portable tablet, we could connect to our catalog and compare the device's information against our collection records, which meant we could immediately see which items were checked out versus those that might be misshelved or even lost.

I walked into the stacks and located Zelda in the cookbook section. She was leaning against the shelves, flipping through one of the books, but snapped it shut and reshelved it as I approached.

"Is that the new toy?" she asked, her light-brown eyes bright with enthusiasm.

That wasn't surprising. Zelda was enthusiastic about everything.

"Yes, and it's actually pretty easy to use," I replied, biting back another grimace as a sharp blade of pain pierced my temple. "The device does most of the work."

Zelda looked dubious, but took the tablet and reader from my hands. "Lydia said you had a devil of a time setting it up, though."

"That was no fun." I made a mental note to remind my aunt that sharing anything with Zelda meant it was no longer a secret. "But once we figured it out, it worked like a charm."

I leaned over her shoulder and walked her through the use of the device while she chattered about the latest news, including the pie recipe she intended to enter in the county fair.

"Oh, don't tell me that," I said in mock horror. "I don't want to accidentally share any of your secret ingredients with Aunt Lydia. We need to make this a fair fight."

Zelda snorted. "Fair? When is going up against Lydia or Jane Tucker going to be fair?" Her eyes twinkled with mischief. "But I may have a trick or two up my sleeve."

"I bet you do."

"Oh, I forgot to ask about Richard's performance yesterday. Lydia was raving about Saturday night, but I bet you were there for the Sunday show too."

"Yes, and he and Karla were just as brilliant on Sunday as they were on Saturday. They received standing ovations both days." Knowing how information shared with Zelda always seem to travel farther than I could ever imagine, I didn't add that Meredith Fox had not received such an honor. Instead, I pointed my finger at the tablet. "Now, you just have to press that tab, and see—easy as pie."

Zelda tossed her crisp curls. "I've said it before, and I'll say it again—in my experience, pie is never easy."

"Easy to eat, maybe. Not to make. But anyway, I think you have the hang of it now. You can start in the one hundreds, and just go through as many sections as possible in an hour or so. It doesn't have to all be done today."

"Okay, dear, I'll do my best."

"I'm sure you will. And thanks again for volunteering for so many hours this fall."

"No problem at all." Zelda gave me a sly smile. "Part of it is to free up Sunny, you know. To allow her to do more canvassing of Taylorsford and other campaign work."

Despite my thundering headache, I managed a smile in return. "At least she doesn't have to worry with managing the Heritage Festival this year. That donation we got back in the spring means we don't need to raise money during the festival this year. So, thankfully, no yard sale."

"I'm sure you're happy about that," Zelda said, testing the reader over a shelf of books. "My, my, it does work well."

"It's definitely going to make inventory and shelf-reading much easier. And yes, I am thrilled to escape having to set up and run a library sale this year. Instead, we can participate in a more literary fashion."

"That's right, you've organized some sort of read-in?"

"A read-a-thon," I said. "We have Emily Moore reading some of her poetry, which will be the real highlight, but we've also invited patrons to read from their favorite books. There will even be some special time slots when town leaders and others will read selections from books written by people from the area."

"Including Paul Dassin, I hope."

"Oh yes. I have a special reader lined up for that."

Zelda glanced over her shoulder. "Richard, of course."

"Yeah, along with Aunt Lydia. I'm surprised she hasn't told you that yet."

Zelda waved the wand reader through the air. "She may have mentioned it. The truth is, I've been so consumed with Sunny's mayoral campaign that I tend to not pay as much attention to other things these days."

"Well, see if you can focus on the shelf-reading, okay?" I forced another smile before adding, "Find Sunny if you need help. She'll be at the desk. Meanwhile, if you'll forgive me, I must go and take care of some back-office tasks."

I didn't tell her I needed to rest my throbbing head. That wasn't something I really wanted to share. If Zelda knew it, Aunt Lydia soon would, too.

She hadn't seen me stagger in the night before. Fortunately, when Richard brought me home, Aunt Lydia had already been in bed. He'd managed to guide me up the stairs and into my bedroom without waking her.

After I'd changed into a nightshirt and crawled into bed, Richard had placed a full glass of water and a couple of aspirin on my nightstand before promising to lock the front door behind him on his way out.

A true gentleman, despite my unappealing behavior, I thought, as I made my way into the workroom. *I need to thank him again today. Several times, if necessary.*

Before settling in to tackle a waiting pile of interlibrary loans, including one for myself, I swallowed down some additional aspirin with a full bottle of water. After sending off my special request for a copy of Emily Moore's elusive first book of poems, I examined the stack of books I needed to mail out, as well as the printout detailing the additional items I needed to request from other libraries. *But first*, I thought, *I'd better check the mailbox to make sure there aren't some additional ILLs.*

The mailbox was mounted on the stone exterior wall of the library, right outside the staff door. It was an old metal box, with a slit in the top that would accommodate only letters or other flat mail. Any packages had to be delivered inside, which often made our postal person grumble. But I refused to change over to a newer, larger box. I didn't want anyone depositing books or other library materials in the mailbox instead of the exterior book drop.

Unlocking the metal box, I yanked out a handful of items before slipping back into the workroom and allowing the door to slam behind me.

It was mostly ads and catalogs. I tossed those in the recycling bin before sorting through a few invoices for book and media purchases, a letter requesting information from the archives, and an electric bill. At the bottom of the pile was a piece of mail addressed directly to me.

That was odd. I held the envelope up to the fluorescent light hanging over the worktable. It was printed, not handwritten, but there was no stamp or return address.

I ripped open the envelope and pulled out a single sheet of paper. The text was also printed, and there was no signature.

Cease your investigations and research into the Jeremy Adams case unless you want to suffer the same fate, as well as put your friends and family in danger, it said.

I stared at the page for a moment before opening my fingers and allowing the paper to flutter to the surface of the worktable. Rigid as an automaton, I slipped my cell phone from my pocket and hit the quick-dial button to reach Chief Deputy Brad Tucker.

Chapter Fifteen

Brad told me to slide the letter back into the envelope and store it somewhere safe until he could stop by and collect it.

"But fingerprints," I said, clutching my phone like a lifeline.

"We can eliminate yours, so as long as no one else touches it, we should be good." Obviously sensing my anxiety, Brad used his most soothing tone. "I'll drop by the library as soon as I can get away from the office."

I did as he instructed, then wandered out to the circulation desk, abandoning any work on the interlibrary loans. They'd have to wait—I was too dazed after receiving such a direct threat to process anything properly.

Afraid she'd guess my distress, I asked Sunny to take over the children's story hour I was supposed to present.

"Still too woozy?" she asked.

I agreed with her guess before shooing her away and collapsing onto the tall stool we kept behind the circulation desk.

Brad appeared about fifteen minutes later.

"Can you grab that item for me?" he asked casually, after glancing around to make sure no one was lurking near the desk.

I nodded and fetched the envelope. Mutely sliding it across the desk, I looked up into his strong-featured face. A tall, well-built man in his early forties, Brad had short-cropped dark-blond hair mostly covered by his sheriff's department hat. Laugh lines radiated from the corners of his light-blue eyes, and his skin still bore traces of a summer tan. "I hope you can figure something out. It looks like it was printed from a computer, and there's no signature or return address."

"Also no stamp," Brad said as he surreptitiously pulled a small plastic evidence bag from a pocket inside his uniform jacket. "Here, can you just drop it in this? I don't want to touch the envelope without gloves."

He pocketed the bag before looking me over. "You doing okay?"

"Sure. I'm getting pretty used to death threats at this point," I replied, trying to make a joke of it.

Brad didn't crack a smile. "Well, you shouldn't. This isn't something to fool around with, Amy. Whoever this is, they know what you're up to and where you work." He fiddled with the gold star pinned to his uniform. "Thank you again for dropping off that CD Ruth Lee gave you, although I'm not sure how it might tie in with our investigations. But I appreciate you handing it over. Now—along those lines, you need to promise to come into the office and share what you know with me as soon as possible."

"Me? What do I know that you don't?" I fluttered my eyelashes in an attempt at innocence, which obviously succeeded as well as my joke.

"I'm aware of your visits to former commune members, so don't try that act with me." Brad's glare was uncomfortably stern. "I did ask for your help with some research, which you've already shared, but all this other investigating is unnecessary. Leave that to my department, please. Especially after this." He patted the jacket pocket that held the letter.

"Sorry, but these visits to the commune members were just something I thought I could do to help Carol and P.J. clear their names. Which helps Sunny too, you know. But no more, I promise," I added, lifting my hands.

"Obviously I can't lock you up to stop you from doing so, but please—tell me anything you've heard from those people as soon as possible, would you? Yes, my team is questioning them as well, but they may have told you something they wouldn't share with law enforcement."

"I realize that, and I tell you what—I'll call your office and make an appointment to talk to you as soon as possible," I said, actually planning to allow this to "slip my mind" for a few days.

I will tell Brad everything, I promised myself, *but maybe not quite as quickly as he would like, and hopefully after P.J. and Carol are cleared of any involvement in Jeremy's death.*

"Good." He softened his expression. "That will help Sunny's grandparents as much as anything, you know."

"I hope so." Looking past him, I laid a finger to my lips for a second. "Thanks for stopping by, Brad," I said, as Walt Adams strode through the main doors of the library.

"Hi, Walt," I said, waving him over to the desk. "Zelda's in the stacks, if you're looking for her."

"Yes, thanks, we're meeting for lunch. Hello, Brad," he added, with a nod toward the chief deputy. "Checking up on the library director?"

"I just stopped by to make sure everything was okay here," Brad replied. "With the investigation into the Jeremy Adams cold case and the tragic death of Ruth Lee, there are a lot more reporters and other strangers in town. I like to make sure they aren't bothering our local citizens."

"Right, the investigations." Walt's dark-brown eyes clouded over. "Any new leads? Jeremy was my cousin, you know." He straightened. The two men were approximately the same height, and even though Brad was bulkier and younger, I wasn't sure he had the advantage.

"I'm aware, especially since you gave a statement after his disappearance and then stopped by the department recently to repeat it," Brad said.

"I'm invested in the case, as you can imagine." Walt ran one hand over his cropped hair. "Jeremy was always kind to me, even when I was a little kid and pestered him constantly to play one more song."

Brad tipped his hat. "My sympathies, Mr. Adams. It is a tragedy to lose someone that young."

"And such a talent." Walt's hands, hanging loosely at his sides, clenched. "A bright light snuffed out by some unknown criminal. Someone who didn't even have the decency to allow his family to know what had happened to him. It broke my poor aunt's heart. I'd like to see someone pay dearly for that."

Brad's eyes narrowed as he studied the older man. "The sheriff's department wants to see justice done too. Best to leave that to us."

"All done, Zelda?" I said, raising my voice to let the two men know Zelda was on her way over.

She placed the library equipment on the desk before slipping one arm around Walt's lean waist. Tilting her head, she looked up at Brad. "Well, hello there, stranger. What have you been up to recently? I sure haven't seen you around much." She wrinkled her pert nose. "You don't have to avoid Sunny, you know. I think she's already moved on."

Brad pushed his hat away from his forehead. "Honestly, I'm just busy with several investigations, on top of the usual departmental duties."

"I guess that's true, especially with poor Ruth Lee and that skeleton they found out at Vista View." Zelda pursed her tinted lips. "You know Sunny's grandparents had nothing to do with that child's death, don't you? I mean, I heard the poor lamb had his skull bashed in. Doesn't sound like something Carol or P.J. would do, now does it?"

Walt took a step to the side, pulling free of Zelda's embrace.

"You know I really can't comment about an ongoing investigation, Ms. Shoemaker," Brad said, scratching at his hairline.

I thought I understood why he appeared nervous—having dated Sunny for over a year before they mutually broke off their relationship, Brad knew P.J. and Carol well. It had to be difficult for him to include them on a list of murder suspects. But Brad Tucker was a man of integrity, as well as a professional. He'd never allow personal feelings to compromise an investigation.

"Like Walt, I'm wondering if there are any new leads," I said, hoping to shift the conversation away from P.J. and Carol.

"Nothing I can share," Brad replied, yanking his hat back down on his forehead before shooting me a conspiratorial look.

I knew he was thinking about the CD and my anonymous note. "There seem to be numerous possible suspects, if you consider all the people who lived with Jeremy Adams back then. Not to mention the drug connection."

"We're looking into all of that, of course," Brad said.

Walt mumbled something before saying, "Everyone keeps bringing up the drugs. I don't think Jeremy was as much of an addict as you all seem to think." He glanced down at Zelda, who was too preoccupied with glaring at Brad to notice. "I never saw him when he was strung out or anything."

"Hardly evidence. You were just a child," Zelda said, without looking up at him. "So anyway, Brad, how about making a statement about numerous leads, instead of allowing everyone to focus on Vista View and its owners? You could easily mention the possibility of other suspects without naming names. That might take the spotlight off P.J. and Carol, which would really help Sunny. It's tough for her to campaign with all the rumors swirling around her grandparents."

"I have to follow where the facts lead," Brad said, meeting Walt's piercing stare.

Zelda tapped her foot. "Sure, but everyone I know seems to think the focus is on P.J. and Carol."

A voice boomed out from the stacks. "Just where it should be."

"Oh great," I muttered as Taylorsford's mayor strode out of the stacks. "When did he get here? I didn't see him come in."

Zelda marched up to face him. "Look here, Bob Blackstone, I know you want to win this election, but you have no business doing so by spreading false rumors."

"Who says they're false?" Bob adjusted the sleeves of his navy suit over his pale-blue shirt cuffs. Although only in his late forties, he always dressed like he was headed to court, with his dark hair slicked back like some 1950s trial lawyer.

"I do, for one." Zelda placed her fists on her hips. "There's no evidence that Carol or P.J. Fields was involved in any crime. Yes, that poor boy's body was discovered on their farm, but that's the only connection."

"Jeremy Adams," Walt said firmly. "Not just some poor boy."

Zelda shot him a surprised glance. "Of course, but you can't assume they were involved in his death, even if he did live with them on the commune for a couple of years."

"Pretty damning coincidence." The gleam in Bob Blackstone's eyes betrayed his joy over this connection.

"But a coincidence all the same," Brad said. "Don't go jumping to conclusions before all the facts are in, Mr. Mayor."

"That's the gospel truth." Zelda stabbed the air with one of her plump fingers. "You just want to use this to derail Sunny's campaign. I bet you've been spreading plenty of rumors yourself, even though you have no proof of anything criminal involving the Fields family. Those of us who know them firmly believe they are innocent." She looked up at Walt expectantly. "Right, dear?"

"Well . . ." Walt shuffled his feet and looked over her head to meet my gaze. "I don't know if I'd go that far."

Zelda took a step back. As she pressed her hand against the edge of the circulation desk, I could see the elation glittering in Bob Blackstone's eyes and concern creasing Brad's brow.

"What do you mean, Walt?" Zelda's fuchsia-painted fingernails scratched across the wooden surface of the desk.

She didn't notice the other patrons hovering at the edge of the stacks, obviously drawn by the raised voices. But Bob Blackstone did.

"What do you say?" he said, turning to face them. "Do you want to elect someone whose grandparents are under suspicion? For murder, no less? Maybe more than one murder, if it comes to that."

"Why, you . . ." Zelda stomped forward to stand toe-to-toe with the mayor. "How dare you use this to further your own career?" She spun around to face Walt. "Tell him, Walt. Tell him, and them, that they shouldn't condemn an entire family for a tragedy they had nothing to do with."

Walt took in one deep, shuddering breath before replying. "I'm sorry, Zel. I can't."

"What do you mean?" Pain swamped the anger in Zelda's voice.

"I mean, although I do doubt they have any connection to Ruth Lee's murder, I'm not convinced Carol and P.J. Fields had nothing to do with my cousin Jeremy's death." Walt met Zelda's glare without flinching. "Not that I necessarily think they killed him, but I do think it's possible they helped to cover up someone else's crime."

Zelda opened her mouth and snapped it shut again before saying anything.

Brad strode forward to stand between Walt and Zelda. "There are other likely suspects. No one should jump to conclusions. Not even you, Mr. Blackstone. You may be the mayor, but you don't have an inside track into the official investigation." He cast Bob a sharp glance. "So why don't we all just go about our business and stop trying to stir up trouble. In a library, of all places."

The watching patrons, abashed, wandered off, while Bob Blackstone made some comment under his breath before whirling around and storming out the front doors.

"Good riddance to bad rubbish." Zelda smacked her hands together as if slapping off dust.

"What's up? I heard a commotion," Sunny said, as she crossed the library to join us. "I could barely finish reading the story to the kids."

Brad shoved his hands into his pants pockets and rocked back on his heels. "Nothing you should worry about."

"Just Walt throwing us under the bus," Zelda said, in a tone I'd never heard from her before. "Thanks for that, Walt. You certainly had my back—too bad you had to go and stick a knife in it."

Walt sputtered some swear word before he replied. "Look here, Zel. I have to be honest. With Sunny as well." He glanced over at my friend. "Sorry, Sunny, but it was my cousin who was murdered. I want justice for him, no matter who was involved, and sadly, I'm not convinced that your grandparents are as innocent as they claim."

"Really?" Zelda stared at Walt, tears welling in her eyes. "You're going to back that crook the mayor over Sunny? Or me?"

"That's not what I mean, and you know it." Walt stepped around Brad to move closer to Zelda.

She swatted away his proffered hand. "I don't know anything, apparently. Certainly not you, Walt Adams."

"Zel . . ."

"Don't you *Zel* me. You just take yourself and your doubts out of here."

"What about lunch?"

"I'm not hungry, and even if I was, I wouldn't want to share a meal with you. Not today." Zelda turned away and pulled a lace handkerchief from the pocket of her slacks. "Go on, then. Maybe if you walk fast enough, you can catch up with the mayor and eat lunch with him," she said, dabbing at her damp eyes.

Walt threw up his hands and strode past her. The library doors slammed behind him as he exited the building.

Sunny hurried to Zelda's side and placed her arm around the older woman's shoulders. "I'm so sorry. I appreciate the gesture, but you shouldn't stand up for me or the grands if it's going to jeopardize your relationship with Walt."

"Doesn't matter." Zelda sniffled and blew her nose.

"Of course it matters," I said. "Why don't you go try to catch him and apologize and . . ."

"Apologize?" The word exploded from Zelda's lips. "I'm not the one who needs to do that, so maybe you should just mind your own business, missy."

I side-eyed Brad, whose face was frozen into a stoic mask. *No doubt achieved with great effort*, I thought, as I attempted to control my own expression.

"Now"—Zelda shoved the handkerchief back into her pocket and pulled free of Sunny's comforting arm—"I'm heading home. I can walk there, thankfully, even if it is a bit of a hike. But I suppose it will give me plenty of time to think things through."

I almost asked *What things?* but just said, "Goodbye."

"Nonsense, I'm going to give you a ride." Sunny glanced over at me. "If that's okay with my boss."

"Sure, sure, take all the time you want," I said, waving them off.

As Sunny led Zelda to the back of the library and the parking lot, I exhaled loudly.

"Yeah, me too," Brad said, before wishing me a good day and leaving by the front doors.

I sank back down onto the stool behind the circulation desk and leaned forward over the desk, dropping my aching head down onto my crossed arms. *Give me one quiet moment*, I thought, just as the parents and kids who'd been in the children's room for story hour bounced up to the desk with stacks of books to check out.

I forced a smile and made pleasant conversation while checking out their books, all the while vowing to never drink so much in one sitting ever again.

Because, I told myself, *you should have learned by now that you never know what the next day will bring.*

Chapter Sixteen

I took advantage of the fact that I was scheduled to work until eight o'clock on Wednesday to sleep in, which definitely helped my mood. I was able to catch up on some much-needed rest and take my time getting ready, instead of my usual habit of rushing around in the morning like a chicken with its head cut off. Arriving at eleven, I found Sunny busy helping patrons in the stacks while Denise, one of our most loyal volunteers, covered the circulation desk.

The day sped by quickly, with enough reference questions and other patron interaction to keep things interesting. I also took advantage of Sunny's presence to spend a couple of boring hours working on the statistical report I'd need to present to the town council at the beginning of October.

Around four, Dan Dane showed up, asking to use the archives. I sent Sunny out to help him, not just because I was busy but also, I had to confess, to encourage what appeared to be a budding relationship.

In fact, when Sunny came back in at five, saying that Dan wanted to keep working until eight, I impetuously requested that she ask Dan to join her, Richard, and me for a late-night dinner and drinks after I closed up the library.

"Richard's picking me up at eight. We're planning to try out that new vegetarian place in Smithsburg," I said. "I thought, since Dan will be researching until late, and he really doesn't know many people in town, maybe he'd like to join us. Along with you, if you don't mind coming back to meet us here."

Sunny fiddled with her silver bangle bracelets as she eyed me with suspicion. "Are you trying to play matchmaker? Because I thought you disliked that sort of interference." She arched her golden brows. "But I guess that's just when it involves *your* love life?"

I flashed a grin. "Yep. Because where you're concerned, I'm going to become just as obnoxious as Aunt Lydia and Zelda."

"Oh heavens, I don't know if I can deal with that." Sunny's smile belied her words. "Okay, I'll ask Dan. And if he says yes, we'll join you and Richard for dinner."

"Even if he says no, you're welcome," I replied, as she turned away.

"The dreaded third wheel? Not likely," Sunny called over her shoulder.

She returned with an affirmative answer from Dan, and I called Richard. I hadn't thought he would mind, and he didn't, although he did poke fun at my matchmaking efforts.

"And you were so ticked off when Lydia tried that tactic on you," he said.

"Only because I wasn't sure I should be dating my neighbor. Just think how badly that could've turned out. What if we hadn't gotten along, or had dated and then broken up or something?"

"Was that the only reason? I seem to recall some other serious doubts on your part, despite my obvious charms."

I laughed. "Is that what you're calling it? I have some memory of that time too, you know."

"You mean you don't think I possess any charm?" Richard said, in a tone brimming with humor.

"I think you possess too much for your own good, and mine, and you know it. But anyway, back to the matter at hand. You know I just want to see Sunny happy, and she does seem to like Dan."

"All right, but I plan to render my own judgment on the guy. If I don't think he's good enough for Sunny, out he goes."

"Maybe not tossed from the restaurant," I said with a chuckle. "Okay, see you later, mister."

"Looking forward to it, miss," Richard said in a starchy voice, adding in a warmer tone, "Love you."

"Love you too," I said, before hanging up.

I held up my left hand, studying my engagement ring. It still amazed me that I'd met someone and gotten engaged in such a short span of time. *But,* I thought as I rubbed the central diamond with my fingertip, *what's more amazing is that I don't have any doubts. Not anymore.*

When Dan called the main-desk phone at seven forty-five to tell me he had completed his research, I slipped out to meet him at the archives and lock the building behind him.

"Thanks for inviting me to dinner," he said as we walked back into the library.

"No need to thank me. I think it will be fun. Now, if you just want to hang out in the reading room or something, I need to check and make sure the building is clear before I lock up."

"Why don't I walk around with you?" Dan's sea-green eyes sparkled with what I hoped was anticipation over spending more time with Sunny. "Just to make sure you're safe."

I shrugged. "Thanks, although I've been closing at eight since I took this job. No problems yet." I cast him a wry smile. "Despite some of the recent murder cases in Taylorsford, it really is a quiet town. We don't see a lot of trouble."

"Murder isn't trouble?" Dan asked as he trailed me through the stacks.

"Sure, but all those cases . . . well, there were significant personal motives that made the killers do what they did. It wasn't like they were just running around offing people for no reason."

"There's always a reason for murder, isn't there?"

"I don't know." After poking my head in the break room, I paused in the center of the children's room. "There are psychopaths who kill for nothing more than the thrill, or so I'm told."

"But in my experience, they always believe they have a valid reason for their actions, as twisted as it may seem to us." Dan met my inquisitive gaze with a shrug. "I did some crime reporting in the past. Talked to some people I expect you'd call psychopaths or sociopaths or whatever. They always had their own logical reasons for what they'd done, flawed as that logic might appear to you or me."

"Interesting. You'll have to expound on that later." I stopped at the circulation desk. "I just need to make sure the workroom door is shut tight, and then we can head out the front doors. Oh, I forgot to ask—do you want to ride with Richard and me, or drive your own car and follow?"

Dan rubbed the back of his neck with one hand. "I thought I'd drive. That way I can just head to my motel afterwards."

"Good, then Sunny can ride with you." I winked at him. "That way no one has to sit in the back, at least on the way over."

His lips twitched. "Good thinking."

"Richard and I will drive her home, though. She called a little while ago to tell me her grandfather was going to drop her off." I tipped my head to one side and looked him over. "I'd say you could escort her home as well, but since I expect your motel is closer to Smithsburg, that would mean backtracking. Not too many places to stay right in Taylorsford."

"True," Dan said. "There are a few B and Bs, but they're expensive, as is the inn on the edge of town. And that one motel near the strip mall . . ."

I gave a fake shudder. "Ugh, no one wants to go there." I circled around the desk and double-checked the workroom, grabbing my jacket and purse before meeting up with Dan again in the small front lobby.

"You don't need to lock those doors?" He pointed to the interior main doors.

"No, only the exterior ones have locks," I said, as I used my keys to set the tumblers on the front doors. "Just head on out. They'll lock behind us."

Sunny was already waiting on the sidewalk in front of the library.

"Hi again," she said, fastening the zipper on her electric-blue suede jacket. "It's a bit colder than I expected."

I looked her up and down, taking in the spiky high heels and the short stretch of dress, black lace over midnight-blue silk, that poked out from under the long, lean jacket. Her loose hair flowed down her back like a river of gold. She looked spectacular, which I suspected was not for my or Richard's benefit.

"Dan's going to follow, so we thought you could ride with him," I said, as Richard's copper-colored sedan pulled up in front of the library. "But Richard and I will still drive you home."

"Sounds good." Sunny made a face at me and mouthed *I know what you're doing* as Dan turned away.

"I'm parked in the back," he said. "Sunny, just wait here while I bring my car around."

I gave him basic directions in case he got lost following us, then crossed over to climb in the passenger's seat of Richard's car.

Richard raised his eyebrows. "Sunny's not coming with us?"

"She's riding with Dan."

"Ah, the plot thickens."

Refusing to take this bait, I craned my neck and glanced in the rearview mirror. "There's his car now, pulling up behind us. We can go as soon as Sunny gets in. But take it slow. Dan needs to be able to follow us."

"I promise not to use my getaway driver skills," Richard said dryly.

I wrinkled my nose at him. "Very droll."

"You bring it out in me." Richard leaned over to give me a quick kiss before checking the rearview mirror. "Looks like Dan's ready to go, so let's head out. I'm starving."

"Aren't you always?" I said as I fastened my seat belt. "Oh, by the way, I need to tell you something that happened yesterday. As long as you promise not to freak out."

As he drove toward Smithsburg, I filled him in on the anonymous note I'd received the day before.

"You didn't think to mention this last night when we talked on the phone?" he asked, frowning.

"I thought it would be better if we discussed it in person."

"But Brad is checking it out? For sure?"

"Yeah, and you know how dogged he is about chasing down any leads. I'm sure he'll find the culprit soon enough." I laid my left hand on Richard's right knee. "Don't worry too much, okay?"

"Why not ask me to fly to the moon?" Richard's lips twisted into a sarcastic smile. "Not worry? That'll be the day."

"I said *not too much.* I know you'll worry, no matter what I say."

"You got that right." Richard steered the car onto a side road on the outskirts of Smithsburg. "Keep an eye out for the place. It's supposed to be somewhere on this street."

We located the restaurant without any trouble and waited for Dan and Sunny to join us before heading inside.

After a light but delicious meal accompanied by pleasant conversation, Richard ordered coffee for everyone. With my fingers wrapped around my steaming mug, I looked across the table and caught Dan's eye.

"I did want to ask you a little more about your crime-reporting days," I said, before taking a sip of my coffee.

Dan tapped his spoon against the rim of his ceramic mug. "What do you want to know?"

"How you got into that, I guess. And what was your most interesting interview."

Sunny rolled her eyes. "Haven't you had enough of crime for one lifetime, Amy?"

"I'm just curious." I cast Dan a warm smile. "I am rather inquisitive, I'm afraid."

Richard set down his mug so hard that coffee splashed over the rim. "Now, there's an understatement," he said, reaching for a napkin.

Dan met my gaze, his eyes narrowed. "I got assigned to that beat when I first started out. Not my choice, but it did turn out to be more interesting than I expected."

"Did you really interview murderers?" Sunny asked, lifting her mug to her mauve-tinted lips.

Dan sat back, pressing his head against the wooden back of the bench seat. The shaded light fixture hanging over our booth faded the green from his eyes, leaving them as dark gray as storm clouds. "Yes. Even some serial killers."

Sunny shivered dramatically. "Oooo, not sure I could do that."

Dan shrugged. "It isn't what you think. The people I talked to didn't act like crazed maniacs. In fact, they seemed as normal as anyone at this table."

"Assuming that we're all normal." Richard offered Dan a little salute with his coffee mug. "You don't actually know that, do you? We could be playing a part, just like your serial killers. Pretending to be calm and rational when we're actually plotting murders." He glanced over at me and winked.

I giggled and Sunny smiled, but Dan fixed Richard with an intense stare. "Good point. I've learned that people can hide their true natures quite easily, especially if you have no reason to suspect them of bad behavior." He shook his head and looked at Sunny. "But I think I'm safe."

"You don't think I'm capable of plotting any mischief?" Sunny's tone was adorably arch.

"None I would mind," Dan said, giving her a warm smile.

I tapped Richard's foot with mine. It seemed that my matchmaking was moving along just fine.

He shot me a side-eyed glance. "I don't think you need to worry about Sunny. Now Amy, on the other hand . . ."

I kicked his foot a little harder. "What about me?"

Richard grinned and took a swig of coffee before replying. "You have that tendency to morph into Nancy Drew at the drop of a hat. Or maybe I should say, *clue*."

Dan tore his gaze from Sunny's lovely face long enough to glance from Richard to me. "Is that right? Of course, I did read about the assistance you provided the authorities on some other investigations. But I thought that was mainly behind-the-scenes stuff."

Sunny widened her blue eyes. "Oh no, sometimes Amy jumps right into the middle of things. And occasionally drags me right along with her."

"Much to the dismay of her family and friends," Richard said.

I drummed my fingers against the table. "Don't listen to them, Dan. Honestly, I don't go looking for trouble. Although I must admit that it sometimes seems to find me whether I like it or not."

"Sometimes?" Richard raised his eyebrows and took another slug of coffee.

"It's just that I have this natural curiosity," I said, shooting Richard a dirty look. "I start digging into things and turn up more questions, and that compels me to chase down answers."

"That could be a dangerous hobby." Dan's amused expression sobered. "Knowing what I do, I'd warn against too much amateur investigating. There are many dangerous people in the world, Amy. Individuals who won't let anything stand in the way of what they feel they must do."

"I know. I've met a few of those," I said.

Richard set down his mug and draped his arm around my shoulders. "That's what I keep telling her, but I'm afraid one of her few flaws is that she is—how should I put this delicately?—somewhat stubborn."

I stiffened my shoulders under his arm as Sunny chuckled and said, "Somewhat?"

Richard shared a smile with her. "I was trying to be diplomatic."

"To play devil's advocate, I do understand the need to reveal the truth," Dan said. "It's something that drives me to extremes as well."

"See"—I pointed my forefinger at Dan—"he gets it."

Sunny surveyed Dan, a little smile playing about her lips. "I guess that would be a useful trait for a journalist. But don't you write books too? I mean, novels, not nonfiction. In that case, you aren't seeking the truth, you're fabricating things."

Dan turned to Sunny, his expression animated. "Yes, but I like to think I'm still attempting to be honest. I strive to get to the heart of things and reveal deeper truths."

"Oh? Well, that makes me want to read your books even more," Sunny said, her smile broadening.

"I'd like that." Dan looked from me to Sunny. "To be honest, being the voracious readers that you are, I'm curious about your thoughts on the current state of fiction."

This opening was all it took to prompt Sunny and me to share our thoughts about our favorite books and authors, which led to a lively discussion about contemporary literature, a conversation that continued as we strolled into the parking lot of the restaurant.

"Thank you so much for inviting me to join you," Dan said as he unlocked his car. "I not only had a good time, I also learned a great deal."

"You're quite welcome," I said, nudging Richard when I noticed that Dan was hovering by his car door and Sunny had paused to stand beside him. "Let's get in. It's gotten a little colder than expected this evening."

Richard didn't reply until we were both seated in his car. "Looks like things are heating up to me." He motioned toward Sunny and Dan, who were loitering by the side of his car.

"Yes, isn't it lovely when a plan comes together?" I clasped my hands in my lap.

"Let's just hope this one doesn't backfire." Richard stuck the keys in the ignition and shot me a warning look as Sunny popped open the back door.

"Oh ye of little faith," I said, earning a grin from him.

Sunny slid into the back seat. "Thanks for inviting me along. That was fun, and it was nice to get to know Dan a little better."

"Looked to me like he'd like to get to know you a lot better," I said, clamping my lips over any further comments when Richard pulled out onto the road whistling "Matchmaker" from *Fiddler on the Roof.*

Chapter Seventeen

The weather stubbornly refused to cooperate when I closed up the library on Friday afternoon.

I'd walked to work, trusting the news report that had claimed a thunderstorm wouldn't roll in until after dark. But at five o'clock, as I locked the front doors behind the last patron, the bottom fell out. Sheets of rain created a wall of water between the covered entry and the stone steps that led down to the concrete walk.

I phoned Aunt Lydia and told her I was going to wait out the worst of the storm before heading home. "I have a little office work I need to catch up on anyway," I said, which was unfortunately true.

"We can come and get you."

"No, it's fine. You and Hugh have tickets to that play at Clarion, and I don't want you to miss your dinner reservation beforehand. I don't want to interfere with your plans." I glanced out one of the library's tall windows, trying to spy a break in the clouds, but all I could see was rain pelting the ground. "If this keeps up too long, I'll call Richard. He said he'd be home by six, so I can just have him swing by and pick me up on his way home from the university."

Aunt Lydia reluctantly agreed to this plan. I slid my phone into the pocket of my long gray sweater and walked back to the workroom.

Staring at the pile of printed documents stacked beside my back-office computer, I exhaled a loud sigh. Compiling statistics wasn't my favorite task, but one I needed to complete before my next presentation to the Taylorsford town council. As I compared this month's circulation statistics with previous months, I was happy to see a significant uptick in our numbers. That would placate the council, who were always worried that "all books being digital" meant that the library was "redundant."

A foolish worry anyway, I thought with a wry smile. As I'd told them many times, not everything was available digitally, even today. There were tons of older print materials that could be converted to electronic formats only after an exorbitant expenditure of time and money. Anyway, as I constantly reminded the council, the public library was not simply a repository for books and other materials. It also offered Internet access to those who couldn't afford a computer, furnished research databases that no one could pay for on their own, and provided literacy training, book clubs, children's activities, and homework assistance, among many other community services.

As I finished up my report, a bang startled me, and I spun my rolling chair around to face the open workroom door. That was odd. It had almost sounded like heavy books tumbling off a shelf.

I stood, reaching into my pocket to curl my fingers around my cell phone. Crossing the workroom to reach the area behind the circulation desk, I slid my fingers along the plaster wall until I reached the main switch and flicked on the lights.

Nothing happened. I toggled the switch off and on a couple of times before giving up and reaching under the circulation desk for the flashlight we kept for emergencies. I wasn't overly worried about the failure. It wasn't uncommon to lose power every now and then. The original portion of the building dated from 1919 and the electricity could be problematic, especially in bad weather. We'd upgraded some of the wiring to accommodate computers and other equipment, but we couldn't afford to fix everything. As long as it worked, it didn't get touched.

But it wasn't working now. I gripped the flashlight with one hand, keeping the other in my pocket to retain my grip on my phone. If I saw anything that looked suspicious—like arcing or sparking in any of the lights or outlets—I wanted to be ready to call 911 immediately.

A clunk of wood against wood made me pause in one of the nonfiction aisles and lower my flashlight. It sounded like one of our heavy wooden reading room chairs had knocked against the edge of a table. I stared at the circle of light illuminating a section of the carpet for a second, my thoughts racing, before I flicked off the flashlight.

The lights were apparently the least of my problems. Someone was in the building—that was the only explanation for such a noise. And I didn't want my flashlight to lead whoever it was directly to me.

I tiptoed backward before slipping around the endcap to enter another row of shelving. Pulling the phone from my pocket, I pressed the side button to bring up the screen.

But even that light was a mistake. A book, thrown from the end of the aisle, knocked my cell to the floor.

Cradling the spot where one edge of the book had slammed into my wrist, I dropped down in an attempt to reach my phone before the invader could reach me. As I stood, pulling myself up by grabbing one of the strong metal supports that framed the shelving units, I heard the thunder of footsteps heading toward the back door of the library.

The back door slammed. I turned on my flashlight and crept over to the reading room area, where I sank into a chair. Reconsidering the need to alert all emergency services, I pressed the number I'd programmed to call Brad Tucker instead.

Brad promised to arrive, with backup, in less than ten minutes.

As I waited, I shone the flashlight in an arc over the area, noticing a chair that had been knocked over by the intruder. Crossing over to that area, I stopped in my tracks and stared at the top of the adjacent table.

MIND YUR OWN BIZ was carved into the wood, obviously with a penknife or some other sharp implement. The old table was marred with ink stains and other, older graffiti, but the new cuts, while shallow, shone in contrast to the dark wood.

On a hunch, I flashed the light up across the nearby ivory plaster wall. There was a message emblazoned there as well—STOP YUR SNOOPING OR DIE.

The arc of light swung wildly as I grabbed my upper arms. As I stared blankly at the defaced wall, a bang on the front door sent me running to the entrance, hoping that Brad and his fellow deputies had somehow arrived sooner than expected.

But outside the entry doors, framed in its thick glass panes, I spied a solitary figure—a tall, burly man with water dripping from his mane of white hair.

Brilliant blue eyes stared back at me. "Let me in, Amy!" Kurt Kendrick shouted.

I stared at him through the glass, uncertain if I should comply with this demand. What if he'd been the intruder? He could've fled out the back and appeared at the front doors easily enough.

But would Kurt—brilliant, manipulative, and cunning Kurt—lower his standards to leave such blatant messages? *No,* I thought, *he'd drop cryptic hints, but face-to-face.* And vandalism of a library? Not his style at all.

Besides, Brad would be here any minute.

I unlocked and opened the door, ushering Kurt into the small, ceramic-tiled foyer. "What are you doing here at this time of day, and in this weather?"

Kurt brushed back his hair with both hands, creating a spray of water droplets. "Sorry," he said. "The rain just stopped, but I still got drenched. Let's stay here." He lifted one leather shoe to display the red mud clotted on its heel. "I don't want to stain the carpet."

"Again, why are you here?" I asked, tapping the flashlight against my palm. "I should tell you that the sheriff's department has people headed this way. I called them because there was an intruder in the library just now."

"I know." Kurt used a silk handkerchief to wipe the mud from his shoe. "I saw them run around from the back of the building and sprint off across the street. Could've hit them, to tell you the truth." He looked me over. "Perhaps I should have, given your expression."

"What do you mean?" I asked, puzzling over why he was so sure someone running from behind the library had actually been inside.

"You look haunted." Kurt tossed the handkerchief into a nearby garbage bin. "I have others," he added, obviously registering my surprise.

"I get that you were driving by, but how'd you know the person came from inside the library? They could've been running down the lane beside the building."

Kurt's lips curled into a smile. "That's my girl—always thinking. Actually, I wasn't just driving by. I was parked out front. I stopped when I glimpsed shadows moving inside the library. I knew the building should be closed, so"—he held up his hands—"I thought I should keep an eye on things and be prepared to call the authorities if necessary."

"So you lied. You didn't almost hit them."

Kurt grinned. "Not with my car, no."

"And you're drenched because . . ."

"Because I jumped out of the Jag and pursued them for a few yards before giving up and returning to check on you." He shrugged. "I saw you through one of those big windows when I was heading toward the door. Your flashlight clearly illuminated you."

"Did you get a good look at the intruder? Can you identify him, or her?"

Kurt gazed over my head, his attention apparently caught by something outside. "No. But Amy, we need to talk. Not here," he added quickly, as sirens pierced the air. "Can you come by my house tomorrow? Sometime in the early afternoon? I'd like to . . ." He tightened his lips as Brad and a few deputies strode up the stone steps outside the entry. "We can't talk about it now. Tomorrow, say, around one o'clock?"

I studied his implacable face before turning to open the door for Brad. "All right," I said, calculating how I could slip away the next day without alerting Aunt Lydia or Richard. I did need to pick up some items for Richard's dinner party on Sunday. I could say I could only get the proper things from the fancier grocery store about forty-five minutes from Taylorsford . . .

"Amy, glad to see you're okay." Brad pulled off his hat and held it in front of his chest like a shield. He looked Kurt up and down. "And why exactly are you here, Mr. Kendrick?"

"Just driving by. Ms. Webber flagged me down, and of course I stopped," Kurt replied smoothly.

Flagged him down? I studied my hands to hide my expression.

"Wait—did the guy attack you?" Brad gently cradled my hand in his and examined the darkening bruise on my wrist.

"Not sure it was a guy, and no, not directly. Whoever it was just threw a book at me to knock my phone from my hand. Collateral damage," I added, lifting my hand and holding out my wrist to Kurt.

The older man's eyes glittered like sapphire chips. "So I see. Well, fortunately, they didn't actually lay hands on you."

I met his gaze, and what I read there told me it was fortunate for *them*.

Maybe he has some idea who it was, I thought, as I gnawed the inside of my cheek. *Was he just driving by, or following them, or*—I took a deep breath—*watching me?*

Behind us, lights flared. "Power was just shut off at the junction box, sir," one of Brad's deputies called out from inside the library.

"Did they steal anything?"

I shook my head. "I don't know for sure, but I don't think so. They left something instead."

Brad tightened his grip on the rim of his hat. "Left what?"

"Some graffiti. In the reading room area. Take a look for yourself."

"I will. Deputy Coleman"—Brad motioned at one of the waiting deputies—"with me. As for you two, stay here until we can get statements."

As Brad strode past me to enter the library proper, Kurt said, "Graffiti?"

"A couple of messages, actually." I shot Kurt a sharp look. "A warning."

"Really? What did it say?"

"What you've told me before. That I should stop trying to help the current investigations into Jeremy Adams's death. At least, that's what I assume it meant. The wording was rather primitive."

"Or made to appear so." Kurt looked down at me with a smile that did nothing to warm his craggy features. "I see you've thought of that as well. We definitely need to talk."

"And we will, tomorrow. For now, I want to get these statements over with so I can walk home." I glanced out at the clearing sky. "At least it isn't raining anymore."

"I will drive you home," Kurt said, holding up his hand when I started to protest. "That intruder is still out there somewhere. I'm certainly not allowing you to walk home alone tonight."

"Brad can take me," I argued, as exhaustion swept over me. The last thing I wanted was to keep playing a cat-and-mouse game with Kurt.

"He probably won't be done here for some time. Are you sure you want to wait that long?"

"It's fine. Besides, I'll have to make sure the library is secure before I leave. As soon as you give your statement, you go ahead and take off. I promise to stop by your house tomorrow sometime after one. We can talk more then."

"Yes, we will. And perhaps I can convince you that, despite their rather crude methods, today's intruder actually has the right idea." Kurt's eyes were very bright as he gave me a nod and turned to talk to Detective Carver, who'd come to take our statements.

He interviewed us one at a time in the workroom, and although I'd planned to contradict Kurt's white lie about me flagging him down, for some reason I never did.

Chapter Eighteen

Saturday was one of those lovely September days where everything appeared to be rimmed in crystal. The sky was blue as a fine piece of Wedgwood, and the leaves, still green, were outlined with gold by the bright sunlight. I paused for a moment at Kurt Kendrick's forest-green front door and inhaled a deep breath, enjoying the scent of the late-season roses that filled his cottage garden.

Built in the eighteenth century, Kurt's home was one of the oldest houses in the area as well as one of the most beautiful. Set in a clearing surrounded by hardwood trees and tall pines, its three-story central section was built from local fieldstone. Large, narrow windows, the waviness of the glass betraying their age, were sunk deep into the mottled gray stones. The two-story wings that extended from either side of the central structure had wooden siding painted a pale jade green, and the smaller, square windows of the wings were flanked by black shutters. Ivy draped the largest of the stone chimneys, while the front of the house was enlivened by flower beds separated from the paved driveway by a whitewashed picket fence.

I'd visited this house many times over the past couple of years, but today my visit felt particularly momentous. I had to find out if Kurt Kendrick, known as Karl Klass when he'd first lived in Taylorsford over fifty years ago, had somehow been involved in the death of Jeremy Adams.

Or knows who was, I reminded myself, as I pressed my finger on the doorbell. Kurt hadn't been the only person dealing drugs in the area back in the sixties. But knowing him, I was sure he'd been aware of every other dealer, and their activities, especially if those actions involved a murder.

Kurt answered the door and ushered me inside before striding off down his wide, antiques-and-art-laden central hallway. He headed for a staircase at the back of the house.

"I thought we'd talk up in the study," he called over his shoulder as I jogged to keep up with him.

At the top of the stairs, where the upper hall was open to the floor below, I leaned on the balustrade to catch my breath. I also checked out the art hanging on the opposite wall, especially a small painting nestled between some larger works. A painting that could easily have been mistaken for a Van Gogh by anyone who knew art.

"It's still there," Kurt said, flashing me a toothy smile. "And, as I suspected, no one has guessed its true provenance. At least not yet. Now, come along. The study is this way." He motioned toward a room at the other end of the short hallway.

As I entered, the first thing I noticed was a large oil painting hanging in the one wall space not occupied by wooden bookcases. A landscape, it depicted the Blue Ridge Mountains from a vantage point quite familiar to me.

"That's one of my uncle's pieces, isn't it?" I padded across the thick Persian rug to examine the painting more closely. Although it was painted in a realistic style, it held an air of mystery—as if at any moment something momentous was about to occur in that quiet field bordered by trees.

"Yes. I bought it, and a few others, after the showing of Andrew's paintings I hosted here last December."

I turned to face Kurt. "You were one of the anonymous buyers? Aunt Lydia was surprised that the paintings sold so well, although she was grateful for her cut of the profits."

"I didn't do it out of charity." Kurt's gaze was focused on the landscape. "I genuinely wanted to own more of Andrew's works."

"I'm sure." I sat down in a nearby wingback chair. Sinking into its buttery leather cushions, I surveyed the study, which I would've called a library instead. Books of every size and description overflowed shelves that filled almost every inch of wall space, from the tops of built-in lower cabinets to the high, coffered ceiling.

Kurt grabbed the back of a chair tucked under a rolltop desk built from solid oak. As he rolled the wooden office chair around, I couldn't help but notice that its casters were gripped by feet that resembled the talons of some predatory bird.

How appropriate . . . I cleared my throat. "How about you tell me what you called me here to discuss? I don't want to waste too much time. Richard is throwing a little dinner party tomorrow, and I want to hurry back to help with the preparations."

"Of course. Straight to the point as always." Kurt gave me a wink, but as soon as he sat down, his expression sobered. "But to be blunt—I asked you here to warn you."

"The graffiti wasn't enough?" I threw up my hands as his frown turned into a glower. "Okay, okay, I know you had nothing to do with that. Not your style."

"Definitely not. I'd never deface any building, much less a library." Kurt stretched his long legs out across the muted blue–and–rose gold pattern of the rug. "But I have been doing a little digging of my own—contacting some old acquaintances through my more discreet associates and so on. What I've heard is not encouraging."

"You mean former drug-dealing acquaintances?"

"Yes." Kurt rested one elbow on the wide arm of his chair and balanced his chin on the back of his hand. His gaze held a mixture of ferocity and fondness. "I've never pretended that I was an angel in my youth. Or anytime in my life, for that matter. But I do care about you, Amy, as well as many people in your circle of family and friends. I don't want to see any of you come to any harm."

"And you think that could happen?"

"It's possible, given the people involved. Most have moved beyond their criminal pasts, but not all."

"You believe Jeremy was killed by a drug dealer, not someone he knew at Vista View?"

Kurt lifted his head and leaned against the curved back of his chair. "I don't have absolute proof yet, but that makes the most sense to me. Mainly because I can't think of any real reason why one of the commune members would want him dead, and a thousand reasons why a dealer might've desired that outcome."

"I tend to agree with you. I did glean a few motives from the former commune members, but they all seemed rather . . . weak." I drew a circle with my forefinger in the soft leather of my chair arm. "Although I have found that sometimes people kill for strange reasons."

"True. But in all honesty, my contacts have informed me that one of the dealers from back in the sixties and seventies is now working for a larger operation." He narrowed his eyes. "A larger, more dangerous operation."

"Which one? The Weasel?"

Kurt lifted his bushy eyebrows. "You *are* well informed. No, he left the game about the same time I did. The last thing I heard about him was that he'd moved farther south and become an evangelical preacher."

"He found religion?" I couldn't prevent a little smirk. "Unlike you."

"Oh, I believe in a few things," Kurt replied, with a glance over at my Uncle Andrew's painting.

"Who, then?" I curled my fingers into my palm. "Not the woman they called Esmerelda?"

"Yes, that's the one."

"And you think she might've killed Jeremy Adams, then murdered Ruth Lee to prevent Ruth from spilling any information about her previous crime?"

"Don't look so incredulous. You, of all people, should know that women can be as cold-blooded, and as deadly, as men."

"I know they can kill just as easily, but it seems strange . . ." I fixed Kurt with an intense stare. "Were you ever Jeremy's dealer?"

"For a while." Kurt flicked a speck of lint from his tailored wool trousers. "But eventually Jeremy wanted more than I could, or would, offer, and turned to Esmerelda for that stuff. He got in pretty deep, I'm afraid. Which was a shame. He did possess great talent." Kurt looked up and met my sharp gaze with a sigh. "I imagine it's possible that he fell behind on his payments, and . . . Well, perhaps Esmerelda's bosses decided to make an example of him."

"I'd think you would've heard about such a thing, if it had happened that way. Don't you keep tabs on everything remotely related to your business ventures?"

"I do now. Back then, not so much." Kurt tapped the wooden arm of his chair with his short fingernails. "Anyway, I left the area right around the time Jeremy Adams disappeared from the commune. I wasn't aware that he'd ever returned, although apparently that must've been the case."

I slid to the edge of my chair, gripping my knees with both hands. "Yes, and why? That's what I don't understand. He told two people he was headed to, or was in, LA, but then he came back, at least for a brief visit, only a month or two later. Why?"

Kurt shrugged. "My guess is that Esmerelda or someone from her organization tracked him down and told him to come back and pay up or they'd harm people he loved. He had a girlfriend at the commune, you know."

"That was Ruth Lee."

"Yes, and then there was his family, including your friend Walt. If they were threatened, I suspect Jeremy would have rushed back to deal with the situation." Kurt toyed with the gold cuff links on his pale-gray silk shirt. "He may have had a temper, and a drug problem, but deep down he was a kind and decent man. The drugs made him unpredictable, but his heart was always in the right place."

I thought about the songs I'd listened to on Jeremy's demo reel. "I can believe that. I mean, from everything I've heard."

Kurt shot me a questioning look. "Something you want to share?"

"No, no. I did talk to Ruth and some of the others, as you know. It's the way they depicted him, that's all." I clasped my hands in my lap to stop my fidgeting. I had no intention of telling Kurt Kendrick about Jeremy's demo tape. "So basically, you called me in for a chat to warn me off the investigation because you think some still-active criminals might not want anyone digging into their past activities?"

"Exactly."

"You could've just told me all this last night, at the library."

"Not with all those deputies around." Kurt rose to his feet. "I hope you understand—I do not wish to be drawn into this investigation in any way. I prefer my past to remain . . . unexamined territory."

"You're afraid someone might dredge up more than one skeleton?" I asked as I stood to face him.

"If you mean, do I want to keep some things buried? Why yes, I do. Although not necessarily actual bodies."

I considered that *necessarily* for a moment. "I suppose I should thank you for the warning, but really, there's no need. I've completed my mission for P.J. and Carol, and I think I've also exhausted all the research help I can offer the sheriff's department. So it looks like I'm done playing detective. But you"—I met his intense gaze and held it —"could help the authorities a great deal if you shared the information about Esmerelda and her compatriots with them."

"I will talk to someone. Perhaps not Brad Tucker, who, despite his many fine qualities, tends to hold a rather black-and-white view of life. But I do have contacts on the federal level who might be able to assist our good chief deputy." Kurt stepped forward and gripped my forearm. "I hope you won't run to the local authorities with this information I've shared today. I prefer to handle this type of thing in my own way."

I twisted my arm hard to the right, dislodging his fingers. "That's fine. But I'm giving you a deadline."

Kurt's eyebrows shot up under the fall of his thick white hair. "Oh, really?"

"Yes, really. You go to your FBI pals or whoever and share what you know by the end of next week, or I tell Brad what you've just shared with me."

Looking me up and down, Kurt chuckled. "This takes me back. Do you know how much you look like your great-grandmother Rose when you get riled up?" He winked. "'Though she be but little, she is fierce,' indeed."

I'd heard enough harrowing stories about my great-grandmother to make me bristle at any mention of our resemblance. "I don't care for that comparison, you know."

"I said you looked like her, not that you behaved in the same manner. Which, thankfully, you don't. I only knew the woman when I was young, but I can assure you that your personality is a great improvement upon hers."

"I should hope so." I waved my hand toward Uncle Andrew's painting. "Do you also want me to keep silent about your purchase of Andrew's work? Around Aunt Lydia and Hugh, I mean."

"If you don't mind. I don't want Lydia to feel beholden to me."

It was my turn to chuckle. "Don't worry, I doubt she'd ever feel that."

Kurt flashed a smile. "Probably not. But I'd prefer she not know about my purchases, just the same."

"All right, you have my promise to keep that quiet. Now—if you feel I'm sufficiently warned off the Adams case, I really should be going. Like I said, I need to help Richard with his dinner party prep." I crossed to the door but paused to look back at him. "Oh gosh, I suppose we should've invited you. It's a party to celebrate Fiona Muir's birthday, and since you were her uncle's foster son . . ."

Kurt joined me in the hall. “Nonsense. You needn’t worry about that. Anyway, I have other plans.”

“Still, I should have thought of it before this,” I said, glancing over at that small painting, worth a great fortune, that hung so innocently on the wall. “But to be honest, Hugh Chen is going to be there, which would probably make it uncomfortable for you.”

“Yes, Hugh does like to quiz me about all my art dealings,” Kurt said as we made our way down the stairs. “He believes he’s bound to catch me in a lie someday. Something he can prove, I mean.”

“Hope springs eternal,” I said, following his swift progress to the front door.

“‘Man never is, but always to be, blest,’” Kurt replied, as he opened the front door. Before I could step out onto the portico, he laid a hand on my shoulder. “Remember that, Amy. One can eternally hope, and yet always be thwarted.”

I glanced up at him from under my lowered lashes, unsure if he was talking about Hugh’s quest to uncover his less-than-legal art deals, or something else.

Perhaps something like the love he still felt for a man he’d lost so long ago.

“I still think that hope is worth indulging in sometimes.” I reached up and patted his hand before moving away. “Perhaps you should try it.”

He gave me a speculative look. “In what fashion?”

“I don’t know. Maybe hope to meet someone to share this great heap with you,” I said, turning aside so that he couldn’t see my face.

He didn’t reply. When I paused at the picket fence gate and glanced back at him, his face wore its familiar mocking expression.

But whether that sarcasm was directed at me or himself, I couldn't be sure.

"Goodbye, Amy," he said. "Please give my regards to Richard, Lydia, Fiona, and yes, even Hugh. Tell them I wish them all well and hope to see them again soon."

"I'll do that," I said. "Goodbye, and thanks for the information, and the warning. I vow to remain vigilant." I gave him a little mock salute.

His expression sobered. "As, I promise, will I."

Which made me wonder, as I started up my car and headed down his long, tree-shaded driveway, just how long and how seriously he'd been keeping tabs on some of his former acquaintances.

It also struck me, as I turned onto the gravel road that led back to town, that perhaps Kurt's driving by the library last night had not been an entirely random occurrence.

Chapter Nineteen

Watching Fiona Muir examine the dining setup for her birthday dinner involved a great deal of swallowing words and tongue biting.

"I suppose this works," she said, her forehead crinkling. "Although a folding table isn't exactly my idea of elegance."

"There is a linen tablecloth." Richard circled the table, placing silverware at each setting.

The stack of wooden salad bowls I carried clattered as I crossed the living room. Richard, who'd sacrificed a formal dining room for his studio, had spread a large beige-and-tan-patterned wool rug over the wooden dance floor and set up a folding banquet table covered by a white tablecloth. The chairs, pulled from the kitchen table and other locations in his house, might have been a motley assortment of styles, but they were all sturdy and perfectly suitable.

"I think it's a very clever way to provide a bigger dining space," I said, handing the bowls to Richard. "We usually just eat in the kitchen, but there isn't room for a larger crowd at that table."

Fiona smoothed back a strand of dark hair that had escaped her smooth chignon. "I hope you're going to be happy with this arrangement in the long run, Amy. There isn't space in this house to add a real dining room, and I imagine that you'll regret this rather peculiar setup after a while."

I met her imperious gaze. Her beautiful gray eyes, enough like Richard's to give me pause, were narrowed between her thick black lashes. "Oh, it'll be fine. We don't plan to do much formal entertaining. If the group's too large for the kitchen, we'll just have a buffet."

"But holiday dinners . . ." Fiona said, before Richard cast her a sharp glance.

"I have plans to convert the back porch into a dining space eventually," he said, banging the last of the salad bowls down beside a dark-blue ceramic plate.

"That's a good idea," his mother said, her expression brightening. "Just let me know when you plan to start that project. I'm acquainted with a great interior designer, if you decide to go that route."

"Thanks." Richard caught my eye and raised his eyebrows. "We'll keep that in mind."

"Do." Fiona tugged a tiny wrinkle out of the tablecloth. "When is this friend of yours arriving, Richard? I thought we were eating around one." She stared pointedly at her delicate gold wristwatch.

"She'll be here," Richard said. "And she isn't just *some* friend. You know her, Mom. You met her years ago."

"Right, the husky, very tall girl. The one you used to dance with so often. But then she just disappeared." Fiona fluttered one of her fine-boned hands. "I hope she's not still so flighty."

"Excuse me, I need to check on something in the kitchen." Richard strode across the room, grabbing my hand and pulling me along with him.

"Do you need any help?" Fiona asked.

"No, just take a seat in the living room, Mom. We'll only be a minute," he told her as we headed into the hall.

"You knew this would be difficult," I said when we entered the kitchen.

"Problems?" Aunt Lydia, who was standing at the tall, oak-topped table that functioned as a kitchen island, waved a carrot at us.

Richard released my hand and headed straight for the counter that held an open bottle of white wine. "No more than usual," he said, pouring himself a full glass.

I walked forward and leaned against the other side of the island. "Fiona is being a little . . ."

"Critical?" Aunt Lydia chopped the carrot into thin slices.

"You could say that." I picked up a loose head of leaf lettuce and began tearing it into bite-sized pieces.

"As always." Richard took a long swallow of wine.

Hugh, who was using a fork to fluff some curry-spiced couscous in a saucepan, cast us an amused glance over his shoulder. "She does know what she likes."

"And doesn't," Aunt Lydia said, sharing a glance with me.

"And there's the doorbell," Richard said, finishing off his wine in one gulp. "I'd better get out there before Mom greets Karla in some less-than-flattering way." He plunked down his glass and dashed out of the room.

"That woman," Aunt Lydia said, dicing a piece of celery. "And she's not nearly as bad as her husband. How Richard turned out as well as he did is beyond me."

"That is the ultimate mystery," I agreed.

"Where is Mr. Muir, by the way?" Hugh asked. "Lydia may have told me, but I'm afraid I don't recall what she said."

"Because you were distracted by that news on the TV about some famous lost painting being recovered after twenty years," my aunt said, meeting Hugh's abashed gaze with a smile. "It's okay. I found that story pretty fascinating too."

"Jim Muir is away on a business trip. Fortunately." I held my finger to my lips. "Don't repeat that."

"Our lips are sealed, although I'm sure Richard would agree." Aunt Lydia tipped up her Lucite cutting board and dumped the chopped vegetables into a large wooden bowl. "Throw in the lettuce and let's get this tossed. It sounds like Karla is here, so I expect Richard will want to eat soon."

Hugh covered the saucepan with its glass lid. "In that case, I'm going to wash up. The couscous is ready. I think if we leave it covered it will stay warm enough."

"Thanks." I crossed over to the stove and gave a pot of orange-glazed carrots a stir. "Everything's ready then, except for the salmon, and Richard didn't want to grill that until closer to serving time."

Aunt Lydia slipped her white apron over her head, revealing an elegant rose-pink natural-silk jacket-and-skirt ensemble. She folded the apron and laid it on one of counters. "I think I'll just wash my hands in here, since Hugh's using the hall powder room." She patted her short cap of white hair. "But since there's no mirror—do I pass muster?"

"And then some," I said, glancing down at my own outfit. I'd made the concession of wearing a dressy jade-green blouse over my black slacks, just to please Richard's mother. Although, based on the expression on her face when she'd arrived and looked me over, I'd apparently failed in that mission once again.

When Aunt Lydia stepped aside, I washed my own hands in the kitchen's deep farm sink before grabbing the wooden salad bowl and tongs. "I've got this. If you could just bring the dressing, that would be great. But please watch that you don't spill anything on that lovely suit."

"I'll be careful." Aunt Lydia picked up the silver-plated serving tray that held three different salad dressings in crystal cruets. "Are we waiting to carry in the rest of the meal?" she asked as she followed me into the living room.

"Yeah, salad first. Richard and I will serve everything else later."

As we crossed over to the table, I noticed that Richard was introducing Hugh to Karla, while Fiona stood off to one side.

Making judgments, I thought, then chided myself for being so catty. While it was true that Fiona Muir tended to be opinionated and overly critical, she was still Richard's mother. I had to eventually learn to get along with her, one way or the other.

"Looks like we're ready to start on the salad course," Richard said. "Please, everyone, take a seat at the table. I just need to grab the water pitcher and fill glasses, and then we can have dinner."

"Need help?" I asked him as he paused beside me.

"No, go ahead and sit down. I'll take care of it." He gave me a smile. "Besides," he added, leaning in so that he could whisper in my ear, "someone needs to keep Mom in line."

"Gee, thanks," I whispered back, but kissed his cheek before he moved away.

"Hi, Amy, so good to see you again." Karla enveloped me in a hug. Since she towered over me, I had to tip my head back to look up into her broad face.

Karla's hazel eyes were bright and clear, her dark-blonde hair cut in a sleek bob that just grazed her jaw. As always, her lovely but larger-than-life features reminded me of a statue of the goddess Artemis brought to glowing life.

"Good to see you too. Glad you could make it." I stepped away but kept my arm around her waist as we crossed to the table. "Here, you sit between me and Richard." I motioned to one of the chairs. "And Fiona, please sit at the head of the table, as you are the guest of honor."

I put Hugh on Fiona's right, while leaving a space for Richard on her left. That allowed Aunt Lydia to sit beside Hugh, facing Karla, while protecting both Karla and me from Fiona's direct regard. A little measure I thought wise, given the circumstances.

Part of my reasoning was based on Karla's slouchy gray tunic worn over a pair of black leggings, along with ballet flats and no socks. It was an outfit not at all to Fiona's taste, especially for a dinner party, and I was anticipating at least one snide comment on the dancer's attire from my future mother-in-law.

Fortunately, my fears were unfounded. Fiona, charmed by Hugh and Aunt Lydia, spent most of the meal talking to them, with a few asides to Richard. She glanced at Karla once or twice, but that was it.

Richard and I were pouring coffee by the time Fiona finally addressed me. Of course, it was yet another attempt to coerce me into considering her choice for wedding and reception venues.

"And speaking of the ceremony," she said, after taking a dainty sip of coffee, "what size wedding party are you planning to have? Large or small? It will make a difference in terms of what church might work best, you know."

"Small," Richard said firmly.

"I suppose that's best, given your ages. One doesn't want to make too much of a spectacle when the bride is over thirty."

I choked on my coffee, then waved my hand to silence the murmurs of concern from around the table. "Just went down the wrong way."

Richard, meeting my gaze over the rim of his cup, widened his eyes comically, which made me cough to cover up a burst of laughter.

I pointed at my cup. "Hot."

Fiona's gaze rested on me, her eyes narrowed. "So, two or three attendants, then?"

"Just two," I said, after clearing my throat. "Sunny Fields is my maid of honor, of course, and an old friend from library school has agreed to be the other bridesmaid."

"You'll need two attendants then, Richard," Fiona said, tapping his arm with one buffed fingernail. "To balance things out."

"All taken care of," he replied, after wiping his mouth with his napkin. "Amy's brother Scott is going to be a groomsman. And as for the best man"—he glanced over at Karla—"well, we're doing something a little different. Your best man is supposed to be your closest friend or a brother, and since I have no siblings, I decided to ask my best friend. Although," he added, folding the napkin and carefully placing it in his lap without meeting his mother's eyes, "that means I will have a best woman instead of a best man."

I clasped Karla's hand and gave it a squeeze. "Oh, you did say yes!"

Aunt Lydia opened her mouth but closed it again without saying anything, while Hugh looked across the table, gracing the three of us with a warm smile.

"Such an interesting idea," he said, before turning to Fiona. "It will make the ceremony that much more unique, don't you agree, Fiona?"

My future mother-in-law sputtered something unintelligible before she was able to spit out, "But you can't do that."

Richard draped his arm across the back of Karla's chair. "I don't see why not. It's my wedding, and I want my best friend to stand beside me. Where's the harm in that?"

"But whatever will she wear?" Fiona's voice slid up almost an octave on the final word.

Richard sat back in his chair and crossed his arms over his chest. "A gown, of course. She's not going to masquerade as something she's not."

"Amy," Fiona said, in a tone that made me jump, "are you okay with this?"

"Of course," I said. "I think it's a lovely idea. And it's what Richard wants, which is what matters."

"It is unusual, but certainly not unheard of," Aunt Lydia said, turning her most charming smile on Fiona. "And as Amy said, it's what the bridal couple wants that matters the most, don't you think?"

Fiona's gaze swept over the table. She was obviously looking for someone to back up her opinion. Finding no one willing to do so, she sank back in her chair and pressed one hand to her forehead. "Goodness, I'm feeling a bit light-headed all of a sudden. Would you escort me over to a more comfortable chair, Richard?"

"Of course," he said, rising to his feet and offering her his arm with what looked like exaggerated gallantry.

But Fiona didn't seem to notice any sarcasm in his words or actions. She stood slowly, took his arm, and allowed him to guide her across the room. Seating her in one of the upholstered armchairs, Richard leaned in and solicitously asked her if she would like him to bring over her coffee cup.

"Oh no, that's quite all right," she replied, fanning herself with one hand. "I think perhaps the coffee overheated me, to tell you the truth."

Richard, who'd turned back to face the table, pulled a comical face and said, "Yes, I'm sure that was it."

I pressed my napkin over my lips to silence a giggle, as Hugh pushed back his chair and rose to his feet.

"Allow me," he told Aunt Lydia, pulling back her chair so she could stand up. "Why don't we join Fiona while the table is cleared?" he suggested, with a nod toward the living room area.

"That sounds like an excellent plan," Aunt Lydia said, sharing a knowing look with me.

With Fiona occupied with company, Karla, Richard, and I set to work gathering up dishes and other items from the table and carrying them into the kitchen.

"We'll wash everything up later," Richard said, when the last load of dishes was placed in the sink. "For now, I suggest a glass of wine."

"Sounds good," I said as he uncorked another bottle.

"Just let me take out this bag of trash. I assume the can's out back?" Karla kicked open the door to the screened-in back porch.

"Wait!" I tried to dash forward fast enough to close the door before Loie and Fosse, who'd been relegated to the porch for the afternoon, slipped through Karla's legs.

But I was too late. Richard swore as the two kittens dashed through the kitchen and bounded into the hall, making a beeline for the living room.

"I'll grab Fosse and you capture Loie," I told him, as we left Karla standing at the back door laughing, and ran after the cats.

Skidding into the living room on the slick soles of my loafers, I gasped as Loie leapt directly into Fiona's lap. Fosse, not to be outdone, immediately jumped up onto the arm of the chair and threw his furry body on top of Loie's arched back.

Fiona shrieked and leapt out of the chair, sending kittens flying. With the dexterity of their kind, both cats flipped in midair and landed on their feet on top of the coffee table, but that action sent magazines sailing toward Aunt Lydia and Hugh, who were seated on the sofa.

Aunt Lydia threw up her arms, while Hugh batted away the magazines with his fists. Fiona, her hands waving like she'd been attacked by bees, kept repeating something that sounded like "furry fiends." As Richard strode into the seating area, Fiona's flailing fingers caught in her hair and pulled a chunk free of its carefully twisted updo.

I stopped short as Richard chased the kittens toward me. As I spun around to try to snag one of them, my foot slipped out from under me, and I ended up on my backside on the floor.

Richard scooped up Loie while I just sat there, frozen in surprise at my tumble. After a minute, something nudged my arm, and I looked down at Fosse gazing up at me, his amber eyes wide and innocent. "You little stinker," I said, pulling him into my lap.

Richard, who'd apparently already deposited Loie back onto the porch, reappeared. He gazed down at me and Fosse, who had begun to purr and knead my upper thigh with his paws.

"Troublemaker," he said in an indulgent tone, before lifting the kitten from my lap. He held out his other hand to me and pulled me to my feet. "Nothing broken or bruised, I hope."

"Only my pride," I said, then motioned discreetly toward the center of the room, where Aunt Lydia was helping Fiona pin up her hair. "Looks like I'm not the only one."

"So much for celebrating Mom's birthday in a proper fashion." Richard released my hand and shifted Fosse so that he could hold the kitten up before his face. "You and your sister have made a very bad impression, you know."

Fosse reached out and bopped Richard on the nose.

"I don't think your tough talk is working," I said.

Karla stepped up behind us. "Here, let me take the little monster and put him back on the porch. You two had better go make nice with Fiona. And Rich, I'd also suggest that you take your mom out to some fancy restaurant, just the two of you, in the next week or two. Someplace where you'll spend a great deal of money on some tiny plates of food." Karla winked. "Just a suggestion."

Richard handed the kitten off with a sigh. "And not a bad one, I'm sorry to say." He glanced over at me. "You don't mind if I do that someday soon, do you, sweetheart?"

"Not at all," I said, sliding my arm around his waist. "Whenever you want to spend time with Fiona without me is fine."

"I know," he said glumly, as Karla chuckled and carried Fosse toward the back porch.

Fiona, sharing some words with Aunt Lydia and Hugh, who both looked pained enough for me to guess the tenor of her remarks, shot us a glare from across the room.

"Perhaps you should go and entertain your mom while I escape . . . I mean, finish cleaning up the dishes." I hugged him a little closer. "I'll make it up to you."

"Will you?" He flashed me a wicked grin. "Do I get to set the terms?"

"Within reason," I said, but couldn't help smiling in return.

"That's fair. Maybe I can make it through the rest of this afternoon now. At least I'll have something to look forward to."

"Richard," Fiona called out, "would you please make sure those creatures don't get out again? Otherwise, I'm afraid I may have to leave early."

Both Richard and I cast longing glances down the hall before looking back at each other.

"I know what you're thinking," I said, tapping his chest with one finger. "And it's a wicked plan."

He shook his head. "You were thinking the very same thing."

"Yes, I was," I said, as we both turned and looked at our guests. Fiona, once again seated, was saying something about the impossibility of getting good help while Aunt Lydia and Hugh practiced their poker faces. "And depending on how things go, I might implement it," I added as Karla rejoined us.

"Leave that to me," she said. "You just give me a signal and I'll release the beasts."

"Richard, are you ever going to join us?" Fiona's shrill tone cut through our sotto voce conversation like a blade.

"Coming," Richard called out, before casting Karla a knowing look. "I stand and point one foot. That's the signal."

"Aye, aye, Captain," she said with a grin.

While Richard strode forward to join the others, I laid my hand over Karla's wrist. "I can see why Richard chose you. Best woman, indeed."

"I've dealt with Fiona before, remember?" Karla's hazel eyes were bright with mischief. "And believe it or not, she's actually mellowed."

Karla plastered on a smile and strode over to sit in the rocker near Fiona's armchair. As I settled in beside Aunt Lydia and Hugh, I gazed over at Richard, who was slumped in the armchair facing the sofa. I cast him a warm smile and mouthed *later* while pointing a finger from him to me.

He grinned and straightened in his chair. "So Mom," he said, "how'd you like the gift from Amy?"

Fiona turned her head to stare at him, suspicion narrowing her eyes. "It was lovely, actually." She cast me a quick glance. "Thank you again."

"You're quite welcome," I said, adding for the others' benefit, "It was an antique cup and saucer."

"Haviland," Fiona said, with a lift of her sharp chin. "Very nice, though I am surprised you remembered that I love old china, Amy."

I bit the inside of my cheek to prevent a sarcastic response. Fiona had mentioned her china collection every time I'd seen her over the last few months. "I hoped you would like it," I said.

"Yes, well"—Fiona fluttered her hands—"it was certainly more appropriate than Richard's gift, I must say." She shot him a sharp glance. "A bottle of cognac, of all things. He knows I don't drink that much."

"I thought we could share it the next time I visited," Richard said, before smoothly shifting the topic to art and engaging Hugh in a discussion of Chinese ceramics.

Later, when all our guests had left and I was snuggled beside Richard on the sofa, I mentioned Karla's comment about Fiona having mellowed over the years. "Is that true?"

"Actually, yes," he replied.

"You poor thing." I stroked his bare forearm with my fingers. "I suppose I should be extra nice to you then. You know, to make it up to you, like we agreed earlier."

"Yes, about that." Richard flashed a devilish smile. "I have some ideas."

"Well, as I've often read in critiques of writers—show, not tell."

"Sounds like excellent advice," Richard said, before proceeding to follow it.

Chapter Twenty

When I arrived home from work on Monday, I walked in on an intervention.

From the central hallway, voices rose and overlapped. I recognized them immediately—the primary speakers were Zelda and Walt, with a few interjections from Aunt Lydia.

"I just want you to be on my side, at least in public," Zelda was saying as I walked by the open door to the sitting room. "Amy, dear. Wait. We need you to help settle this."

I sighed and dropped my keys into the ceramic bowl on the hall side table. "I'm not sure I'm the best person to ask at this moment," I said, hanging my jacket on the coatrack. "The patrons stomped on my last nerve at the library today."

"Oh, fiddle." Zelda appeared in the doorway and motioned me into the sitting room. "All I want is an honest answer to one question."

I glanced at Walt's stony face before catching Aunt Lydia's eye. "Okay, but I retain the right to refuse to answer if I think it might incriminate me."

"Nonsense." Zelda bustled over to the center of the room. "Sit, sit. I'm sure you've been on your feet enough for one day."

I sank down onto the sofa, mentally calculating just how diplomatic I'd have to be to get out of this situation without antagonizing at least two people.

Aunt Lydia, seated in her favorite armchair, cast me a sympathetic smile, while Walt, standing next to one of the built-in bookcases, stared fixedly over my head as if mesmerized by the painting that hung behind the sofa.

"You see, Lydia invited us here." Zelda perched on the padded arm of the room's other upholstered chair. "Separately, I might add. It was quite an underhanded move to pull on old friends."

"It's because you're both my friends that I wanted to bring you together. You needed to hash things out," my aunt said, her tone mild as butter. "You've been spatting too long over nothing as it is."

"Nothing? You call Walt not having my back when that weasel Blackstone was smearing poor, dear Sunny, nothing?" Zelda swung her legs, which were so short they didn't touch the floor, banging her heels into the suede fabric of her chair.

"I call it foolish, and if you don't mind, I'd prefer that you don't punch a hole in my armchair with those spiky heels."

Zelda stilled her legs and threw my aunt a sharp glance. "You weren't there, so how can you know what really happened? But Amy was. You tell her, Amy. Tell her how Walt threw me to the wolves." Zelda's rosebud lips puckered into a pout.

I lifted my hands. "I don't know. I can see both sides of this."

Walt snapped his gaze from me to Zelda. "See. It's not as cut-and-dried as you think, Zel."

"I just mean that I can understand why Walt isn't quite ready to absolve Carol and P.J. Fields of all involvement in his cousin's death." I held up one finger as Zelda opened her mouth. "Let me finish, please. It's not that I think they were responsible for his death, but perhaps they do know more than they're telling. I honestly think they may be harboring some secret."

"What secret might that be?" Zelda asked with a toss of her crisp curls.

"I'm not sure. But knowing P.J. and Carol, I can imagine them covering up an accidental death if they thought they were protecting a friend or the commune." I tipped my head and stared directly at Zelda. "Can't you?"

"I suppose." Zelda slid down off the chair, teetering slightly on her high heels. "But I don't like the mayor using this tragedy—and yes, I do consider it a tragedy," she said, with a swift look at Walt, "to further his own interests."

Walt's expression softened. "We can agree on that point, at least."

"Of course it's a tragedy," Aunt Lydia said. "But what's even worse is how it's driven a wedge between you two." She rose gracefully to her feet. "Which is why you're both here—to work things out instead of sulking in separate corners. And I intend to keep you here until you come to some sort of understanding."

"Keep us here? How do you plan to do that?" Walt strode forward, towering over my slender aunt.

Aunt Lydia lifted her chin and met his gaze with a steely stare. "By appealing to your friendship. If not with one another, with me."

Walt, looking abashed, stepped back. "Sorry," he said, after clearing his throat. "I guess, to be perfectly honest, I've always been more affected by Jeremy's disappearance than I ever let on."

"That's perfectly understandable." Aunt Lydia motioned toward the armchair where Zelda had been perched. "Why don't you have a seat, Walt. No sense standing on ceremony."

Zelda, settling down beside me on the sofa, clasped her plump hands together in her lap. "I guess I didn't realize it was such a big issue with you, Walt. You never talked about Jeremy that much after he disappeared."

Walt slumped into the armchair. "I wasn't allowed to."

"What do you mean?" Zelda asked, her tone softening.

"My family discouraged any talk about Jeremy. I suppose they must've felt betrayed by him as well as concerned. And then there was the worry about the sheriff's office and other legal authorities investigating our family. Related to finding Jeremy, they said, but you have to understand—we were one of the only African-American families in Taylorsford in the sixties." Walt shared a glance with Aunt Lydia, who nodded.

"I remember how it was," she said. "The sheriff's department had only white officers back then."

"Yes, and many of them weren't too keen on investigating the disappearance of some black kid who'd lived on a hippie commune. We had to be cautious, too, because we knew that Jeremy did do some drugs. Of course, I had no idea the extent of his involvement in that scene. I guess my aunt and my parents might've known a lot more, and maybe that's why they didn't force the investigators to dig deeper." Walt frowned. "Strange, it never really occurred to me before, but I imagine they didn't want to implicate Jeremy in any major drug activity, because they hoped he'd come home safe and sound one day."

"You mean they didn't want to push too hard on the investigation because they were worried that if he'd fled due to threats from drug dealers, he'd be arrested when he returned?" I asked, saddened by the realization that Jeremy wouldn't have been likely to receive justice even if his murder had been discovered much sooner.

"Yes, I imagine so." Walt tapped one finger against his chin. "It wasn't like we were always treated with the greatest courtesy by the deputies, either. I got the feeling they were suspicious of our statements and were asking questions that even I, as a kid, felt were more like fishing for something to pin on other members of my family than intended to gather any leads on Jeremy's whereabouts. So we all finally just shut up." He sighed. "Which is what they wanted, I guess. Anyway, when we never heard anything more, it was like my family didn't want to even acknowledge Jeremy's existence. Which also meant that even though I was hurting"—Walt's dark eyes glistened with unshed tears—"I couldn't say anything. Not without a reprimand."

"I didn't know." Tears welled up in Zelda's light-brown eyes. "You've never shared that with me."

Walt roughly brushed the dampness from his cheeks with the back of his hand. "I was trained not to. Even though Jeremy was like an older brother to me, I was supposed to forget him and not care anymore. When I even mentioned his name, my mother would shush me, saying it pained my aunt too much. So I just bottled it all up."

Aunt Lydia nodded. "But you never stopped wondering what happened. And when you found out that he was killed, you wanted justice."

Walt nodded before pulling a tissue from his pocket and blowing his nose.

"Oh, poor lamb," Zelda said. "I can just picture you as a little boy having to deal with such a thing." She bounced up off the sofa and tapped her way across the room to reach Walt's chair. "I'm so sorry. I can see I've been too quick to accuse you of being mean-spirited, dear."

He looked up at her, his expression brightening. "And I've been too judgmental. I should give Carol and P.J. Fields the benefit of the doubt. It's what I'd want someone to do for me, after all."

When Zelda bounced onto his lap, he made a grunting sound. But both of them were smiling.

My aunt rested her hand on the back of her chair and shared an amused glance with me. "So now perhaps we can enjoy some coffee and dessert? What do you say? I made a lemon pound cake just yesterday."

"Sounds lovely," Zelda said, before leaning in to give Walt a peck on the cheek.

"I wouldn't say no to that," Walt agreed, tightening his arms around Zelda's waist.

"Let me go and put that together. No, no, you two stay here. Amy can help me, can't you, Amy?"

"Sure," I said, as my aunt breezed past me and headed into the hall. I jumped to my feet and followed her, while Walt and Zelda continued to intersperse endearments with kisses.

"Good work there, Mrs. Talbot," I said, following her into the kitchen.

Aunt Lydia patted her smooth cap of white hair, a little grin tugging at her lips. "I have some skills. And I can be rather clever sometimes, you know."

I smiled back at her. "All the time, I'd say."

* * *

After assisting Aunt Lydia with cutting the cake, I excused myself, telling her I wanted to head outside. "I thought I'd take a little stroll through the backyard before it gets too dark," I said as I left the kitchen.

Twilight had already dulled the color of the flowers and thickened the shadows in the woods behind the garden. As I walked the white pea-gravel paths, I considered the possibility of using the garden as a backdrop for some wedding photos. We could certainly stop by the house to take a few pictures, regardless of where we held the ceremony. Even Fiona would approve of that.

Absentmindedly spinning my engagement ring around my finger, I strolled past the back edge of the yard and onto the path into the woods. The path, just a beaten track bordered by arching vines and undergrowth, led me to an old wooden arbor draped with wisteria vines.

Richard had proposed to me under the arbor, back in early May. The wisteria had been blooming then, its curling vines dripping with blossoms as purple as amethysts. I smiled, recalling that evening, and thinking that if we timed it right, we might even be able to have some photos taken when the wisteria bloomed again.

Lost in my examination of the arbor, I didn't even flinch when something whistled past my ear. But at the crack of metal splintering wood, I jumped and spun around.

That was a bullet. My mind processed this information with detachment. Why was someone shooting in these woods? It wasn't the right season, and Aunt Lydia didn't allow hunting on her property . . .

Twigs crackled and snapped as someone moved through the woods. The shooter was drawing closer.

Close enough to see that I was no deer or other wild creature. Through a mosaic of leaves, I spied a flash of light bouncing off metal and a distinct circle that indicated a gun barrel.

I dropped to the ground, ignoring the sting of small stones stabbing my flattened palms. Another bullet whistled over my head.

Scrabbling through the undergrowth like a lizard, I crawled toward the edge of the woods. I had to reach the garden before my assailant reached me.

It doesn't make sense, I thought, ignoring the sharp twigs piercing the knees of my light slacks and the vines whipping against my bare lower arms. The shooter had to have seen me. Which meant they weren't simply a befuddled hunter, too quick to fire on anything that moved.

They'd meant to shoot me.

Reaching the point where a narrow strip of grass separated Aunt Lydia's garden from the woods, I debated jumping to my feet. The shooter wasn't an expert marksman or they would've already hit me, but if I stood up, I risked giving them a bigger target.

At that moment, shouts exploded from Aunt Lydia's back-porch stoop.

"What the hell do you think you're doing?" Walt's strong voice sailed across the garden, followed by Zelda's shrieks of protest.

"No shooting allowed on my property!" my aunt yelled, her voice vibrating with anger. "Get out!"

A thump and crackle of boots ripping through the undergrowth echoed through the woods. Assuming the shooter was beating a retreat, I stood up. Swaying on legs that were weak as cooked noodles, I grabbed the closest tree trunk for support.

"Amy!" My aunt raced toward me, arms outstretched. "Are you all right?"

"I'm okay. Physically, that is." As I brushed the leaf meal from my clothes, I noticed that my hands and arms were bleeding from a web of scratches.

"Hang on, I'm coming," Walt said, striding down the path to meet us. "Here, lean on me, Amy. And maybe you too, Lydia," he added, giving my aunt a swift glance.

"I'm fine," my aunt said, through trembling lips. "The authorities . . ."

"Zel's calling them right now. Let's get you both inside before we do anything else."

With Walt's lean arm wrapped around my shoulders, I slowly made my way to the house. "Didn't see who it was," I said as we climbed the back-porch steps to meet a waiting Zelda.

"Oh, my poor lamb! Whatever happened?"

I winced as Zelda grabbed my hands and pulled me over to the wicker fan-backed chair. "Going to bleed all over," I muttered as I slumped down onto the rose-patterned cushions.

"That doesn't matter," my aunt said firmly. "What matters is that, except for some nicks and bruises, you seem to be okay." She leaned over me and tipped up my chin. "Eyes look a little glazed, though. Better raise her feet while I get something to clean her up." She scurried out of the room.

Galvanized by Aunt Lydia's commands, Zelda grabbed some loose pillows from the glider while Walt dragged one of the tile-topped side tables across the cement floor of the porch. They set the table at my feet and balanced the cushions on top.

"Dang fool inexperienced hunters," Walt said as he propped my feet on the pillows. "Probably some idiot who just bought a gun and never took any firearms training. The type that hunts out of season and fires at anything that moves."

"Brad Tucker's on his way, along with some other deputies," Zelda said, as Aunt Lydia reappeared with a small bowl of water. A kitchen towel was draped over her arm.

"Unfortunately, the shooter will probably be long gone," she said. "Now, stay still, Amy, and let me sponge off some of this dirt and grime."

I twitched as she gently ran the damp cloth over my skin. "They must've thought I was someone else. Or maybe they were just drunk and shooting at random. I can't imagine who'd want to take potshots at me."

"Can't you?" My aunt's blue eyes were very bright under her pale eyelashes. "I thought maybe it could be connected to the help you've been giving the authorities recently. And all those visits to former Vista View commune members."

She hadn't been fooled. Of course not. My aunt was, as she'd said earlier, quite clever.

A lot smarter than me sometimes, I thought, grimacing as she scrubbed at the dirt embedded in my scratches. When she finished and stepped away, I lowered my feet to the floor.

Sirens wailed outside. "I'll get the door," Zelda said, trotting into the hall.

Her tapping steps were soon followed by the slam of the front door, voices mixed with two-way radio squawking, and the thud of heavy shoes thundering down the hallway.

"What happened?" Brad Tucker slid aside the small table in front of me before grabbing the nearby rocker and pulling it up in front of my chair.

"It was in the woods," Walt said. "You might want to search . . ."

"I've already sent deputies out to investigate and establish a perimeter," Brad said, his gaze fixed on my face. "I want to know what you saw, Amy."

I pushed my tangled hair behind my ears with both hands. "Not much, I'm afraid. I heard a bullet whiz past me and hit the arbor, then turned and saw a gun barrel some distance off; then I hit the ground before whoever it was got another shot off."

"A rifle, you think?"

"Yeah, that's what it looked like, what little I saw. Long barrel poking out of the shrubbery."

"Good girl." Brad leaned in and enclosed my hands in his. His touch was surprisingly gentle. "Did they say anything?"

"No, nothing."

"They didn't call out your name?"

I shook my head. "No. You think it's possible they didn't know who I was?" I looked up at Brad hopefully. "I'd much rather the shooter be just some loose cannon, taking shots at anything that moved, rather than someone targeting me."

He sighed. "Doubtful. I think they must've been watching and waiting before heading into the woods."

"What makes you say that?"

"Because we got a report from one of your neighbors across the street earlier—something about someone skulking about in their yard. I sent out a car, but the deputies couldn't find anyone and left." He shook his head. "Now I wonder if the intruder just gave my deputies the slip and hid in the woods behind your house."

I slid my hands from his loose grip and crossed my arms over my chest, hugging my upper arms to still my trembling. "You think someone was specifically watching our house? Waiting to see if I'd go outside?"

"Maybe." Brad sat back and studied my face. "Which means you need to be especially careful right now. I'm going to keep a patrol posted on your house tonight. We'll make sure there's a presence of deputies, just to let this shooter know they're the one being watched now."

"Thanks," I said, as Deputy Coleman pushed open the back door.

"Anything?" Brad asked, standing to face the deputy.

Coleman shook his head. "No individuals anywhere in the area, but there was proof that someone was in the woods and took some shots. We gathered up all the casings and other evidence we could find. So at least we can analyze those."

"There may be a bullet stuck in the arbor," I said. "I heard wood splinter."

"Yeah, we found that. Which means we can track the gun, or at least the specific type of rifle. Hopefully." Deputy Coleman shared a glance with Brad. "We'll keep searching until it gets too dark. See what else we might find."

"Good. I want to view the scene, of course, so let's head back to the woods and let Ms. Webber relax with her family and friends." Brad tipped his hat to Aunt Lydia and the others. "I think we can wait until tomorrow for Amy to make a formal statement. We'll keep a watch over the area, though, I promise."

"Thank you," Aunt Lydia said. "Just let us know if you need anything more."

"Sure thing." Brad turned to me. "Try not to worry too much. I'm sure we'll track this perp down soon enough." He gave me a little smile. "Judging by them taking shots at you in your own backyard, they don't appear to be a mastermind."

I mustered up a faint smile in return before he followed Deputy Coleman out the back door.

"Probably time we should be going," Walt said.

Despite my scratches, which were stinging like a bad sunburn, I smiled. He and Zelda were standing close together, Walt's arm draped around her shoulders. "We'll be sure to keep you posted on any developments."

"Please do," Zelda said. "And you take care of yourself, poor lamb."

"She will," Aunt Lydia said firmly. "Once I see you off, I'm going to make sure of that."

Zelda hurried over and gave me a kiss on the forehead as she and Walt said their goodbyes.

When Aunt Lydia returned after escorting her friends to the front door, she looked me over with a critical eye. "I think it's time for a nice, hot bath. That and changing into some comfortable PJs will do you a world of good. No need to worry about dinner—you just relax in your bedroom and I'll bring up something on a tray."

"I'm not an invalid," I said, biting back a yelp of pain as I pushed myself out of the chair and stood to face her.

"No, but you've had quite a shock." My aunt linked her arm through mine. "It's not every day that someone takes a shot at you. Although," she added grimly as she guided me toward the stairs, "in your case it does seem to happen far too frequently."

Chapter Twenty-One

Later, snuggled in my quilt and blankets, a pile of pillows behind my back, I attempted to read one of the many books stacked on my nightstand. But the words kept swimming before my eyes. I finally set down the book with a sigh.

Aunt Lydia knocked lightly. "I can take that tray if you're done," she said through the door.

I fluffed my pillows so I could sit up straighter. "Sure, come on in."

"Also," my aunt said as she pushed the door open, "there's someone here who's demanding to see you."

"Amy, I'm so sorry I wasn't here." Richard reached my bed in three long strides. "Of all the days to work late . . ."

"It's all right," I said as he perched on the edge of the bed. "There's nothing you could've done anyway."

"Well, I can do this," he replied, before leaning in to kiss me.

"Mmm, that does help." I patted the bed. "Come sit next to me. Aunt Lydia won't raise an eyebrow, will you, Aunt Lydia?"

My aunt sniffed as she gathered up the tray and headed for the door. "If I was going to do that, I'd have done it long ago," she said, stepping into the hall and closing the door behind her.

Richard kicked off his shoes before swinging his legs up onto the bed. "You don't look too worse for wear," he said after kissing me again.

"It's mostly just scratches." I held up my hands. "Nothing life-threatening."

"Well, those bullets certainly would've been." Richard slid his arm around my shoulders and pulled me close to his side. "Any news from Brad about the shooter?"

"Not yet." I rested my head on his shoulder. "He did leave some deputies to watch the house."

"I saw, and in fact had to run the gauntlet. They wouldn't let me pass until Lydia vouched for me. Which is good," he added, brushing a strand of still-damp hair away from my forehead.

"It's so weird. Either it was just some befuddled hunter, or someone is deliberately trying to hurt me."

"Or maybe," Richard said thoughtfully, "they were just trying to frighten you off. Like with that anonymous note sent to the library, and the graffiti sprayed on the wall and carved into the table. Perhaps it wasn't meant to hurt you, but just to warn you."

I gave him a nod as I realized the truth of his words. "That actually makes more sense, but why would anyone see me as that much of a threat? Sure, I've been helping Brad with some research and talking to a few of the former commune members, but I don't feel like I know much more than the authorities do. So why specifically target me?"

"Someone thinks you know more than you actually do?"

"I guess so." I threw back the covers. "Here, make yourself comfortable."

"Don't mind if I do," Richard said, flipping the sheets, blanket, and quilt back over his legs, before pulling the covers up to his waist. "A nap sounds like just the thing."

"Not what I had in mind," I said.

He shot me an amused glance. "I assumed you'd be exhausted . . ."

"That's not what I meant either, so behave." I patted the hand he'd laid on my thigh. "What I really need is to try to make sense of things. Do you mind helping me think out loud?"

"Of course not. Fire away." He grimaced. "Sorry, bad choice of words. Let's try this instead—share your theories, Sherlock."

"I only wish I was that clever. But anyway, here's what I know so far. First, Jeremy Adams left Taylorsford, if we believe Walt's story about a phone call from the road and Emily Moore's comment about Jeremy calling and giving her his phone number in LA. I mean, I suppose Jeremy could've called from anywhere, but he does seem to have left the immediate area. Even if he was hiding out somewhere close to Taylorsford, he apparently didn't have any contact with anyone at the commune."

"That they will admit," Richard said.

"Right, we only have their word for it. But regardless, he left the farm and was away for a time, and then returned for some unknown reason. I doubt he'd have popped in for a visit after having ticked off most of the other commune members in some way. Not that soon, anyway. Which makes me think someone forced him to come back."

"Maybe for a secret meeting? He apparently didn't contact his family."

"Right. The only proof of his return is that photo from the Heritage Festival."

"And his body," Richard said dryly.

"Yeah, that too." I lifted my head from his shoulder and leaned back against the pillows, staring at the ceiling. "The thing is, if he was trying to keep a low profile, why did he allow anyone to take a photograph? Or why would he even show up at the festival in the first place?"

"That is odd." Richard absently caressed my shoulder as he too gazed upward. "If I had to speculate, I'd say it proves he wasn't afraid to be seen around town. Which means he didn't come back due to any wrongdoing on his part."

"Nothing he thought of as wrong, anyway." I gave Richard a sidelong glance. "Maybe he was returning to help a friend?"

"Or a lover. You told me he had a couple of those at the commune."

"Yeah, Ruth Lee and Belinda Cannon, for sure." I chewed my pinkie nail for a second. "I suppose it's possible that Ruth contacted Jeremy and asked him to return, and he complied because he felt he owed her."

When Richard turned to me, his eyes were sparkling with interest. "You mean she lured him back?"

He's getting into the sleuthing in spite of himself, I thought with a little smile. "Well, she could've claimed she was pregnant. Or ill. Or maybe she told Jeremy she was in trouble with her drug dealer, and he returned to help her pay her debts or something."

"Any of those things could've drawn him back, I suppose."

"Yeah, but . . ." I twisted a strand of my hair around my finger. "She admitted she was angry when he left. Although I do think she truly loved him."

Richard cast me a wry smile. "Love doesn't always stop people from committing murder."

"I know. It's still possible, though, even if Ruth did call Jeremy back to Taylorsford, that someone else actually killed him."

"True. It could've been connected to her drug use. Maybe Jeremy confronted her dealer and things took a violent turn."

"Always a possibility." I sat up and turned to face him. "I suppose you know that Kurt supplied drugs to some of the commune members."

"Did he? I guess I'm not surprised." As Richard stretched his legs out under the covers, he laid one leg over mine. "He's been pretty open with me about how he got his start. And he's a bit of a scoundrel, no question. But honestly, I doubt he'd ever kill anyone."

"I'm not so sure about that," I said, earning a sharp glance. "But I don't know that he'd have had any reason to kill Jeremy. He told me he wasn't the one who supplied Jeremy with the really hard stuff, so there was at least one other dealer in the picture."

"Which is another person who might have contacted Jeremy and forced him to return. Perhaps he had to pay off some debts himself? If he owed money and skipped town, the dealer could've threatened his family unless he returned and paid up."

"I think that's Kurt's current theory, to be honest." I flopped back against my pillows. "But we shouldn't forget the other suspects. From what I've heard, most of the commune members had believable motives to kill Jeremy."

"Such as?"

"For starters, there's still Ruth Lee. She was his lover, but he betrayed her. First with Belinda Cannon and then by leaving town."

"So a crime of passion? But if we follow that lead, then why was she killed?"

"That doesn't fit the theory, but playing devil's advocate, that could've actually been a robbery gone wrong."

"I don't think you really believe that."

I shrugged. "I'm not convinced, but I guess we can't discount it entirely. Getting back to the other commune members, there's also Dean Bodenheimer. Ruth thought he was furious because Jeremy reneged on a promise to include him in his band."

Richard frowned. "Would someone kill over that?"

"It's no stranger than other motives for murder we've encountered."

"True. And Bodenheimer is still alive, which means he could also be Ruth's killer."

"Yeah, I wouldn't discount that," I said. "The guy gave off some seriously bad vibes."

Richard lifted his eyebrows. "Vibes? You're really getting into this sixties stuff, aren't you? Going to start reading auras next?"

"Yeah, yeah, laugh it up, smart guy." I made a face at him before settling back against my pillows. "Anyway, Bodenheimer definitely seemed to be hiding something, although it could be that he's just a habitual liar."

Richard wrinkled his brow. "At this point, it seems like it could've been any of them. Which is a little unnerving, especially since someone is obviously gunning for you."

"Yeah, too many possibilities. I mean, there's Pete O'Malley as well. He didn't seem to have any particular beef with Jeremy, but according to everyone, including Pete, he was pretty strung out most of the time. And he supposedly has a temper. Maybe he lost control when he was high and struck Jeremy in a fit of anger."

Richard rubbed at his jaw with the back of his hand. "Then there's Emily Moore and that Stanley Owens guy. Although honestly, I can't see Emily Moore as a suspect. Can you?"

"It seems unlikely, but she did lie when she told me she and Jeremy were just casual acquaintances. Even though I don't entirely trust Dean Bodenheimer, I do think he was telling the truth when he contradicted that claim."

"Maybe she was in love with him too?" Richard gave me a questioning look. "Could've been a love quadrangle instead of the typical triangle."

"Hmmmm . . . I didn't get that impression, but I've been wrong before." I tapped his lower arm with my fingers. "You left out Belinda Cannon. She left the commune abruptly, then went missing from her home not long after Jeremy disappeared. Who's to say she didn't run away after murdering him?"

"And is now picking off the rest of the commune, one by one? Sorry, but that sounds too much like a Hitchcock film to me."

"I know, but we have to keep her on the suspect list, along with Stanley Owens."

Richard slapped his forehead with one hand. "Not another one. I thought he died in an accident."

"I know, and given what the others have said about his timid personality, it does seem unlikely he'd kill anyone." I twisted my lips as a thought occurred to me. "But Ruth told me he was in love with someone who rejected him. If that was someone Jeremy stole from him and then abandoned, Stan could've snapped and killed Jeremy for revenge. That might also explain the breakdown he suffered right before leaving the commune."

"But he was dead long before Ruth was killed."

"True, but we've established that Jeremy's killer doesn't necessarily have to be the same person who murdered Ruth."

"Back to the robbery theory, then?"

"Could be, except there is something I find odd about Stan's death." I filled Richard in on both Ruth's and Dean's comments about Stanley Owens's intense fear of heights. "I keep wondering—what was he doing on that footbridge?"

Richard exhaled a gusty sigh. "Don't tell me you think he was murdered as well."

"I think it's a possibility. Which means . . . nothing, really. Even if he was murdered, it could be totally unrelated to the Jeremy Adams case. Being a lawyer, I'm sure he must've made enemies." I pressed my palms against my temples. "And one more thing occurred to me. Maybe someone killed Jeremy by accident. It might have been manslaughter rather than murder, but then the commune covered it up."

"Or Jeremy simply died by accident and they hid that?" Richard's forehead furrowed in concentration.

"His head was bashed in."

"Which could've happened in a bad fall, especially if he hit something like an anvil or rock."

I sighed. "I hadn't thought of that angle, but it would explain why everyone has been telling different stories and being secretive. Even P.J. and Carol."

"You did tell me they seemed evasive when you spoke with them," Richard said thoughtfully.

"Right. If Jeremy died accidentally, but it was somehow related to drug use and happened on their property, they might have covered it up to protect the commune."

"This is quite a tangle. There are far too many possibilities." Richard lifted my hands and clasped them in his warm fingers. "Which is why you should stop digging and allow Brad and the other investigators to do their work. You've helped enough."

"Okay, but if someone is going to take potshots at me, I want to know why," I said, allowing him to pull me into his arms. "I hate unsolved mysteries, you know."

My ear, pressed against Richard's chest, vibrated from his burst of laughter. "I know only too well," he said, as I lifted my head to look up into his face. "I blame those."

Following his pointed finger, my gaze landed on the collection of old Nancy Drew titles that filled the lower shelf of a white bookcase.

"Oh now, you can't blame poor Nancy," I said, laying my head back on his chest. "I was terribly inquisitive long before I picked up one of those stories. Just ask my parents."

"No need, I believe you." Richard tipped up my chin with one finger. "You are quite a bit more adventurous than the usual librarian."

"Hold on," I said. "You can't prove that. First, I don't think you know that many librarians, and second, lots of librarians are quite adventurous, and third"—I took a deep breath—"while I do like to solve mysteries, it's not like I'm some wild woman, always seeking thrills."

Richard tapped my lips with two fingers. "Now that I *can* dispute. At least in some areas." He grinned. "Fortunately for me."

Chapter Twenty-Two

I finally received my interlibrary loan copy of Emily Moore's first book of poetry on Thursday, but we were so busy at the library that I decided I'd have to check the contents later. As I shoved the large manila envelope under my purse on a shelf in the workroom, Sunny poked her head around the door and asked me to come out to the desk to help one of our elderly patrons, Carter Scott, who was conducting ongoing research about the history of the churches in Taylorsford.

"What was that ILL, anyway?" she asked, after we'd guided Mr. Scott to the proper resources. "It didn't feel like a book."

"It isn't. No one would lend the actual book," I said, searching the desk computer to see if I could find any online information to share with Mr. Scott. "It's photocopies of the poetry from Emily Moore's first book. The one I couldn't buy, remember?"

"Oh right. The rare one." Sunny absently twirled her bangle bracelet around her wrist. "But at least you found a library that would help."

"I didn't ask them to copy the illustrations—that would've been too much trouble. But they were happy to provide photocopies of the pages containing the poems." I glanced up to meet Sunny's inquisitive gaze. "I want to be able to introduce Ms. Moore properly when she does her reading here in a few weeks. I thought it would be nice to reference her earliest poems as well as the later ones."

"Makes sense." As if suddenly aware of her fidgeting, Sunny pressed her palms against the top of the circulation desk. "By the way, Dan told me something yesterday. It's an interesting tidbit he uncovered in the course of his investigations."

"What's that?" I asked, closing down my search. I already had a page of jotted notes that I planned to share with Mr. Scott. Knowing how some people shut down when presented with too much information all at once, I didn't want to overwhelm him before he had a chance to assimilate any information he'd found on his own.

"Dan says that a couple of sources told him Stanley Owens—the guy from the commune who died in that fall—was supposedly in love with Belinda Cannon, but it was unrequited. Belinda only had eyes for Jeremy."

"Really?" I recalled Ruth's words about Stan's unfortunate love affair. *So the object of his affection was Belinda Cannon. Definitely one of Jeremy Adams's lovers. Interesting.*

"Yes, and that he basically had a breakdown right before the commune dissolved. That was after Jeremy left, of course."

I didn't tell Sunny that I'd already heard this from Ruth, or that it was information I'd already shared with Brad. "I'm not sure what that has to do with the missing-persons cases, though."

"Well, Dan thinks that maybe Stan killed Jeremy because he was jealous or something. You know, a crime of passion. Then Stan was overcome with guilt. Thus the breakdown."

"Not so overcome that he confessed," I said. "And Stan's death is also a bit questionable, don't you think? Ruth Lee and Dean Bodenheimer both mentioned his fear of heights."

Sunny frowned. "I remember you telling me that. Which does make it weird for him to be on that footbridge. Unless it was a suicide. Maybe the guilt finally overwhelmed him."

"That seems an odd way to go, when he was so afraid of falling. You'd think he'd pick another method. And then there's the fact that he was already dead when Ruth was killed, so he couldn't have had anything to do with that." I gave Sunny a side-eyed glance. "I believe Dan's theory is wrong, at least in this instance. It seems to me more likely that Stan was killed because he knew too much, just like Ruth. He could've easily been aware of the dealers who supplied Jeremy with drugs."

Sunny slipped her bracelet off and rubbed her wrist. "So you think Stan might've known something about Jeremy's death but kept quiet for some reason?"

"Yeah, maybe because confessing would've implicated him? I mean, if it involved buying or selling drugs, Stan could've been in a lot of trouble, especially back in those days. Or maybe"—I rapped my fingers against the top of the circulation desk—"Stanley Owens was scared to talk because he knew it would put his own life in jeopardy. But, after all these years, he just couldn't deal with hiding the truth anymore, no matter the cost. Ruth told me that he seemed to be suffering from guilt when they bonded after Jeremy left the commune. Maybe, later in life, Stan finally had enough of keeping a terrible secret and planned to tell the authorities what he knew about Jeremy's death."

"And you think if the actual killer got wind of that somehow, Stan could've been murdered in a way to make it look like an accident?" Sunny asked.

"Yes, and then the killer murdered Ruth when she threatened to talk after Jeremy's body was found. That upped the ante and made the killer take a risk, shooting Ruth instead of taking the time to try to stage another accident, like he or she did with Stan."

Sunny looked thoughtful. "Because without the body it was still a missing-persons case, but with it—especially given the way Jeremy died—it became a murder?"

"Right. And there's no statute of limitations on prosecuting a murder."

Lines furrowed Sunny's brow. "But if someone is killing people who might know anything about Jeremy's death . . ." She bit her lip and cast me a worried glance. "The grands could be in danger."

"You really think they *do* know something?"

"No. Yes. I don't know." Sunny shoved her long hair behind her ears with both hands, then kept her palms pressed to her temples as if trying to contain her thoughts. "They continue to give me evasive answers when I ask direct questions about that time. It's gotten worse since Ruth Lee's death, and frankly, I'm unsure about everything now."

I mustered up a smile that I hoped didn't look as forced as it felt. "You know they didn't murder anyone."

"But what if they covered up a crime? I could see them doing something like that, if it would protect their other friends, or the commune." Sunny dropped her hands to her sides. "They don't really trust the legal system or any civil authorities, even now, and they were more radical back in the sixties."

"I see your point," I admitted reluctantly.

"And when I talk to them about anything to do with the Jeremy Adams case, they always shift their eyes so they aren't looking directly at me. Like they're ashamed of something. I'm pretty sure they have something to hide. Of course, they won't confess anything, because they don't want to involve me." Sunny blinked away the tears that had welled in her eyes. "They want to protect me."

"Look," I said, reaching out to clasp her hand. "There's no point in making yourself sick over *what-ifs*. Just be honest with the authorities about what you know, and allow your grandparents the freedom to make their own decisions. I'm sure, knowing them, that they'll make the right choice in the end."

I was glad, at that moment, that I hadn't shared the CD containing Jeremy's demo reel with P.J. and Carol. At least that was one thing they wouldn't have to lie about.

"I suppose you're right," Sunny said as I released her hand. "I just don't want to see them go to jail. They could be charged as accessories after the fact if they actually covered up a murder."

"It won't come to that, I'm sure," I said, although I wasn't certain of anything. "Now—let me take these notes over to Mr. Scott before he has to leave. He said he only had an hour free for his research today."

"Okay. I'll hold down the fort here," Sunny said, giving me a wan smile. "And I'll try not to worry."

"Good, but maybe"—I cast her a speculative glance—"you should warn Carol and P.J. about the possibility that someone is tracking down people who might know anything about Jeremy's death. Just to be safe, you know?"

"Trust me, I will," Sunny replied fervently.

As I crossed behind the desk, clutching the paper containing my notes to my chest, I made a mental note to ask Kurt—who I was convinced was keeping tabs on me, as well as probably Richard and my aunt—to have some of his associates also keep an eye on Carol and P.J. Fields.

* * *

After sharing a light supper with Aunt Lydia, I headed upstairs to my bedroom to read over the photocopies of Emily Moore's earliest poetry.

I sat on my bed, popped in my earbuds, and scrolled through the music player on my phone until I reached the file containing Jeremy Adams's songs. *A perfect accompaniment to Emily's poems*, I thought, *especially considering they were created around the same time.* Although, to be precise, I reminded myself, Jeremy's music must've been written at least a year or two before the publication of Emily's first book. Which didn't mean she hadn't written the poems earlier, of course. Perhaps even during her stay on the commune.

I glanced over the note the librarian had sent along with the photocopies. It outlined what I'd already learned through my own research—Emily Moore, then called Daisy, had moved directly to New York City after the commune at Vista View had closed its doors. She'd immediately been taken up by Andy Warhol's crowd, and had lived at the Factory off and on for a few years. It was during that time that several unnamed artists had created illustrations to go along with her poems, prompting Warhol to have the slender volume of poetry and art published by a private press.

Even though the book had been distributed primarily through hand-selling at concerts and other events, it had developed a cult following that propelled Daisy—under her Emily Moore name—to fame. Only a year after the release of her first book, she acquired a literary agent and a prestigious publisher and began a career that had continued to the present day.

I set aside the explanatory document and settled back against the pillows I'd piled up against my headboard.

Jeremy's voice reverberated through my headphones. Despite his gravelly tone, his clear pronunciation of the lyrics allowed me to understand all the words.

"Definitely a true talent," I said, as if Jeremy were sitting in the room with me. "Such a shame you died so young, before everyone could appreciate your work."

I focused on the pages of poetry. Almost immediately I could see why it would've appealed to the flower-power generation. Mystical, cryptic, yet somehow hypnotic, it evoked the mysteries of nature as well as an obviously drug-fueled exploration of consciousness.

But I could also see why Emily Moore had not bothered to have this particular volume reprinted. It was an artifact of its time. Today it seemed naïve and almost embarrassingly revealing.

As I picked up another page, Jeremy sang something about stars and fireflies, and how both filled the night with flickering light.

I blinked and stared down at the paper in my hand.

The same words—in my ear and on the page. The very same.

I sat up, pausing the music. After pulling a pen from my nightstand drawer, I scrolled back to restart the file containing Jeremy's demo reel.

Song by song, I matched Jeremy's lyrics to the poetry. There were more poems than songs, but every lyric on Jeremy Adams's demo reel was one of the poems in Emily Moore's first book.

As the final song concluded, I pulled out my earbuds and dropped the player on top of the scattered photocopies that blanketed the bed. Jumping to the floor, I paced around my bedroom.

There were only a few conclusions I could draw from my discovery. Emily could have collaborated with Jeremy while he was writing his songs—willingly supplying him with the lyrics. Or conversely, Emily could have taken Jeremy's lyrics and presented them as her own work.

I gnawed on the nail of my little finger. The poetry was different enough from Emily's later style to make that a possibility. Perhaps she'd worked with Jeremy on his music, then taken the lyrics and used them to ignite her own career. Without giving Jeremy any of the credit.

But the reverse could also have been true. If Emily, who Dean claimed had been "tight" with Jeremy, had shared her poetry with the young musician, maybe he'd used the poems as lyrics without obtaining her permission.

I gathered up the pieces of paper from my bed, stuffed them back into the manila envelope, and carried it over to my dresser. Glancing at the wall clock, I decided it was too late to call Brad over something so tenuous. But I would call him tomorrow and share what I'd discovered. Perhaps he'd think the poems were as peripheral to his investigation as the demo reel CD I'd already given him, but I still had to share this discovery.

Because, while I had no absolute proof of anything but a collaboration between the musician and the poet, it certainly seemed—from the lack of attribution on both the demo reel and the book of poetry—that one or both of them had used the other's work without giving their co-creator proper credit.

Which is, I thought, as sadness filled my chest, *as good a motive for murder as I have ever stumbled across.*

Chapter Twenty-Three

The next day I was grateful for the county fair, which seemed to have drawn everyone away from Taylorsford. Or, at least, away from the library. Even though it was a Friday, I'd given Sunny the day off so she could help her grandmother prepare for the next day's baking competition.

My aunt was also busy baking, but I knew she'd prefer that I stay out of the kitchen while she worked, so I'd volunteered to cover the library with only one volunteer. On a normal Friday, that could've meant chaos, but we ended up seeing so few patrons that, when Denise left at four o'clock, I wasn't worried about managing the library on my own.

In fact, it was quiet enough that I was able to use the last hour to do some research. Diving deeper into any information I could unearth on Emily Moore, I finally discovered an article that had been digitized from a now-defunct literary journal. It was an interview with Emily, conducted right after the Factory had published her first book of poetry.

Overlooking the new-age mysticism threaded throughout the interview, I discovered that Emily had credited another artist at the Factory with the discovery of her poetic talent. This individual, who'd gone by the name Aqua, happened to be an old school friend of Stanley Owens. While traveling between Florida and New York, she'd used this connection to secure a bed at Vista View for a couple of nights, where she'd heard Emily read some of her poems.

Aqua had then convinced Emily to share copies of her poetry. When Aqua had shown them to Warhol and others at the Factory, they'd issued an invitation for Emily to join their community in New York City.

I mulled over this information, considering how it shed light on the time frame surrounding Jeremy Adams's death. Emily Moore had not headed north simply because of the collapse of the commune. She'd known about Warhol's interest in her poetry prior to leaving Taylorsford. Which meant that she would've had a compelling reason to call Jeremy Adams back from LA before she left Taylorsford. If the Factory had promised to publish her work, she wouldn't have wanted him shopping around his songs, with her uncredited lyrics, at the same time.

I tapped a pencil against the top of the circulation desk. Whether or not he was willing to give her credit, if Jeremy had refused to change the lyrics to his songs, I could imagine an ambitious young woman snapping and striking him in anger. Perhaps she'd had no intention of murdering him. He could've hit his head against something when he fell, or she could've accidentally hit him with some object that caused more damage than she'd anticipated.

But even if it was unpremeditated, it would still be murder.

I sighed and circled behind the desk. It was almost five—time to make a last check for patrons before closing up the library. Walking through the quiet space and seeing no one, I locked the front doors. As I strolled back across the main section of the library, I pondered my latest theory. If Emily had killed Jeremy, someone had helped her hide her guilt. She was unlikely to have been able to drag his body, let alone bury him, on her own. And wherever the murder had occurred on the farm, it was certain to have resulted in a significant loss of blood. Someone, or perhaps several people, had to have been involved in cleaning up—and covering up—the crime.

Which led me back to Carol and P.J. and their reluctance to talk about Jeremy Adams or anything related to that period of time.

I double-checked the children's room before heading to the back of the building. Flipping through my key ring, I didn't notice the shadow moving behind the frosted glass of the back door.

When I glanced at the door, I realized that the emergency alarm was turned off. That was a breach of library protocol. For fire safety reasons, the back door had to remain unlocked when patrons were in the building, but we were supposed to keep the alarm on so that people couldn't leave the building with materials they hadn't checked out.

As I made a mental note to remind the volunteers that the door should remain armed unless they were taking people to the archives, the door opened. On the stoop, her face shadowed under the hood of a dark raincoat, stood Emily Moore.

My inclination was to slam the door in her face, but Emily stepped inside before I could reach for the doorknob.

"Amy." When Emily pushed back the hood of her coat, the static caused strands of her dark hair to fly up and surround her face like Medusa's snakes. "I'm sorry to accost you like this, but I tried the front doors and they were already locked. Then I walked around the building and noticed that your car was parked in the lot and thought perhaps I could still catch you before you left."

"It's closing time," I said, gripping the key ring in my palm, with one of the keys poking out between two of my fingers. It was an instinctive gesture, honed by years of walking alone as a woman on campus and elsewhere.

"Yes, I know, but I had to tell you . . ." Emily moved forward, forcing me to step back. "That is, I wanted to warn you to be careful."

"What do you mean? Careful about what?"

"All this digging around in the past." Emily took a deep breath. "It might not be worth the danger."

"Is that a threat?" I thrust my free hand into the pocket of my jacket. If I could reach my cell phone . . .

Emily's dark eyes widened. "You think I'm threatening you?"

"Aren't you?"

"No, I'm simply warning you." Emily swept the back of her hand across her forehead. "I feel threatened myself, and your research into the past isn't helping my sense of security."

"Why might that be?" My fingers curled around my phone.

"Someone is stalking me. Oh, you can say I'm paranoid, but I'm sure of it. It's been getting worse over the last week or so."

I slipped my hand, holding the phone, out of my pocket. "Excuse me? You think *you* are being followed?"

"I know I am." Emily grabbed my arm.

I instinctively jerked my arm away, which caused my grip to fail. My phone fell onto the carpet. "Don't you come any closer," I said, waving my fist clenching the keys in Emily's face. "I'll stab you in the eye if I have to."

"Good heavens, Amy." Emily took two steps back. "You needn't act as if I'm the culprit. I only came here to alert you to the possibility that someone might be watching you."

"Like you, perhaps? Don't pretend you're trying to do me any favors. I've been caught in this type of situation before."

Lines creased Emily's forehead. "Me? Why would I wish to harm you?"

"Because I know about you and Jeremy Adams. I know that you wrote the lyrics that he used for his original songs. And I suspect he didn't want to give you credit, leading to a confrontation between you."

Emily worked her mouth as if searching for the right words. "Yes, that is true. How did you . . . ?" She narrowed her eyes. "I suppose it doesn't really matter. If you know, you know. Yes, Jeremy and I worked together on his original songs, and he used my poetry as the lyrics. At first I didn't care. I thought it would be cool. I even had this foolish notion that maybe I could make a name for myself if he got a record deal. But then"—she clenched her fingernails into her palms—"I heard from Ruth that he was claiming to have written the lyrics as well as the music."

"So you called him back to Taylorsford to settle the matter."

"I asked him to return, but only after I found out that the Factory wanted to publish my poems."

"Yeah, I already figured that out."

"Very clever, but you don't have everything right . . ." Emily thrust her hands into the pockets of her raincoat.

A gun, you idiot, I thought, frantically considering my best avenue for escape. *She probably has a gun. Just like the others you've confronted in similar circumstances.*

I knelt down for my phone, leaping back to my feet as soon as I grabbed it. "I have the sheriff's office on speed dial," I said as I turned on the phone. "So don't try anything."

Emily reached back and kicked open the door with her foot. "I don't know what's going on here. I just came here to warn you, that's all." She gave her glasses, which had slipped forward, a fierce shove up to the bridge of her nose. "Stop messing around with things you don't understand."

"I think I understand only too well, and trust me, I intend to share my thoughts with the sheriff's department."

Emily lowered her head until I couldn't see her eyes. "You're very clever, Amy, but perhaps not quite as astute as you think. Your assumptions could place you in grave danger, as I believe they have in the past. Think about that, why don't you, after I leave."

My cell phone lit up. I held it out, my finger poised over the screen. "You'd better get going, then. Because I'm just about to call the authorities."

Emily shot me a fierce glare before she turned away and headed outside, her shoes striking the back steps like gunshots.

I waited until she reached her car and drove away before I slammed the door and locked it. Leaning against the hallway wall to steady my trembling legs, I called Brad.

He didn't answer, so I left him a message to call me urgently. I considered calling 911, but with Emily gone, the situation didn't seem to merit such a drastic response. As I ran back to the workroom to grab my purse, I reviewed the encounter in my mind.

Sadly, I had to admit I didn't really have any damning evidence to share with Brad or anyone else. I realized Emily's words could be interpreted in many different ways. She hadn't directly threatened me, and I hadn't actually seen a gun. I paused at the staff door in the workroom and tapped the phone against my palm.

Perhaps she really was simply trying to drive me off the case. Another warning, like the anonymous letter, the graffiti, and the gunshots in the woods. In the last two instances, the perpetrator could've easily hurt me, but they hadn't. Maybe it really had been Emily, or someone she hired, simply trying to frighten me off. Even if she'd murdered Jeremy, it was possible it had been an accident, or at worst manslaughter. She might not be a true cold-blooded killer like some I'd encountered. She might be determined to protect herself without murdering anyone else.

But the information about her connection to Jeremy's songs, and her confession confirming that she'd asked Jeremy to return to Taylorsford, were still facts I'd need to share with Brad. Maybe they'd persuade the authorities to question Emily Moore more thoroughly, even if they weren't enough to lead to an arrest.

Staying in the shadow of the large forsythia bushes as I crept to the back of the library, I peeked around the corner of the building and confirmed that my car was the only vehicle in the lot. I stepped out under the parking lot lights, sweeping my gaze from side to side as I made my way to my car. I kept my phone gripped in one hand and my keys in the other, ready to call for help or defend myself. When I was finally seated in my vehicle with the doors locked, I released a gusty sigh of relief. I was safe, at least for now.

A rap on my side window made me jump and drop my keys into the cup holder between the front seats. Turning to face the window, I recognized a familiar face.

Kurt Kendrick spun his hand in a circular motion. I stared at him for a moment, considering whether I should honor his request to roll down my window, or instead grab my keys, start the car, and speed off.

Common sense won out. I rolled down the window. "What in the world are you doing here—keeping tabs on me?"

"As a matter of fact, I am." Kurt crossed his arms over his broad chest. "Although I admit my initial target was Emily Moore. But when she drove here at closing time and seemed so determined to speak with you, I thought I'd better hang around rather than follow her."

"You know her, don't you? From your dealer days, I suspect."

"Yes. I'm not sure she'd recognize me today, but I don't want to test that theory. Which is why I've been maintaining a low profile while keeping an eye on her." He dropped his arms with a shrug. "To be more accurate, I've had some of my people keeping tabs on Emily. Tonight I decided to do a little surveillance on my own."

I grabbed my keys from the cup holder. "Why? Because she knows too much about your connection to Jeremy Adams?"

"No, because I know too much about hers."

I paused with my hand poised to insert the keys in the ignition. "What do you know?"

"Something you may have already discovered, if your research skills are even half of what I imagine them to be. Jeremy used Emily's poetry for the lyrics to his original songs, and when she was offered a book deal, she demanded that he return the rights to her."

"And she called Jeremy back to Taylorsford to ensure that he would," I said, meeting Kurt's intense gaze.

"Yes, she was the impetus for his return. But I'm not convinced that she killed him."

"Is that because you know who actually did?"

"Not exactly. And I could be wrong. Maybe Emily did kill Jeremy, but even so, she had help covering it up. I have my suspicions as to how that might have played out, but I need a little more time to check with a few contacts . . ."

"Wait," I said, cutting him off. "You want me to say nothing to the authorities about her visit here tonight, then?"

"If you wouldn't mind."

"I do mind. I think Brad Tucker should know that Emily is a more viable suspect than she may have first appeared. As soon as I can, I will tell him so."

Kurt reached in the car and grabbed my left hand, pinning it to the steering wheel. "Don't."

I scooted back in my seat, struggling to loosen his hold. "Let go of me, please."

"I will when you're willing to listen to reason."

"All right, spin your story. I promise to keep an open mind."

"Very well." Kurt leaned over and whipped the keys from my other hand before releasing me and stepping back. "Insurance," he said, dangling the keys.

I fixed him with a cold glare. "I could have you arrested for that."

"But you won't." Kurt dropped the keys into his other hand. "Now, let me explain. It's true that I've been watching Emily

Moore for some time, as well as a few other people. Individuals I knew from back in my days as a dealer. Many of whom could have had a reason to kill Jeremy Adams." He bared his teeth in a wolfish grin. "All of whom could identify me as the Hammer."

"And that's what really concerns you, I suppose."

"Exactly. It wouldn't be beneficial for my current businesses if that little tidbit from my past was revealed. Not that I don't feel sorry for Jeremy, or his family. But I also don't want to be pulled into the investigation of his death by well-meaning, if misguided, attempts to reveal the truth."

"The truth should be told."

"Of course, and I'll gladly help make that happen. But without allowing the investigation to veer off onto, shall we say, irrelevant tangents."

"If you know anything, you should share it with the authorities."

"I intend to, once I have collected all the information I seek. To do so before that"—he bounced my keys in his open palm—"will simply send the guilty party or parties scurrying underground."

"You really think another dealer was involved somehow, don't you?"

"Perhaps." Kurt held out his hand, offering up my keys. "But I can't prove it, and until I can, I don't want to spook my sources. If they find out that I've been in touch with the authorities, my search for the truth will dry up before it yields the proper results."

"But it won't be you contacting the authorities, it will be me."

"They'll still suspect a connection, especially if the sheriff's office starts focusing more intently on Emily Moore." Kurt dropped my keys into my open palm. "So I implore you, Amy—keep quiet about what you've discovered about Ms. Moore. Just give me a few more days. I have someone on the trail, and I think . . ." He shook his head. "Never mind that. Just promise me to say nothing for a day or two."

"You really think your investigations will yield the truth?"

"Yes, I do."

"All right. I'll wait a few days to talk to Brad about Emily Moore. But only because you've risked your own life to save me, and those I love, in the past. I guess I owe you that much." I pointed a finger at him. "But if you don't provide the sheriff's office with some useful intel, and soon, all bets are off."

"Fair enough." Kurt looked me over, his expression unreadable. "I really do want justice for Jeremy, you know. I liked the guy, and even more importantly, admired his incredible talent. The world shouldn't have been deprived of his music. I'll do whatever I can to make sure someone pays for that crime."

"I should've known you'd be more broken up over the loss of some form of art than a person's life," I said. "But as long as the truth is served, I suppose it doesn't matter."

Kurt backed away. "One more thing," he said. "Please promise me to stay out of this investigation. You've done enough to help, put yourself at enough risk. Given the sort of people who may be involved, I'm afraid it could turn even uglier."

"Good night," I replied, and rolled up my window.

By the time I drove off, Kurt had melted into the shadows and disappeared. I tightened my lips. Despite the times he'd helped me or my loved ones in the past, I could never be sure whether the art dealer truly wanted to protect us, or just himself.

Which meant that while I would stay quiet about Emily Moore's connection to Jeremy Adams's return to Taylorsford for a few days, I certainly wasn't going to promise anything else.

Chapter Twenty-Four

The minute I saw Richard on Saturday, I decided that Kurt's admonition to stay silent didn't apply to him.

"I'm not sure I agree with keeping quiet about Emily Moore's possible connection to Jeremy's death," he said as we crossed the county fair's gravel parking lot. "But I get where you're coming from in terms of owing Kurt a favor. I suppose he could be right about a possible accomplice going undercover, especially if they're an accomplished criminal. And if he can uncover the truth"—Richard took my hand—"that puts any target on him or his associates instead of you, which is fine by me."

I tugged my maroon cotton sweater down over the top of my jeans. "I don't want him to get hurt, though."

"Kurt can take care of himself," Richard said. "Now, let's try to enjoy the day. I'm looking forward to some disgustingly unhealthy fair food and cheering Lydia to victory."

"Don't get your hopes up. Jane Tucker is a formidable opponent, and Carol is no slouch either."

"I'm surprised Lydia didn't enter some of the other baking challenges this year," Richard said as we strolled through the open gates that led into the fairgrounds.

"She said she didn't have time to perfect a new cake recipe along with the pies. I can believe that, since she's been spending a lot of time with Hugh, and that doesn't leave her much time to experiment with her baking. Hugh loves her cooking, but he's not so much into the sweet stuff." I sniffed. "Speaking of food—take a whiff of that."

Richard audibly inhaled before giving me a grin. "Deep-fried delight."

"For a healthy guy, you sure do like your occasional indulgence."

"Of course. That makes it even more enjoyable."

I squeezed his fingers. "And you'll run or dance it off tomorrow, of course." I pressed closer to him as we encountered the crowds clustered around the brightly painted food trucks and booths.

Richard released my hand and slid his arm around my shoulders. "I'll try. Oh look—there's Brad and Alison. Guess they're both off work today."

"Surprising, with all that's going on," I said, as Richard maneuvered us through the food lines that had snaked out onto the packed-dirt main path.

"I guess even Brad gets a day off now and then." Richard apologized to a cluster of teenage girls wearing shorts with combat boots as we squeezed past them. "That's a different look," he said, when we were out of earshot.

"They might have the right idea. I've already had my toes stepped on twice." I raised my right hand and waved it in front of my face. "And it's pretty warm for the last weekend in September."

"True." Richard lifted his arm off my shoulders and waved. "Hello, Brad, Alison."

"Hi." Alison Frye was a petite young woman who typically slicked her dark hair back into a low ponytail or tucked it up in a loose bun. But today it spilled over her shoulders in a shining fall of dark waves.

As I smiled and said hello, I noticed she was also wearing lipstick, a touch of blush, and a T-shirt with a pair of distressed jeans. Of course, Alison—who'd once worked with Brad but was now a deputy in a neighboring county—was not on duty today.

"Nice day for it," Brad said, after shaking hands with Richard.

"A little warmer than I expected," I said, plucking my sweater away from my collarbone. "You had the right idea, Alison."

"We always seem to have these hot spells right before fall really hits," she replied. "Are you going to the food pavilion? Brad says we need to head that way to cheer for Jane in the pie competition."

"Well, not cheer, exactly." Brad gave me an abashed smile. "The judges have already been around, if I have my timing right. But I bet they haven't awarded the ribbons yet, so we can give the contestants some moral support while they wait."

Alison elbowed him. "You'd better be giving all that support to your mom, if you know what's good for you." When he glanced down at her, she popped up on tiptoe and swiftly kissed his lips.

"I suppose," Brad said, after Alison dropped back down onto the soles of her feet. He was wearing a loose white cotton shirt and jeans instead of his uniform, which made him look younger than usual.

Or maybe, I thought with a grin, *it's the flush of embarrassment rising in his cheeks after Alison's public display of affection.*

"I guess we should stop by the food pavilion first," Richard said, casting one longing look at the blooming onion a fairgoer was balancing on a paper plate. "I assume we don't actually get to taste the pies?"

"No, only the judges get to do that," I said, grabbing his hand. "Come on, let's see if they've handed out the ribbons yet."

"You mean, whether we have to congratulate or console Lydia?" Richard asked, as we plunged back into the milling crowd to follow Brad and Alison.

The rise and fall of a multitude of conversations filled the air, along with the aroma of fried dough and the smoky odor of meat sizzling over charcoal. But as we wove our way through the crowd, the smell of food was replaced by the sharp tang of manure wafting out of the cattle and horse barns.

Near one of the wooden barns, we dodged children chasing two goats that had escaped from their pen.

"My money's on the kids," Richard said, as the goats clambered up a tightly packed tower of straw bales. He flashed me a grin. "And I don't mean the children."

The goats bleated and leapt off the bales as soon as the children climbed up to reach them.

"Not going to take that bet," I said, laughing when the goats dashed into the building housing the poultry and rabbit exhibits, setting off a cacophony of caws and peacock shrieks.

"Glad I'm not on duty today," Brad called back over his shoulder. "Or I might feel compelled to help."

Alison tugged on his sleeve. "Maybe we should anyway?"

"Nope," he said, as we walked beyond the animal exhibit area. "I heard nothing; I saw nothing. That's my story and I'm sticking to it. In fact, I'm not even going to answer my phone today. Like I said, I'm not on duty, so for once someone else can deal with any emergencies."

"Good plan," Richard said.

The crowd thinned out on the edge of the fairgrounds, where a pair of cement-block buildings housed the food and craft exhibits. Brad and Alison walked into the food pavilion, but Richard stopped short, turning at the sound of hard-soled shoes thumping against wood.

I immediately realized what had caught his attention. Off to one side of the permanent buildings was a temporary stage shaded by a green fabric sun screen.

On the stage, cloggers practiced their steps to the sound of fiddle music, their feet rhythmically tapping and stomping while their upper bodies remained perfectly still.

Naturally, Richard would be captivated by this traditional form of dance. *Or any type of dance*, I thought with a wry smile. I tapped his arm. "Go ahead, keep watching," I whispered. "I'm just going to go in and say hello to Aunt Lydia and the others."

"Thanks," he said, without taking his eyes off the stage. "I'll be right here."

I patted his arm. "Of course you will. See you in a minute."

Leaving Richard outside, I strolled into the food pavilion. The interior was dim after the bright sun, but I didn't mind. Large fans spun overheard, cooling the air. As my eyes adjusted to the change in the light, I noticed that the rough wooden shelving that filled the open space was arranged in sections, some areas laden with jewel-toned jars of canned fruit, vegetables, and preserves, and others piled high with gourds, corn still in the husk, and other fresh vegetables. At the far end of the building, where the shelves were draped in white tablecloths, cakes, cookies, pies, and other baked goods were proudly displayed.

I caught sight of Aunt Lydia, Walt, and Zelda. Waving, I jogged over to meet them.

"Any ribbons given out yet?" I asked, after saying hello.

"No," said Jane Tucker, a big-boned woman with short white hair and pale-blue eyes. Brad, standing nearby, was only a few inches taller than his mom. "The judges are still deliberating, from what I hear."

I smiled as I studied Brad and Jane. Anyone would've known they were related, while Alison, who stood between them, looked like an elfin maiden caught between Nordic giants. "But where's Carol?" I asked, my smile fading. "I thought she was planning to enter some pies."

"She was, and we're a little worried." Zelda twisted her hands together as she glanced up at Walt. "I even tried to call the house, but neither she nor P.J. answered."

"That's weird," I said, sharing a concerned look with Aunt Lydia. "Sunny's covering the library today, but I know she was planning to drive out here after work to meet up with her grandparents. Maybe I should give her a call."

"Good idea," my aunt said. "She might know why Carol and P.J. couldn't make it. I know Carol put a lot of work into preparing her entries this year, so it's odd for her to not show up."

"Maybe one of them is under the weather or something," Walt said, giving Zelda's shoulder a pat. "That would explain things."

I glanced over at Brad, whose forehead was creased with concern. "I'm sure it's something like that, but let me check with Sunny."

Brad followed me as I stepped away to make my call. "Let me know if anything sounds wrong," he said quietly.

I nodded but held up my forefinger as Sunny answered.

"What's up?" she asked. "I was just getting ready to leave. Bill and Denise said they would cover the last hour and lock up so I could head out early."

"I was just wondering if your grandparents had decided to stay home today. I'm here at the fair with Aunt Lydia, Walt, Zelda, and a few others, and apparently Carol never showed up with her pies. We were a little worried. Are they ill or something?"

"Not them, but yeah, I'm not surprised. One of the cows went into labor this morning, and apparently the grands were concerned she might have some difficulty. They even called the vet, and you know they don't do that lightly. They probably got stuck at the farm today."

"Oh, okay." When I held up my hand, forefinger to thumb in an *okay* gesture, Zelda let out a sigh of relief and Brad moved back to stand with his mother and Alison. "We just wanted to make sure they weren't in any trouble."

"No, I don't think so. But maybe I'll swing by the farm and check on things before I head out to the fair. I'd still like to meet up with you and Richard, if that's okay."

"Sure. Just give me a call when you get here so I can tell you where we are," I instructed her, before saying goodbye.

Walt draped his arm around Zelda's shoulder. "Glad to hear everything's fine with Carol and P.J.," he said, after I explained what was going on.

"Hopefully the poor cow mama is okay, too," Zelda said, before her gaze focused on me. "Speaking of people not being here, where's that fiancé of yours?"

"Distracted by the dancers outside, of course." I pocketed my phone. "In fact, maybe I should go and join him. We'll pop back in a little bit to check about those ribbons." I winked at Aunt Lydia.

"Take your time. I think it may be a while yet," she replied. "The baking judges were still evaluating the cakes the last time I saw them, and I don't think they've even started on the cookies yet."

Brad shuffled his feet. "In that case, I think Alison and I will head out too. We want to check out some of the other exhibits. If that's okay with you, Mom."

"Sure, sure," she said, shooing them off with a wave of her hands. "No use wasting a nice afternoon. Go and have fun. We'll still be here for a few hours, I bet."

"That goes for you too, Amy," Aunt Lydia said.

Brad and Alison and I left, with promises to return later. Outside, I glanced over at the cloggers and noticed that Richard was now on the stage, being shown some steps by a couple of the dancers.

"You two go on," I said, with an exaggerated roll of my eyes. "Looks like we're going to be a while."

Brad threw me a grin before he and Alison walked off, arm in arm.

Catching Richard's eye, I waved.

"Learning something new," he called out.

"I see that." Sensing his enthusiasm, I pointed toward the building housing the craft exhibits. "Carry on. But I think I'll just take a look over there and meet you back here in a few."

Richard flashed me a brilliant smile and a thumbs-up gesture before turning back to listen to the cloggers.

I wandered around the arts-and-crafts building for quite some time, admiring the array of talent on display. There were sections devoted to drawing and painting, which included everything from adorably primitive works by young children to exquisite pieces by local professional artists. Glancing around after I admired a collection of handmade furniture and other examples of woodcraft, I noticed a display of quilts. Hanging on a sturdy line strung between two wooden supports, they created a brilliant splash of color against one of the building's whitewashed walls.

An older woman bustled about the display, smoothing the wrinkles from the smaller pieces draped over the tables beneath the hanging quilts.

"Hello," I said as I drew closer. "Are any of these yours?"

The woman's hazel eyes sparkled as she met my gaze. "A few. But I'm mainly keeping watch so nothing goes missing. I'm a member of the local quilting club, you see. We're taking turns manning the exhibit." She looked me over. "Don't think I know you, do I?"

"Maybe not. I'm Amy Webber, the library director in Taylorsford."

"Pleased to meet you. I'm Sandra Everhart. I live over in the Smithsburg area, so I don't get to Taylorsford much. Don't know many people there, to be honest."

"Well, I just moved to the county a couple of years ago, so I don't know a lot of people in the wider area either."

Sandra Everhart narrowed her eyes. "Webber? I never heard of any family by that name in Taylorsford."

"It's my mom's family, actually. The Littons and Bakers."

"Oh, okay. Them I've heard of." Sandra's lips twitched, making me wonder exactly what she knew about my family.

"Beautiful work," I said, as I took in the intricate patterns and varied colors incorporated into the quilts. Looking down, I noticed the elegant freehand stitching on one—so perfect that it looked like writing on paper.

Each block of this quilt included a different flower or bird, along with a name and dates. Birth and death dates, I realized, as my finger traced the stitching.

"That one is mine," the woman said. "It's a memory quilt, commemorating members of my family."

"It's lovely," I said, before inhaling sharply when my finger slid over a name I recognized.

Belinda Cannon.

"But you've included a death date," I said. "I thought she was missing and never found."

The quilter's expression darkened. "No, that's just what the family allowed everyone to believe. She was found, all right. Dead in an alley from a drug overdose." She met my inquisitive gaze with a lift of her chin. "I'm Sandra Cannon Everhart. Belinda was my older cousin, and I know all about her death, because I was there when the family got that news, as well as the first time she almost died."

"The first time?" I stared back down at the quilt. Sandra Everhart had pieced and stitched a blooming sprig of rosemary as the decoration on Belinda's memory block.

"Yes. When those hippies from that commune dumped her off at my aunt and uncle's house, sick as a dog." Sandra sniffed. "She'd overdosed on something, you see, and they decided to just abandon her on her parents' doorstep rather than take her to the hospital."

"Hippies?" I yanked my hand back and clenched a fist to hide the trembling in my fingers.

"You know, those folks from that organic farm. Vista View, they call it."

"Carol and P.J. Fields? They dropped her off?"

"Them and that young black guy. The one that got himself killed not long after, it seems, if those bones they found out there on that farm are any indication." Sandra squinched up her face, accentuating her wrinkles. "Good riddance to poor rubbish, is all I have to say."

I backed away from the table. "You're talking about Jeremy Adams."

"Yep. And let me tell you, lots of people in my family would rather thank whoever killed him than lock them up."

"That seems harsh," I said, when I recovered my ability to string words together.

Sandra side-eyed me. "You think so? My cousin Gail wouldn't agree. That's my other cousin, the one that was my age. She was Belinda's little sister, and let me tell you, she never got over Belinda's death. It messed her up real bad."

"But Belinda Cannon didn't die from that first overdose, did she?"

"No, but it was that Jeremy Adams and those other hippies that got her into drugs in the first place. She never touched that stuff until she joined up with that commune." Sandra Everhart crossed her arms over her breasts. "I was there, like I said, when those losers dropped her off like a bag of dirty laundry. They tried to sneak away, too, but Gail and I were playing outside and we saw them."

"You're sure it was Carol and P.J. Fields and Jeremy Adams?"

"As sure as I'm standing here. It was dark, but Gail and me, we were running around with sparklers left over from the Fourth of July. So we saw what they did. Gail knew who they were right away, because she used to visit Belinda in that commune from time to time. Well, she was furious, let me tell you. She even ran after them, screaming that it was all their fault. Of course, she was mainly mad at Jeremy Adams. Gail figured he was the one most to blame, because Belinda was so in love with him and would do anything he asked. So Gail attacked him. Threw a real fit." Sandra rubbed her forehead with one hand, as if trying to erase the memory. "I'll never forget that scene. Gail swore she'd kill Jeremy if anything happened to Belinda."

"Belinda survived, though."

"That time. But after she recovered, she up and took off one day without telling anyone where she was going. We never heard nothing from her until the police came by the house a few weeks later and said they'd found her body." Sandra grimaced. "Another drug overdose, and this time there was no coming back from it."

"That doesn't really implicate the commune members, though. I mean, she did choose to leave home again."

Sandra snorted. "Because she was an addict by that point. My aunt and uncle tried to help, but they were clueless about that sort of thing. Gail's always said that if those hippies had just taken her to a hospital the first time, she'd probably have been forced into a detox program and that could've saved her. But no, they were too afraid of getting in trouble with the law themselves, I guess."

I shoved my hands into my pockets, my fingers searching for my cell phone. "Is your cousin Gail still alive?"

"She is. I guess she's seventy now, same as me." Sandra tipped her head and surveyed me, the lines bracketing her thin lips deepening. "We keep in touch, but it's been more difficult recently. She doesn't live in the area anymore. Moved into the city when she married. She's in pretty poor health and housebound, and I don't drive in the city, so . . ." Sandra shrugged.

"That's too bad," I said as my fingers curled around my phone. "If you'll excuse me, I need to go join my fiancé outside. I'm sure he's wondering where I am." This was a lie. If Richard was learning a new dance style, he'd probably forgotten I existed. But it was as good an excuse as any. "Thanks for showing me the quilts. They really are lovely."

"Thank you for stopping by." Sandra Everhart looked like she wanted to say something more, but at that moment a group of women walked up to the quilt display and started peppering her with questions.

I took the opportunity to slip away. Heading outside, I paused outside the building to search the Internet on my phone.

If my calculations were correct, Gail Cannon would've been only fifteen or sixteen when Jeremy Adams was murdered. But that didn't necessarily mean she could be eliminated as a suspect. According to her cousin, she'd sworn to kill him, which was enough to add her to the growing list of people who might've had both motive and opportunity.

A few months after he'd left the commune, Emily Moore had asked Jeremy to return to Taylorsford, and he'd obviously honored her request. He'd even attended the Heritage Festival. Which drew visitors from all over the area.

Which meant Gail Cannon could've seen him there, after Belinda died. And lured him somewhere to kill him. But that still didn't answer all the questions. Even if Gail was somehow connected to Jeremy's death, it seemed unlikely that an older, housebound invalid could've been involved in the more recent murders.

Scrolling through various iterations of Gail's name, I finally landed on one that seemed promising in terms of age and other factors.

But it was the last name that made me gasp and slump back against the concrete block walls of the exhibit building.

Dane. Gail Cannon Dane.

Chapter Twenty-Five

I hastily searched the article that included her name. It was an older piece, highlighting her work with her local garden society. But buried in the middle of the interview was the mention of her husband and child.

One child—a son named Daniel.

I pressed the phone to my breastbone and took a few deep breaths, my thoughts racing. It seemed more than a coincidence that Gail's son was investigating past disappearances around Taylorsford, which allowed him a reasonable excuse to talk to the Vista View commune members. Perhaps he was telling the truth about writing a news story, but he had definitely withheld information about his aunt. Now that I thought about it, I realized he'd been very careful not to mention her name, or her connection to the commune at Vista View.

I wondered what else he'd fabricated and, more importantly, where he was today. I frowned as I realized I had no idea of his location. Despite the fact that I'd talked to him several times recently, he'd never mentioned exactly where he stayed when he was conducting research in the area—or where he actually lived.

Shoving my phone back into my pocket, I hurried over to the temporary stage. I was relieved to see that the cloggers had finished their rehearsal, and Richard was now engaged in a conversation with a man I took to be their troupe leader.

"Sorry to interrupt," I said when I reached Richard's side. "But I need to talk to you. Now."

"No problem," said the leader of the clogging group. "We were just exchanging info. Mr. Muir is interested in having us come in and give a demonstration to some of his students."

"That's nice." I flashed the man a tight smile before tugging on Richard's arm. "This is urgent."

He glanced down at me, eyebrows raised. "Okay. I'll be in touch," he said to the dance troupe leader, before following me as I strode away.

Pausing under the shade of an apple tree planted between the stage and one of the animal barns, I looked up at him. "Again, sorry for dragging you away like that, but I think you should know what I just found out."

I related what I'd heard from Sandra Everhart and what I'd discovered through my Internet sleuthing. "So now I wonder if Dan is somehow mixed up in all of this."

Richard rubbed at his jaw with the back of one hand. "It's a reasonable assumption, but maybe Brad and his team should follow up on that lead." His gray eyes narrowed as he stared intently into my face. "I'm not sure you should try to approach the guy, or even locate him. Leave that to the professionals."

"I will, but we need to find Brad first. I'd prefer that he receives the info directly, because he knows all the details of the case. If

I call the sheriff's department when he's obviously not there, I might get someone who won't understand the significance of this latest development."

"All right, I'll tell you what—you wait here with Lydia and the others, and I'll find Brad. He said he wasn't going to answer his phone today, so I guess I'd better go track him down."

I stood on tiptoe to give him a kiss on the cheek. "Thanks, that will be a great help."

Richard pulled me into an embrace and gave me a proper kiss. "That's a reminder to stay safe. For my sake, among other things."

"I promise," I said, when he released me. "I'm just going to check on that quilt one more time. I think I'll try to sneak a photo with my phone so I can share that with Brad too."

"Okay." Richard tapped my nose with one finger. "But then go join up with Lydia in the food pavilion. I'll meet you there once I find Brad and Alison."

"Yes, sir," I said, giving him a mock salute.

"Enough with the sarcasm; it's my duty to worry about you," he said, before kissing me again.

* * *

Back in the arts-and-crafts pavilion, I headed to the quilt section, but stopped at the adjacent pottery display to make sure Sandra Everhart was nowhere in sight.

Fortunately, it appeared that she'd been replaced by another quilt society member. I strolled over to the table that held the memory quilt and pulled out my phone.

"Just wanted to snap a few photos for my mom," I said, when the woman watching over the display shot me a questioning look. "She loves quilting, and I like to collect pictures of unique ideas for her."

That was a lie, of course. My mother, a marine biologist who loved scuba diving and other outdoor activities, had no interest in crafts of any kind. But considering the importance of establishing some proof of Belinda Cannon's death, I didn't care.

"Fine work, isn't it?" a familiar voice said in my ear.

I spun around to face Dan Dane.

"What are you doing here?"

Dan's sea-green eyes glittered. "Visiting the fair, of course. You know, collecting some local color to add to my stories."

"Or following me?"

"Why would I want to do that?"

"I don't know. You tell me," I said, with a surreptitious glance at my phone. If I could get my finger over the button that would dial 911 . . .

Dan reached out and deftly knocked the phone from my hand. "Oh, terribly sorry. Let me get that," he said, diving for the cell before I could reach it. He plucked it off the floor and shoved it into his pocket in one swift move.

My gaze darted among the various clusters of visitors in the building. "I could scream."

Dan lowered his voice. "You could, but I don't think you will. Not when I tell you about your friend Sunny and her grandparents."

I swayed slightly. "What do you mean? What have you done with them?"

"Nothing, yet." Dan gripped my arm and steadied me. "They're just enjoying a little quality time together at the farm."

I allowed him to pull me to his side. "But they're free to leave?"

Dan slipped his arm through my crooked elbow and turned me around. "No, I'm afraid not. Now, let's take a little stroll." He marched me toward the back exit of the pavilion. "And I'd advise you not to alert anyone we meet, if you want your friends to have any chance for survival."

"Someone will find them eventually," I said, considering whether to scream despite Dan's threats. Surely if he was arrested, the authorities could then free the Fields family from wherever he had stashed them. "People are already concerned that they didn't show up today."

"Perhaps. But will they find them before their air runs out?" Dan glanced down at me, his eyes icy as an arctic sea. "Debatable."

I glared at him from beneath my lowered lashes. "I don't understand. You like Sunny. You flirted with her, and I thought . . ."

"That I'd fallen for her? Maybe I did, or would have, if she hadn't been the granddaughter of Carol and P.J. Fields." Dan tightened his grip on my trembling arm. "But sadly, I couldn't allow my feelings to get in the way of justice."

I ground my teeth before replying. "Justice? Is that what you're calling it?"

"Yes, because it's the truth. Now shut up and move." Dan lengthened his stride, forcing me to jog to keep up with him.

"You can't possibly get away with abducting me," I muttered as we crossed an empty stretch of grass.

Dan halted before an old gate in the fence surrounding the fairgrounds. "Looks like I am." He broke open the rusted latch on the gate with his fist, then kicked the gate wide open. "Keep walking. My car's just over there, behind that dumpster."

"I just don't understand why you think this is a good idea," I said as Dan shoved me in the driver's seat of the car, forcing me to crawl over to the passenger side.

I reached for the door handle as I heard a click. *Power locks*, I thought, shooting Dan a furious glance.

"Good idea? No, it isn't. It's a terrible idea, actually. But I had to do something. You and the authorities were backing me into a corner. And you see"—he cast me a humorless smile—"like you, I'll do anything to protect those I love."

His mother. I didn't dare say that aloud, although it was clear to me now that, somehow, Gail Cannon had followed through on her threat to murder Jeremy Adams.

Jeremy would've met Gail somewhere, especially if she'd told him she had an important message from her sister. Because Jeremy was basically a nice guy who would've wanted to help a former lover. And because, since her family hadn't shared the news, he wouldn't have known Belinda was dead.

I gnawed on my pinkie fingernail. Jeremy Adams had been tall, but thin, and probably not trained in fighting or self-defense. Gail could have killed him, given the right weapon and circumstances. And Jeremy wouldn't have been expecting violence, not from a young girl, even if she had threatened him before. He would've been caught unaware. I squirmed in my seat as Dan drove away from the fairgrounds. I could try the same thing—take Dan by surprise. Unbuckle and lean over and punch him and grab the wheel . . .

One thought stopped me—Dan's threat about Sunny and her grandparents running out of air. Maybe it was another lie, but if it wasn't and he'd trapped them in a box or barrel where they might die before they were found, I had to stay silent. I couldn't take the risk that Dan would clam up and refuse to reveal their whereabouts when he was captured. I had to find out where he'd hidden them before I attempted any escape.

But that didn't mean I couldn't consider all my options. I gave Dan a side-eyed glance. "Were you ever planning to write a story about the disappearance of Jeremy Adams and the others?"

Dan didn't take his eyes off the road, but a little smile quirked his lips. "No, but it was a clever cover, wasn't it?"

"You are a journalist, though, or was that a lie too?"

"Yes, of course." His fingers tightened on the steering wheel. "Although I guess I'll have to change professions after this. I suppose I can still write books under a pseudonym. And I have made some preemptive plans to acquire a new identity. It will be tough, throwing away my old life, but I suppose I'll manage."

I ignored this disgusting plea for sympathy. "What did you want from Carol and P.J., anyway?"

"The truth."

I snorted. "Says the liar."

Dan casually threw out one hand and slapped the side of my face, slamming my shoulder into the locked car door. "Why don't you keep your mouth shut, Miss High-and-Mighty. Not like you haven't kept plenty to yourself after all that snooping through the archives and searching the Internet, not to mention your chats with former commune members."

I winced as I fingered my jaw. Nothing broken, thank goodness, although I knew the soreness would probably only increase over time. "I didn't keep it to myself, actually. I shared what I found with Chief Deputy Brad Tucker."

Dan swore and shot me a furious glance. "You really are the most interfering . . ." He cleared his throat as he focused back on the road. "Never mind. I doubt whatever you told him links anything directly to me."

I didn't reply. Let him think whatever he wanted—I wasn't about to ease his mind. *Richard will know something is wrong when he doesn't find me with Aunt Lydia and I don't answer my phone. Not to mention he'll have Brad with him, and they'll both know about my discovery of Dan's connection to the case. So don't panic, Amy. Hang on to that knowledge. Be glad it's information your adversary does not possess.*

Dan spun the steering wheel hard to the right, making the wheels squeal and sending gravel flying as we turned onto Vista View's driveway.

I sneaked a glance at his hawk-nosed profile as we rattled our way toward the farmhouse. He hadn't murdered Jeremy Adams, but I wasn't ruling out the possibility that he *had* killed Ruth Lee. And maybe even Stanley Owens.

It made sense, if I considered everything I'd learned from my research and talks with the other commune members. Stan had loved Belinda Cannon. I could imagine him helping her little sister cover up the murder of the man she felt was guilty of luring Belinda into the drug addiction that had ultimately killed her. Because, although she might've been able to kill him on her own, someone had to have aided Gail in burying Jeremy and cleaning up the crime scene.

Stan had still been living on the farm at the time when I suspected the murder had taken place. Gail would've known him from her visits to the commune, and maybe even guessed his feelings for her sister.

It also explains Stan's breakdown, I thought. His rash actions and subsequent feelings of guilt would've created more trauma than a broken heart.

But I wasn't going to raise the specter of his mother's guilt with Dan. That seemed like a good way to get myself killed. Instead, I decided to try another tack, hoping I could throw him off his game by offering an alternative killer. Maybe he'd see me as less of a threat if I convinced him I'd come to a different conclusion than the one he feared.

"You know, I was thinking about Stanley Owens's accident," I said, as Dan pulled the car into the small gravel lot beside the farmhouse. "It seems so weird, him being on that footbridge when he was supposedly so afraid of heights. It makes me wonder if maybe he killed Jeremy Adams, and the guilt ate away at him over the years until he couldn't live with it anymore." I caught Dan's eye and held up my hands. "You see, that would explain things. He didn't fall; he jumped."

"Stanley Owens? You think he had the guts to kill anyone?" Dan grunted and leapt out of the car. He circled around the hood and unlocked and opened the passenger door before I could do more than unbuckle my seat belt. Clamping his hand onto my arm, he dragged me out of the seat and forced me to stand beside him. "Not as clever as you think, are you?" He gave my arm a shake and fixed his cold gaze on my face. "Of course he didn't jump, you idiot. I pushed him."

Chapter Twenty-Six

I froze. If Dan was admitting this, he didn't intend to let me live.

"I can't believe that," I said, as he again linked his arm though mine and yanked me close to his side.

"Why not? You don't really know me, now, do you?"

"Apparently not."

Dan jerked my arm. "And I have a very good reason to silence people like Stan."

"He wanted to confess?" I tripped over my own feet as Dan dragged me along.

I could see that we were headed toward the old barn, the one used to store extra hay and straw. It was located beyond the more modern barn that housed farm equipment and fresh produce like apples and potatoes. It was also hidden behind a grove of trees, and probably wouldn't be the first place searched if Brad and his team canvassed the farm. I grimaced. Which meant that Sunny, Carol, and P.J. could be in real trouble if Dan was telling the truth about their limited air supply.

And now you could be in trouble too. I blinked rapidly to chase the tears from my eyes. I couldn't fall apart. I had to hold it together and figure out some way to save my friends as well as myself.

"You said you were protecting your family. I can understand that. Was Stan going to put them in danger?"

"Yes, simply to ease his own conscience." Dan pulled me along the narrow path that led through the stand of trees hiding the old barn.

He didn't have a gun, as far as I could tell. I could've tripped him and tried to make a getaway. But that wouldn't help me find where he'd trapped Sunny and her grandparents. I had to bide my time until I knew exactly where they were—in the old barn, or elsewhere. I knew there were a few other abandoned outbuildings on the farm. I had to be certain which one they were in before I attempted an escape.

"So he killed Jeremy Adams, but your aunt or your mother helped him cover it up?" I asked, still hoping to offer him a way to avoid confessing his mom's guilt.

Dan snorted. "Hardly. My aunt was already dead. She ran away and OD'd not long after Jeremy and your pals dumped her off at my grandparents' house. Like garbage, my mom said. They treated her like garbage."

I wanted to dispute this but held my tongue.

"My mom vowed to get justice. She was only fifteen at the time, but she was braver than all the rest of those losers combined. They just covered everything up. Mom said if they'd only taken Belinda to the hospital in the first place, maybe she would've gotten the help she needed and lived."

But the addict has to want to change. No one could've forced Belinda Cannon to do that, even if she had been hospitalized. One glance up at Dan's furious face made me decide to keep that thought to myself.

"Your mom told you she killed Jeremy?" There was no point in being subtle anymore. I simply had to keep him talking so he'd take me to the place where he'd stashed the others.

"Yes. Not when I was a child, of course. But when Stan Owens contacted her and said he wanted to go to the authorities and confess his part in the murder, she had a breakdown." Dan cast me a sharp look. "She was already in bad health at that point, and Stan's stupid notion about atoning for his guilt sent her over the edge. That's when she finally told me. She didn't know what to do, how to keep him quiet."

"Which meant you took care of the problem to protect her," I said, as Dan kicked open the weathered side door to the old barn. "I can understand that. You didn't want her to have to face a trial, and prison. I might've done the same." This lie slipped easily off my tongue. I wouldn't have done anything of the kind, but there was no point in further antagonizing Dan. I had my own loved ones to protect.

Dan shoved me inside the barn. I stumbled forward when he released me but quickly regained my footing. Sunny and her grandparents had to be here somewhere. Now that I knew where to send any searchers, perhaps it was time to take action.

I spun around to face Dan, who pulled his hand away from a shelf formed by one of the wooden beams bracing the barn wall.

Too late. Now he had a gun.

"All right, turn around and walk over there to that door in the back corner," Dan said. "And in case you have any doubts, I've already used this weapon on someone else who wanted to share a little too much with the authorities. Believe me, I have no hesitation about using it again."

Ruth Lee, I thought, as I dodged stacks of bales to cross the barn. Dan had killed Ruth, like Stan, to keep her from implicating his mother in Jeremy's death. I didn't understand why Dan would've thought Ruth knew anything about it, except . . . Ruth had comforted and supported Stan during his breakdown. Maybe Gail had found out about that relationship. It wouldn't have been surprising for Gail to have stayed in touch with Stan over the years in order to keep tabs on her accomplice, and if she'd ever suspected that Stan had confessed anything to Ruth, that could've been enough to put Ruth on Dan's hit list.

I gnawed the inside of my cheek. The sad truth was that it was unlikely that Ruth had known anything about Stan's or Gail's involvement in Jeremy's death. As far as I could tell, she'd had no knowledge that he'd even died. But obviously, Dan had felt he couldn't take that chance. Which didn't bode well for me, or Sunny and her grandparents. Looking around for any sort of weapon, I tripped over a loose floorboard and fell against a rough wooden door that led to a storage area.

Grain bins, I thought, remembering exploring this barn with Sunny as a teen.

Dan yanked me away from the door and opened it. "Inside."

I moved forward slowly, the muzzle of the gun pressed into my back, guiding me. On my right sat rectangular grain bins the length of a bed and the height of an upright washing machine. All the lids had been thrown back against the rough timber wall except for the one at the far end. That one was closed. A shiny, new padlock fastened its lid, locked through the metal latch.

A thump rattled the closed lid. "Sunny!" I shouted, before Dan came up behind me and slapped his free hand over my mouth.

Instinct kicked in. I bit his palm.

Dan yowled and thrust me aside. I fell to the dusty floor, catching myself with my hands before my head hit the wood planks.

The banging on the grain bin lid resumed, reassuring me that Sunny was alive. *Or at least one of her grandparents*, I reminded myself as I sat up, my stomach churning.

Dan looked me over, his mouth twisted into a sneer. "I should shoot you right now, but I don't have time to do a proper cleanup. I was planning to wait for nightfall to take care of the others. That is, if any of them were still breathing. Guess I'll have to do the same with you."

I yanked a large sliver of wood from my palm with my teeth and spat it out, aiming for his expensive running shoes. "You'll have trouble locking me in with the others. It'll be four against one at that point."

"Two old people and a thin woman, all of whom have been crammed in a box and deprived of adequate oxygen for a few hours? And you"—Dan nudged my foot with the tip of his shoe—"a shorty who doesn't look like she packs much muscle. I think I can manage. Besides, I have a gun."

I glared up at him. "Yeah, that makes you extra brave, I guess."

He leveled the revolver at me. "I'd keep that smart mouth of yours shut if I were you."

"To keep you from shooting me? Wait—I think you plan to do that anyway."

"Not necessarily. I actually haven't decided yet."

Another lie. I bit my lower lip. “Go ahead, open up that bin and toss me in with the others. At least it will give them a breath of fresh air.”

“Not for long, I’m afraid. But I’d advise you to behave and climb in with them like a good girl. Unless you want me to shoot you right here and now.” Dan pointed the revolver at my forehead. “The alternative offers you at least a ghost of a chance. Who knows? Maybe I’ll just disappear before the authorities suspect anything, and you might live. That is, if someone finds you in time.”

“Open it. I won’t try anything,” I said, furiously thinking of a way to throw Dan off guard.

Once the bin was unlocked and Sunny and her grandparents were freed from their wooden tomb, I could fling myself at Dan’s legs. Try to topple him. Sure, he might shoot me, but if it gave the others a chance . . .

“On your feet,” Dan commanded.

I complied, and he knelt down in front of the bin, keeping the gun trained on me while he fiddled with the lock with his other hand.

Sliding the padlock from the latch, he dropped it to the floor before leaping to his feet. The lid of the bin popped up a few inches, and I spied a slender wrist.

“Sunny!” I dashed forward and flung the heavy lid up. It hit the wall with a thud.

Lying pressed together on the bottom of the bin, Sunny’s grandparents were still as corpses. Sunny struggled and sat up before turning to check on Carol and P.J.

“Breathing’s shallow,” she said in a voice as hoarse as the caw of a crow. “But still alive.”

"Thank heavens," I said, meeting Sunny's bleary-eyed gaze.

"Enough chatter. Get in," Dan said, poking the gun into my ribs.

"Okay, okay." I lifted my foot, as if preparing to climb into the bin, but instead swung it to my right, slamming the heavy rubber heel of my sneaker into Dan's shin.

He howled and grabbed for me with his left hand. But Sunny, fueled by adrenaline, jumped up and dove out of the bin, body-slamming him like a professional wrestler.

I'll have to ask her where she learned that move, I thought, swallowing a burst of hysterical laughter.

Dan hit the floor with Sunny on top of him. Throwing her off to one side, he sat up, still clutching the gun. He narrowed his eyes and trained the barrel on Sunny.

At that moment, music blared from Dan's jacket. And not just any music—one of Jeremy Adams's songs.

Startled, Dan hesitated with his finger on the trigger. He fumbled with his other hand to silence the music, which rolled in waves through the confined space of the storage room.

My phone. Somehow, pressed inside Dan's jacket pocket, it had come to life. I chased away the thought of the improbability of Dan accidentally turning it on and activating the music player.

"Thanks, Jeremy," I whispered, before I flung myself against Dan's back as he once again aimed the gun at Sunny. My action threw off his aim, and the bullet whistled over Sunny's head and lodged in the wall. With my ears ringing from the report of the revolver and with Jeremy's music still blasting from my phone, I latched onto Dan's wrist with both hands, forcing his arm down.

But I knew I couldn't hold him forever. "Run!" I shouted at Sunny. "Get out of here. Get help."

She shook her head as Dan twisted his arm, loosening my grip. With a sharp swing of his arm, he tossed me to the side.

Dan jumped up and reached into his jacket with his free hand, yanking out my phone and flinging it against the wall. The music died in a crack of plastic and tinkle of breaking glass.

"Run!" I screamed, my gaze glued to Dan's hand. To the gun. I didn't care about my phone, or my own safety. All I could think about was the ease with which Dan could now lift the revolver and shoot my dearest friend.

Another wail echoed mine. But this was no voice. It was the scream of sirens, racing closer and closer.

Dan swore and ran, shoving Sunny aside so he could dash through the storage room door. His footsteps echoed throughout the old barn as he fled.

"Are you all right?" Sunny asked, gripping the doorframe with white-knuckled hands.

"Fine. But you"—a hiccup bubbled up in my throat—"you should've run. You could've been killed." I clambered to my feet, locking my knees to keep my rubbery legs from buckling.

"And leave you and the grands here?" Sunny released her hold on the doorframe and tossed her tangled blonde hair behind her shoulders. "What kind of person do you think I am?"

I crossed the room and threw my arms around her quivering shoulders. "A brave one. An amazing, foolish, courageous one."

She hugged me back, and we stood locked together for a moment before Sunny pulled away and cast an anxious look toward the bins. "The grands need help. You have your phone?"

"No. That was the one playing music. The one Dan shattered."

"He took mine too." Sunny wavered slightly.

"But the sirens mean help is coming," I said, placing a hand on her arm. "You go to Carol and P.J. and see how they're doing. Now that they have air, hopefully they can breathe more freely. I'll run out and try to find Brad or another deputy."

"Be careful. Dan's out there somewhere, and he still has a gun."

"I think he's making for the hills, if he has any sense, but okay. I'll be on my guard." I patted Sunny's arm. "Stay with your grandparents . . ."

Coughing from the far side of the room sent Sunny flying to the bin before I could say anything more. She climbed back in and immediately thrust up her hand, giving me a thumbs-up gesture.

Satisfied that Carol and P.J. were regaining consciousness, I headed into the main room of the barn.

The sirens continued to wail outside. I jogged over to the side door that Dan had kicked open and ran outside.

"Over here!" I yelled, waving my hands above my head. "Need help here!"

"Amy!" a familiar, beloved voice called back.

Two people crashed through the shrubs rimming the small grove of trees—Alison Frye and Richard. He spotted me first and outpaced her, sweeping me up in his arms before Alison could reach the barn.

"Thank heaven you're okay," Richard murmured, stroking my hair with one hand. He pressed a lingering kiss on my lips before setting me down on my feet. "And Sunny? Is she here too?"

"She and her grandparents," I said. "But they need some medical assistance. At least they need to be checked out." I glanced over at Alison. "Did you guys bring along any paramedics?"

"Yeah, Brad thought we should, just in case." Alison held up her phone. "I'm not official here, but I can call someone and guide them to this location. You can go back and wait with Sunny and her grandparents, if you want."

I offered her a warm smile. "Thanks. Yeah, I think I'd like that. In the barn," I added, pointing to the open door. "Back in the corner, there's a storage area, with grain bins. That's where we'll be."

"Got it." Alison barked the information into her phone as Richard and I walked back into the old barn.

"It was Dan Dane?" Richard asked, as he slipped his arm around my waist and pulled me close.

"Yeah. He locked Carol and P.J. and Sunny in a grain bin. I think he planned to let them die from lack of oxygen. Guess he thought it would involve less mess than shooting them, although he did have a gun."

Richard called Dan some colorful names, using a few words I knew he'd never say in front of Aunt Lydia.

"Absolutely agree," I said. "And then some."

Pausing just outside the storage room door, Richard lifted my hands and gently kissed the scraped skin on each of my palms. "He'd just better be glad the authorities will find him before I will."

"Let's leave that to Brad and his team," I said, leaning my head against his chest for a moment. "I doubt they'll allow him to get too far. His car was parked near the house, and I'm sure there's a tight perimeter around that area by now. Which means he's trying to escape on foot." I stepped back and gazed up at Richard. "The only path Dan could've taken that wouldn't be out in the open would've led up into the mountains. And I doubt Dan Dane possesses the skills of experienced hikers and trackers, like many of Brad's deputies."

"Very true. They're bound to catch him, sooner or later. Although, if he were to tumble off a cliff, I wouldn't mind."

"Me either, but I guess we should let the law take its course. Now, come on—let's go tell Sunny help is on the way. She was very brave, you know," I added, as we walked into the storage room. "Fought back all she could."

"I suspect she wasn't the only one," Richard said, looking me over.

"I may have hit or kicked him a few times. And bit him once," I added, as we walked into the storage room arm in arm.

Richard grinned. "That's my girl."

Chapter Twenty-Seven

As we waited for the paramedics, Carol and P.J. shared the secret they'd kept for over fifty years.

"It was foolish, and selfish," Carol said, leaning into Sunny, who'd slumped down on the floor beside her grandparents.

"We just panicked." P.J. pressed the back of his head against the rough boards of the wall behind them. "Jeremy came to us, freaking out because Belinda had fallen unconscious. They'd been outside, watching the sunset from the top of the spring field hill, and yes, they'd been dropping LSD. But what Jeremy didn't know was that Belinda had already taken something else not long before."

"Did anyone else at the commune know about this?" I asked, gripping Richard's hand. We were standing together, bracing ourselves against one the crossbeams on the wall.

"Everyone did," Carol said. "And Stan, to his credit, begged us to take Belinda to the hospital. But"—Carol wiped the tears from her cheeks with one grimy hand, creating streaks in the dust that veiled her face—"the rest of us overruled him."

P.J. sighed, his breath rattling in his throat. "That's the way we handled things on the commune. Everyone had a vote on major decisions."

"You decided to just drop Belinda off at her parents' house?" I asked, sharing a concerned glance with Richard. P.J.'s breathing still sounded far too labored.

"Yes, to our shame. We thought if we took her to the hospital, the law would get involved. We were terrified that they'd connect her to the commune and then the sheriff would send out deputies to investigate the farm. Which wouldn't have been good for any of us. I mean, we all had stashes of illegal substances, not to mention the marijuana patch hidden in one of the back fields," Carol said.

P.J. shared a sorrowful glance with her. "Carol and I loaded Belinda in our old van, with Jeremy watching over her in the back seat, and drove to her family home. We planned to leave her on the porch, ring the bell, and get out of there."

"But her sister and a young cousin were outside and saw you," I said.

Carol dipped her head, staring at the weather-worn, hard-working hands she'd clenched in her lap. "Yes. And Gail Cannon attacked Jeremy, threatening to kill him if Belinda didn't recover."

"But then Belinda's parents appeared, and we beat a hasty retreat." P.J. rubbed one of his upper arms. "Sorry, cramp."

"No wonder, with you all crammed into that bin," Richard said, rolling his shoulders as if the thought caused him sympathy pains.

I looked from P.J.'s stoic face to Carol's crumpled one. "But you didn't know anything about Jeremy's death?"

Carol shook her head. "No, no. We assumed he'd left for LA, like he'd told us he would."

"And he did, but then he came back at Emily Moore's request," I said, before explaining about Jeremy's use of her poetry in his demo reel. "I suspect she just wanted him to rewrite the lyrics so she could have her poetry published. At any rate, he must've been willing to return to talk it over with her."

Sunny massaged her grandmother's shoulder. "But then Gail Cannon saw him around town."

"Probably at the Heritage Festival," I said. "There was a photo taken of Jeremy there."

P.J. looked thoughtful. "And I guess Gail contacted Jeremy and asked him to meet her somewhere on the farm. Probably told him she had some message from Belinda, because it was common knowledge that she'd disappeared before he left town."

"Maybe they even met up here, since both of them would've known that this barn wasn't typically used by the other members of the commune," Carol said, glancing around as if trying to picture the scene.

P.J. shook his head. "The thing is, Jeremy never stopped by the house when he came here to see Gail, so we didn't know anything about any meeting. We always thought he went missing out west somewhere."

Sunny's gaze shifted from P.J. to her grandmother. "Your recent anxiety and evasiveness were because of the Belinda incident?"

"Yes." Carol patted Sunny's hand. "We didn't want that bad behavior revealed, especially not when you were running for mayor. It was hard enough that Jeremy's body turned up on the farm, but we knew that was a temporary situation. Since we were innocent, we were sure we'd eventually be cleared of any involvement in that case. But if the sheriff's department dug deep enough, we thought they might discover how we'd failed Belinda." She sniffed back a sob. "Gail Cannon wasn't wrong, you know. If we'd taken her to the hospital, if we hadn't been so concerned for our own skins . . ."

"But she didn't die," Sunny said. "Not then. And she made the decision to run away from her parents' house and fall back into the drug scene. You didn't have anything to do with it."

Carol cleared her throat before replying. "It was still wrong. Maybe if she'd gotten the help she needed that first time, she could've gotten clean."

"But it would've only worked out that way if she'd wanted it for herself," Richard said. His somber expression didn't surprise me, since I knew he'd dealt with fellow dancers and students with addiction issues. "She would've had to be the one to make the choice whatever you did or didn't do."

"It was still a terrible mistake," Carol said. "I've come to see that, over the years. But the secret wasn't just ours to keep."

Sunny cast her grandparents an understanding smile. "You were concerned about how it would affect the other commune members."

"Yes. We were worried it would drag them all into a legal tangle. And then, when we dissolved the commune several months later, after Daisy left for New York and Stan had his breakdown, we decided it was best to continue to keep quiet." He shook his head. "We kept the secret all these years. I even went to see Ruth not long before she was killed to ask her to remain silent, but I saw you there, Amy, and ran off instead. I thought I'd just come back another day, but sadly Ruth didn't have many days left. More fallout from our misguided actions." P.J. reached over and clasped one of Carol's hands. "Keeping our secret was the expedient thing to do—not the right thing—but even before the commune dissolved, the lie was too firmly entrenched. And, in our defense, we didn't have all the details when we made our choice. Sure, we'd heard that Belinda had fled her parents' house and disappeared, but we never did hear that she'd died. I like to think we might've come clean if we'd known that."

"The family covered it up," I said.

Carol sighed. "I guess they preferred to allow people to think Belinda was a missing person, rather than a junkie who died of an overdose. I can understand that, although it certainly set poor Jeremy up for tragedy."

"And deprived the world of his music, as well as his life," I said.

Sunny shot me an inquisitive glance. "Speaking of music, what was that I heard on your phone? It certainly blasted out at the right time, as far as I'm concerned."

I tapped my foot against the floorboards for a moment as I considered my reply. "That was music from Jeremy's demo reel," I admitted at last. "I downloaded it from a CD Ruth Lee shared with me. But how the phone came to life in Dan's pocket, and then how the music app also turned on automatically, I have no idea."

Sunny shared a knowing look with both grandparents. "I think Jeremy Adams helped save us. Or at least saved me from a bullet."

I groaned. "Not your ghost theories again."

"It is an odd occurrence, you have to admit," Richard said.

"Okay, but to assume Jeremy Adams's spirit somehow intervened seems farfetched," I said, fighting to maintain my sense of normalcy.

No matter how close you felt to him when you viewed his photo and listened to his songs. I beat back this errant thought as Sunny expounded on her own ideas.

"This was probably the place where he died, so it makes even more sense," she said, as Carol and P.J. nodded their agreement.

Before I could argue with this theory, which I had to admit I half believed, heavy shoes hitting wooden boards alerted us to the arrival of the paramedics.

"In here," Alison said. "The three sitting on the floor. They were locked up in one of these bins for a few hours without adequate air."

Richard looked down at me. "What about you? I know you were knocked around quite a bit."

"Oh no," I said. "No more hospitals. I just need to clean out a few scrapes with hydrogen peroxide and slap on some antibacterial cream, and I'll be good as new." This wasn't exactly true, as I could already tell I was going to suffer some stiffness and pain from bruised limbs and pulled muscles, but I preferred to keep that to myself. I'd spent far too much time in emergency rooms over the past couple of years.

"If you'll step aside, please," one of the EMTs said to Richard and me.

We complied, after assuring Sunny and her grandparents that we'd check in on them at the hospital later.

"So now what?" I asked as I followed Richard out of the barn.

"Now we leave the rest of this situation to the professionals and head home to let Lydia know you and the others are okay," he replied, slipping his arm around my shoulders.

I fought my urge to wince when his fingers caressed my bruised upper arm. "And see what ribbons she might've won."

"Oh right. I'd almost forgotten about that." Richard guided me through the grove of trees masking our view of the newer barn and farmhouse. "We do need to remember to ask, although I suspect Lydia doesn't much care about that at this point."

"You might be surprised. She's worked hard to beat out Jane Tucker this year," I said as we approached a circle of sheriff's department vehicles.

"Any news?" I asked the uniformed man standing guard over Dan Dane's car. Having met this officer several times before, I hoped he'd share some particulars.

"Dane's still in the wind," Deputy Coleman replied. "But the sheriff has Chief Deputy Tucker and a crack team scouring the mountain, and others are setting up a perimeter around the farm, so I don't think the guy stands much chance of evading capture."

"Good to know." Richard gave Coleman a nod of recognition. He'd made the deputy's acquaintance before as well. "Excuse me, but would you mind taking this young lady's initial statement so I can get her home?"

"Sure." Deputy Coleman pulled out a pocket-sized tablet. "Go ahead, miss."

I filled him in on everything that had happened since Dan accosted me in the arts-and-crafts pavilion at the fair.

But I didn't say anything about Carol and P.J.'s confession concerning Belinda Cannon. That wasn't my story to tell.

Chapter Twenty-Eight

While Richard followed the ambulances taking Sunny and her grandparents to the hospital, I called Aunt Lydia. I let her know the pertinent news, reassuring her that Sunny and her grandparents seemed to be in good shape, all things considered.

"And you're okay too, I assume?" she asked.

"I'm fine. But I'll probably get in late. We're going to wait at the hospital for more news on Sunny, P.J., and Carol."

"That could take a while."

I sighed, knowing all too well the truth of her words. "I know. But I want to see Sunny again before we go home."

At the hospital, Richard and I headed for the emergency department's waiting room.

"The problem is that we're not family," I said as we slumped into two of the room's uncomfortable chairs. "I don't know if they'll even let us see Sunny, or get any news from the doctors. But still, I want to be here."

"Of course." Richard lifted my right hand off the hard metal arm of my chair and held it in his own. "Hopefully they'll release Sunny after a quick checkup. She seemed to be in pretty good shape."

"Physically, anyway," I said, my thoughts haunted by the image of three people locked inside a wooden bin.

"Yeah, they might need some psychological counseling. I sure would." Richard lowered our clasped hands onto his thigh. "I really didn't see the evil in that Dane guy. Guess I need better radar."

"I don't know," I said, squeezing his fingers. "It wasn't like I noticed anything either. Or Sunny. Although, come to think of it, he did talk a lot about killers always believing they had a good motive for their dark deeds."

"That's true. I remember him mentioning that when we went out to dinner. I thought it was just a journalist's tendency to look at all sides of an issue, but maybe he was subconsciously trying to tell us something."

I leaned back in my chair. The bars under the thin cushions pressed against my rib cage, but I didn't mind. The discomfort would keep me alert. "Yeah, I wonder if he somehow wanted us to guess that he was behind Stan's and Ruth's deaths. I don't think he's really the type of killer who feels no guilt or remorse."

"No, I don't think he is. Sounds like he started out trying to protect his mother, then things escalated. After Stan's death, which might've been more of an unpremeditated thing, I guess he felt he might as well continue to silence anyone who could endanger his mom."

I stared up at the ceiling, noticing how the perforations in the white tiles looked like tiny bullet holes. "Seems like he managed to maintain his cool after killing Stan, but when Jeremy's body was discovered, he panicked."

Richard lifted our hands and kissed my knuckles. "That was probably because of your involvement, sweetheart. You told me he'd read about how you'd helped the authorities with those other murder cases. Working with you in the archives, he must've realized you were getting a little too close for comfort, what with your research and your interviews of the commune members. I bet that's why he was keeping tabs on you."

"I guess so. It seems likely that he's the one who sent that anonymous letter, broke into the library and left that graffiti, and then took those potshots at me in the woods. But I expect that was all just meant to scare me off. I mean, he could've actually hurt me in the library or in the woods if he'd wanted to."

"You don't think he meant to kill you?"

"No, not until he caught me talking to Gail's cousin at the fair."

Richard shot me a questioning glance. "I wouldn't cut him too much slack. That had to be premeditated. He'd already trapped Sunny and her grandparents in that bin, so he must've been on a mission to track you down. I bet he heard you were going to be at the fair from someone at the library. Whatever he was trying to do before, tracking you there wasn't a spur-of-the-moment decision."

"True." I laid my head on Richard's shoulder. Releasing a deep sigh, I reveled in the comfort of his presence, despite the wooden arms of our chairs pressing into my waist.

Richard kissed my temple before releasing my hand and sliding his arm around my shoulders. "Anyway, I'm just glad things turned out well for everyone."

"Not poor Ruth Lee," I murmured. "Or Stanley Owens. Or even Dan, I suppose."

"He made bad choices. I understand a compulsion to protect a family member, but murder is never the way to go about it."

"Of course not. But I don't think he set out to become a cold-blooded murderer. It wasn't like he was killing for gain, like some others we've run across."

"I'll give him that. But after he killed the first time, it seems like he threw all morality to the winds."

I caressed the hand Richard had placed on my left shoulder. "Funny. Kurt mentioned something about that to me recently. How having killed once, it's much easier to do it again."

"He wasn't speaking from experience, I hope."

"Who knows? I did ask him that question, but as usual he didn't respond." I lifted my head. "He was conducting a little side investigation of his own, you know. But surprisingly, he missed the mark on this one. He truly believed that the killer, or at least the killer's accomplice, was a drug dealer who had ties to Jeremy Adams in the past."

"I suppose even Kurt Kendrick can't be right all the time." Richard smiled. "Lydia will be pleased to hear that."

"You think? They seem to be getting along better these days." I sat up without dislodging Richard's draped arm.

"Maybe so, but I bet she'll enjoy hearing that he doesn't always know quite as much as he thinks he does. I expect Lydia won't mind seeing that expansive self-confidence of his punctured a little."

"Come to think of it," I said, with a little smile, "neither will I."

"There you go, something to look forward to." Richard shot me an answering grin. "Just make sure I'm there to see it."

"Of course. Oh look—there's Sunny." I pulled free of Richard's arm and jumped to my feet.

Richard also stood up as Sunny crossed the room to meet us. "I've gotten the all-clear," she said, after I hugged her. "But the grands have been moved to regular rooms for now. The doctors want to keep them under observation overnight."

"That makes sense," Richard said.

I laid my hand on Sunny's arm. "You're fine, though?"

"Yes. Perfectly fine." Sunny smiled, but I couldn't help but notice the dark circles under her eyes. "I wanted to stay, but the grands insist that I go home and rest. Maybe I will. I can always come back later and check on them."

"But your car's still at the farm, isn't it?" I asked.

"Yeah, I guess it is." Sunny rubbed at her temple. "Sorry, it seems my mind's not firing on all cylinders yet."

"No problem. We'll drive you home," Richard said. "We can even stop and grab some comfort food on the way."

"And sit with you until you're ready to drive back here," I said.

"No, no. That isn't necessary."

"Necessary has nothing to do with it," I said firmly.

Richard linked his arm through Sunny's. "You heard the boss. We're driving you home and making sure you eat something, and we don't want to hear any arguments, young lady."

Sunny's lips curled upward as she glanced from his face to mine. "I can see I have no choice."

"Absolutely none," Richard agreed. As we strolled toward the exit, he gave Sunny a wink and added, "Besides, why would I ever complain about spending time with two beautiful women?"

"Behave," I said. Catching his expression, I couldn't contain a burst of laughter that made the other people in the waiting room look up with interest.

"There you go," Richard said. "Now half of Taylorsford will be gossiping about the three of us before morning."

"And you think they don't already?" I asked, before throwing my arms around both of them and pulling them into a group hug. "Might as well give them something to gossip about," I added when I stepped back.

"That should do the trick," Richard said, as Sunny giggled. "But just in case it doesn't, why not confuse them further," he added, before pulling me close and kissing me with a passion that was certainly something to talk about.

* * *

After we left Vista View, with Sunny's promise to call later to report on her grandparents' condition, Richard and I debated about stopping in at Aunt Lydia's.

"Honestly, I think I'd like to just spend a little quiet time with you and the cats," I said, as Richard parked in his driveway. "She knows I'm okay and has the basic news about the Fields family. I can fill her in more later."

"Suits me," Richard said. "I wouldn't mind having you to myself for a while."

We were greeted by Loie and Fosse, who'd apparently bonded over the utter indignity of their human forgetting to feed them at the proper time. Their combined yowls filled the air as Richard attempted to make his way into the kitchen without injury while both cats wove in and out of his legs.

I plopped down on the sofa and sank back into the cushions, propping my feet up on the coffee table. Exhaustion battled the ache of my bruises and scratches for my attention, but I was more concerned about the sharp tang of dried sweat rising from my sweater.

"Now that the cats have been fed, a treat for you," Richard said, holding up one of the two glasses of wine he was carrying. "I suspect you'll be almost as grateful as those ravenous beasts."

"Bless you," I said, after he crossed the room and handed me a glass. "But I need to ask another favor. Do you think I could grab a shower and you could lend me a T-shirt or something? I'm afraid today's adventures have turned me rather rank." I pulled the sweater away from my neck and gave an exaggerated sniff. "Yikes. You should've told me I smelled. There I was, sitting in the hospital and at Sunny's, stinky as moldy cheese."

"It isn't that bad," Richard said, "and you've put up with my exercise-induced sweat often enough. But sure, head upstairs and use the guest room shower. I'll find you something." He set his glass down on the coffee table next to mine. "I assume you want some sweatpants too?"

"They'll be far too long," I said, surveying his legs.

"You can roll them up." He looked me over. "I'll even help you up the stairs. I noticed you were moving a little stiffly climbing the steps to the porch. Which doesn't surprise me, given what you went through today."

I gave him a thumbs-up gesture, wincing when my fingernails hit my scraped palm.

As soon as I finished my shower, I changed into the clothes Richard had left outside the bathroom door. Dressing involved more wincing and some sotto voce swearing, but I managed to throw on one of Richard's endless supply of black T-shirts and a pair of gray sweatpants. I had to roll up the legs several times to keep from tripping, but I figured anything was better than my dusty jeans. Leaving my shoes and socks in the bathroom, along with my sweat-stained bra, jeans, and sweater, I padded down the stairs, pausing in the hallway when Fosse dashed in front of me and flew into the living room. He was followed by Loie, sprinting like a cheetah. When they'd reached the center of the room, Fosse spun around and leapt onto Loie's back, and the two kittens turned into one spinning ball of feet and fur.

"You two," I said indulgently as Loie jumped away, arching her back and lowering her little black nose to the floor. Ears flattened to her head and tail swishing like a metronome, she faced off with Fosse.

The younger kitten appeared quite unperturbed by this show of ferocity. Lifting one orange marmalade–colored paw, he simply reached out and bopped Loie on the nose.

"Watch out," Richard called from the sofa. "Another kitten battle's under way."

"So I see." I waited as the cats streaked past the bottom of the stairs, heading back down the hall toward the kitchen.

"Oh, by the way," Richard said, when I toddled across the room and joined him on the sofa, "I just got a text from Brad. They've taken Dan Dane into custody, so you don't have to worry about him anymore."

"That's great, but I'll still have to see him, because I assume I'll have to testify. Again." I sighed. "But ignoring that for now, I must admit that I feel much better. The hot shower did wonders for my stiff muscles. Not to mention, I'm sure I'm much less aromatic."

Richard sniffed. "You'll do," he said, flashing me a grin.

I grabbed my wineglass off the coffee table and downed a long swallow of Chardonnay. "This is the best medicine."

"You think so?" Richard set down his glass and reached out to rub my temple gently with his fingers. "I give great massages, you know."

"Hmmmm . . . tempting. But I think I want to finish off this glass, and maybe another, first."

"All right, we'll save that for later." Richard leaned in and brushed a kiss across my forehead. "I'm just glad you're safe. I was so worried when I couldn't find you at the fair."

"I was sure you'd figure it out," I said, finishing off my wine and setting down my glass before snuggling closer to him. "If you didn't see me with Aunt Lydia and the others, and I didn't answer my phone, I knew you'd alert Brad that something was wrong." I glanced up at him from under my lowered lashes. "But how did you guess so quickly that we were at the farm?"

"I don't know. It just seemed odd that no one from the Fields family had shown up at the fair, and then Sunny wasn't answering her phone either, so"—Richard slid his arm around me and pulled me closer—"both Brad and I felt like that was the first place to check."

"Thank goodness you're both smart men," I murmured.

Richard smoothed my damp hair away from my forehead with gentle fingers. "Are we?"

"Of course. Neither Sunny nor I would fool around with stupid guys." I leaned into Richard's hand, pressing my cheek against his palm. "Although Sunny doesn't date Brad anymore, which is sad, don't you think?"

Richard caressed my cheek before lowering his hand, allowing my head to rest against his chest. "Oh, I don't know. I expect she'll meet someone else. And Brad and Alison make a good couple."

I yawned. "They do. I like Alison, you know."

"She's a fine woman." Richard's lips brushed my ear. "You're falling asleep, aren't you?"

"Uh-huh. Mind?"

"Not at all." Richard adjusted his position so that I could rest more comfortably in his arms. "You just rest. I'll be here when you wake up."

"Best news I've had all day," I muttered, before I drifted into a blessedly dreamless sleep.

I woke while it was still dark. My hand brushed fur and I realized that Fosse, curled up in my lap, was snoozing quietly. Glancing over at Richard, I noticed that he'd also fallen asleep, as had Loie, who was stretched across his upper thighs. His eyes closed, Richard's light snores created a gentle counterpoint to her rumbling purrs.

Laying my head back on his chest, I concentrated on the steady drumming of Richard's heartbeat. Despite my own heart filling with so much love that I was afraid it would burst, I allowed Richard's warm embrace and the kittens' purring to lull me back to sleep.

Chapter Twenty-Nine

It was a month and a half later, after many interviews with the authorities and a few with reporters, that I finally felt I could put the whole business of Dan Dane and his murder spree behind me. Until the trial, of course. An event I was definitely not looking forward to.

But in the interim, we had something to celebrate. Sunny, her family name cleared, had easily won the mayoral race, and Aunt Lydia had arranged a casual party in honor of this achievement.

"I really shouldn't be happy," I said as some of the guests gathered in our sun-room to toast Sunny's win. "Since she's only going to be working part-time for me now, which means I have to find someone else to cover those extra hours."

"Oh, you'll do fine," Sunny said. "I've mentioned the job to a couple of people who I think would be perfect, like Denise and Samantha Green. Either one of them would be great. And since it's part-time, you don't have to jump through quite as many hoops to hire someone."

“True.” I took a sip of wine and stared out the back windows. The garden was mostly dormant now, although the rosemary bush sprawling across one bed was still covered in needlelike leaves, and spindly pines offered bright pops of green amid the bare trees and shrubs of the woods.

Zelda, seated next to Walt on the glider, waved her hand at me. “I know it’s a sacrifice, losing Sunny’s help full-time, but just consider what Taylorsford has gained.”

“Of course it’s the best thing for the town,” I said, shifting my gaze to Aunt Lydia, who’d just returned from the kitchen. She was bustling about the tall side table. “Need any help?”

“Everything’s under control,” she replied, setting down two plates of hors d’oeuvres.

“I’m sure it is, but I’m happy to bring out something if there’s more in the kitchen.”

“It’s fine, I already have the perfect waiters,” Aunt Lydia said, tilting her head toward the door that led into the hall.

Richard appeared, balancing an ice bucket and several glasses on a silver tray. He was followed by Hugh, who was carrying two open bottles of wine.

“Oh, I see,” I said with a grin. “You prefer the help to be good-looking.”

“Doesn’t hurt.” My aunt’s serious expression was belied by the upward twitch of her lips.

“Here you go,” Richard said, placing the tray on the side table.

“Thank you, and you too, dear,” Aunt Lydia said, offering her cheek up to Hugh for a kiss after he set down the wine bottles.

Sunny stepped forward to fill her glass. “Now tell me, Lydia, where can I find this type of help? I might need some handsome waiters for my mayoral events.”

"I'm happy to share, but I'm not sure you can afford them," my aunt replied as she sat down in her wooden rocker.

Richard joined me at the back windows. "What are you talking about? You know all it takes is a couple of good meals. Right, Hugh?"

"Absolutely." Hugh pulled the wicker chair closer to Aunt Lydia before sitting down.

"That sounds doable," Sunny said, casting smiles at both men. "I can get my grandma to help. You know what a great cook she is."

"Yes." Aunt Lydia swirled the wine in her glass. "It's such a shame she couldn't compete in any of the baking contests at the fair this year. I know she spent a lot of time preparing for them."

Zelda wrinkled her pert nose at my aunt. "What, so she could break the tie for all the ribbons between you and Jane Tucker?"

"Not all," my aunt demurred.

"Only the categories you entered." Zelda tossed her head, bouncing her crisp blonde curls. "Meanwhile, I went home empty-handed."

Walt patted her hand. "You had me."

"True, love, true. I suppose I shouldn't complain." Zelda clasped his hands in hers.

"I sure wouldn't," Sunny said. "Especially after the last guy I sort of fancied turned out to be a murderer." She gave a mock shudder.

"We all missed the red flags on that one." Richard slipped his arm around my waist. "By the way, has anyone heard anything about his trial?"

"Not scheduled yet, as far as I know," Sunny said. "I think they may sentence his mother first. I guess you heard that she pled guilty to murdering Jeremy Adams."

"So strange." Walt shook his head. "I suspected lots of people, but never a fifteen-year-old girl. Do you think her age at the time of the crime will be a mitigating factor?"

"Maybe." I finished off my wine and handed my glass to Richard, who placed it beside his on the table. "And her current age and poor health might come into play too. But I suspect she'll be sent to some sort of prison, if not a maximum-security one."

"Unlike Dan, who really has no excuse," Sunny said. "I know he claimed to be protecting his mom, but it seems like he must've had some dark tendencies already, the way he took to killing and hurting people."

"I'd say we all harbor those tendencies," said the man walking into the sun-room carrying an expense bottle of liquor.

"Of course you would," I told Kurt Kendrick. "But I think you're wrong on that point. Can you really imagine Sunny ever murdering anyone?"

Kurt crossed the room and set the bottle of cognac on the side table before replying. "Sorry I'm late. Unforeseen complications with a sale," he added, addressing Aunt Lydia before turning to Richard and me. "And yes, I can picture Ms. Fields killing someone. In self-defense, of course, but I think she has the strength of will for the job."

"That's true," Sunny said, flipping her hair behind her shoulders. "If it was me or them, I'm going to take care of myself."

I met Kurt's amused gaze with a lift of my chin. "Well, sure, but that's not the same as cold-blooded murder."

He shrugged. "It's still taking a life. Something all humans will do when necessary."

"In your opinion," Aunt Lydia said. "Now, let's change the subject, shall we?"

"I don't know if we should." Hugh thoughtfully tapped his chin. "I'm intrigued by Mr. Kendrick's opinions on murder."

Kurt shot him a sharp glance. "No, Lydia is right. It's not the proper topic for a celebration." He poured a couple of fingers of cognac in a glass and lifted it to salute Sunny. "Brava, Madame Mayor."

"Thank you," she said.

I was surprised to see a little color rising in her cheeks. "Yes, we should be talking about Sunny's victory, not vile killers."

"Although I do have some news related to Jeremy's case," Walt said. "Good news," he added, sharing a smile with Zelda.

"Oh, what's that?" Aunt Lydia asked. "I'm certainly glad to hear that anything good came out of that tragedy."

Walt straightened, pulling his back away from the glider's cushions. "Well, I think it's great news. Emily Moore approached me about releasing Jeremy's demo reel as an album. She's willing to allow the family to use her poetry for the lyrics, and even volunteered to help raise the funds necessary for remastering and other production costs."

"That's wonderful," Sunny said. "I'm sure the grands will be delighted to hear that."

"It is a great idea," I said. "His music is really good. It deserves to be heard."

"Interesting." Kurt set down his glass and turned his intense gaze on Walt. "I'd like to talk to you about contributing something to that cause, Walt."

Walt's eyes widened. "Why . . . sure."

I stared speculatively at Kurt, wondering how much of his offer was motivated by his love of supporting the arts and how much by guilt for his former illegal activities. "You were wrong, you know, about some drug dealer or gang being behind the murders, or even being an accomplice."

He looked me over, amusement brightening his craggy face. "Yes, I was. I admit it—sometime even I make mistakes."

"Now there's a first," my aunt said under her breath.

"But, that aside, I am happy to help with any efforts to get Jeremy's music out into the world." Kurt pointed at Walt. "Let's make sure to talk later."

"Sounds good," Walt replied.

Aunt Lydia shared a glance with Hugh. "Now, actually changing the subject—Hugh and I were talking last night, and we have a suggestion for Amy and Richard."

"Really? What might that be?" I asked.

"Well, we know how you've been conflicted about where to hold your wedding and reception," Hugh said.

"Especially with Fiona in the mix," Aunt Lydia interjected.

Hugh nodded. "Yes, especially considering the family interference. Anyway, we were sitting out here last night, and something occurred to both of us."

"The garden." My aunt waved a hand toward the back windows. "It would be perfect for a reception. Especially if you're planning on a May wedding."

"Oh, that would be splendid," Sunny said. "Lots of flowers in bloom then."

Zelda jumped to her feet. "What a lovely idea. Maybe you could hold the ceremony there as well." She caught my eye and winked. "That would avoid the problems with what church is fancy enough and all that."

"It would be beautiful," I said, turning my head to survey the garden, "but there isn't room to seat a lot of people. Not in rows, anyway. You could scatter lots of tables and chairs about, which would be great for the reception, but I'm afraid that wouldn't work for a wedding ceremony."

My aunt rose to her feet and joined us at the windows. She cast Richard and me a sly look. "But that would solve your problem with Fiona trying to choose the venue. Just tell her that you want to hold the event at the home that's been in your family for generations. You can't get more genteel than that, now, can you?"

Richard slid his arm around my waist. "No, and it would be perfect. Especially since Amy does love this garden."

"Yes, I do."

Richard tightened his grip on my waist. "It would also mean we could avoid the pricy rental fees for some other venue."

"It would be perfect," Aunt Lydia agreed. "As long as it doesn't rain."

"That's what tents are for," Sunny said. "And hopefully, you'd luck out on the weather."

"I love it!" Zelda trotted over to stand next to Aunt Lydia. "I can just picture it—the garden in bloom, with some standing urns full of flowers added for extra color."

"Yes, it would be perfect for the reception," I said, as I envisioned the scene Zelda had described. "But what about the ceremony?"

Richard pulled me a little closer. "My lawn?" he asked, his gray eyes sparkling. "It has plenty of room for chairs and some type of gazebo or arbor back near the trees. And with the new gate between the two yards, we could allow the ceremony to flow into the reception easily enough."

"Now that," Hugh said, "is the best idea yet."

“Unless it rains,” I said, already convinced but worried about the fickleness of spring weather.

“I think I can find you some very attractive party tents to have on hand in case rain’s in the forecast,” Kurt said. “I often use similar things for parties at the house, so I have a good supplier.”

“It’s worth taking the chance,” Richard said, looking down at me with a smile. “After all, I’ve been lucky in this relationship so far.”

I wrapped my arms around him. “Me too.”

“It’s settled then,” Aunt Lydia said. “The ceremony will take place in Richard’s yard, and we’ll hold the reception here. Now all we have to decide is”—she widened her eyes—“who will inform the very opinionated Fiona Muir about this plan?”

“Oh, let me,” I said, tipping my head to meet Richard’s warm gaze. “I can pour on the family heritage theme thick as honey. That should do the trick.”

“Brave as well as beautiful,” Richard said, before kissing me.

When we separated, Kurt handed both of us a full glass of wine. “Not champagne, but it will have to do.”

“Thanks,” I said, meeting his sardonic gaze. “And you *are* invited, in case you wondered.”

“I should hope so,” he said as he refilled Hugh and Aunt Lydia’s wineglasses. “I’ll let the rest of you get your own, but fill up. I want to share a little surprise before I propose a toast.”

Richard raised his eyebrows. “Surprise? Why does that make me nervous?”

“It’s a good surprise, for once,” Kurt said, as Sunny carried two glasses to Zelda and Walt. He waited for her to refill her own glass before dramatically clearing his throat. “Amy, one question—have you two planned your honeymoon yet?”

I studied his face, noting the unusual glee in his expression. "No. We were thinking we'd keep it simple. Neither of us has the money to spend on anything too elaborate."

"Good. Don't plan anything. I actually have something I'm arranging for you. Consider it my wedding gift."

"Wait, what's this?" Richard asked. "We can't accept anything too pricy . . ."

Kurt waved his free hand through the air like an orchestra conductor. "Nonsense. You're family, after all. And it isn't costing me that much. As it turns out, I have a friend who owns a place in Tuscany."

"In Italy?" I managed to squeak out.

"Yes, of course." Kurt winked at me. "Is there any other? Anyway, it's a lovely little villa, which he hardly ever visits. He's allowed me to stay there from time to time, so I thought I'd ask him if you two could spend your honeymoon there, and he was delighted to offer it to you. Two weeks, whenever you want it in May or June," Kurt added, as I sputtered something that sounded like *thank you*.

"I"—Richard rubbed at his jaw with his free hand—"I don't know what to say."

Kurt grinned. "Say yes. And don't worry about the airfare. Since the villa really doesn't cost me anything, I'll provide that, along with a little spending money."

Aunt Lydia stood up and gave Kurt a nod of approval. "It is incredibly generous of you."

"Yes, very nice," Hugh said, as he rose to stand beside her.

"Not at all. I'm delighted to be able to offer an appropriate gift," Kurt said. "Now—shall we toast the lucky couple?" He saluted

Richard and me with his glass before turning to face Sunny. "As well as our new mayor?"

"I'll drink to that," Walt said, raising his glass, while Zelda did the same.

"To three delightful, brave, and talented young people," Hugh said, lifting his glass and clinking it against Aunt Lydia's. "Long may they enjoy happiness."

Kurt tapped my glass with his. "And may you never get dragged into another criminal investigation."

"Hear, hear," my aunt said, raising her voice as well as her glass.

"That would be nice." Richard looked down at me with love. "But sadly, I wouldn't bet on it."

I grabbed his glass and set it down on the side table along with mine before standing on tiptoe to kiss him. "You have my word that I won't try to get involved with anything like that again. Not unless I literally stumble over another dead body."

"That doesn't exactly reassure me, but maybe if I keep you preoccupied with other things . . ." Richard said, before returning my kiss with a passion that made our guests break into spontaneous applause.

Acknowledgments

As always, I offer flowers and rainbows to:

My "groovy" agent, Frances Black of Literary Counsel.

My "fab" editor, Faith Black Ross, and everyone at Crooked Lane Books, especially Matt Martz, Jenny Chen, Chelsey Emmelhainz, Rachel Keith, and Ashley Di Dio. You guys are "totally boss."

Lindsey Duga and Richard Taylor Pearson, my "ultra-cool" critique partners.

My husband, Kevin Weavil. "The Force" is definitely with this guy (and so am I).

My "primo" family and friends.

All my readers, with deep appreciation for your continued support of this series. I'm so glad you "dig it"!